and Carina Press

The Boardroom series

Done Deal (Memo #1)
After Hours

The Wicked Play series

Bonds of Trust
Bonds of Need
Bonds of Desire
Bonds of Hope
Bonds of Denial
Bonds of Courage
Shattered Bonds

The Power Play series

Game Play
Back in Play
Penalty Play

And watch for the next books in The Boardroom series, coming soon from Carina Press!

Also available from Lynda Aicher

The Harder He Falls
The Deeper He Hurts
The Farther He Runs

This one is for the spark. That idea that grows and blooms until you have to act on it.

BLIND TRUST

BLIND TRUST

LYNDA AICHER

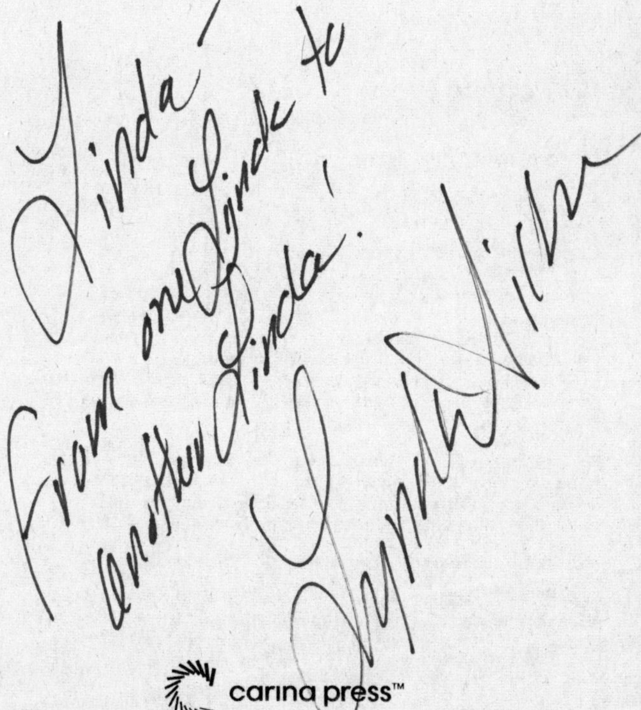

carina press™

Recycling programs for this product may not exist in your area.

ISBN-13: 978-1-335-08070-7

Blind Trust

This edition published by arrangement with Harlequin Books S.A.

www.CarinaPress.com

Printed in U.S.A.

Chapter One

Ryan Burns stepped into the boardroom, looked around. A week's worth of tension slipped from his shoulders on a single, long exhale. "Evening, gentlemen."

"Burns." Cramer gave a nod as he loosened his shirt cuff.

Aaron looked up. "Evening."

"Jacob said he'd be ready in about ten minutes," Ryan told the other men as he draped his suit jacket over the back of a chair that'd been pushed against the wall.

A small table lamp on the credenza at the back of the room provided the only source of light. It dulled the beige industrial carpeting to a muted cream that blended with the pale walls and oak table that ran down the center of the room.

"Did you see the woman?" Cramer asked. He removed his shirt, tossing it with his suit jacket on a chair.

"No." He hadn't wanted to. He preferred the surprise. That was the primary reason why he'd signed on to this scene.

Aaron strolled around the table to lean against the windows. The city skyline jutted up behind him at random heights in a spread of buildings that floated over the low bank of fog that'd rolled in. The sun had set an hour back to leave the city blanketed in the dank, encompassing chill that was common in the summer.

The dim light coupled with the sea of fog brought an intimacy to the otherwise sterile setting. Not that Ryan cared.

He wasn't there for the atmosphere. No, he was there for the sex. And that didn't require romance of any kind. Not for him.

"Did Jacob give you any additional details?" Cramer asked.

He turned his back to deflect the question. The man talked way more than Ryan cared for. He didn't come to the Boardroom to talk or make friends.

"No," Aaron answered. "Not beyond what was posted."

Ryan turned off his phone and slid it into the pocket on his suit jacket, along with his wallet. He left the condoms in his pants pocket, despite spotting a supply of the items on the credenza.

"Do you think she'll be hot?" Cramer persisted.

His jaw tightened around the words he held back. External appearances had never been a requirement within the Boardroom. The exclusive group celebrated the thrill of public sex in safe environments. A willingness to explore, have an open mind and revel in what was otherwise scorned were the primary qualifiers.

Discretion and manners were close seconds.

Aaron crossed his arms, his frown pulling his brows low. He caught Ryan's eye and gave a small roll of his own. Cramer was harmless, but he had an unfortunate knack for annoying others.

Ryan moved around the table, smirking at Aaron as he passed. He rolled the sleeves up on his dress shirt, expectation prickling across his shoulder blades. He rested against the credenza, glanced at the time. He'd removed his tie in the car, and he debated on removing his watch but decided to keep it on.

Jacob had provided minimal information about his female guest. It was her first and possibly only visit to the Boardroom. That alone had been enough to entice Ryan. Add in a grueling week spent huddled over legal contracts with a client who insisted on dismissing his advice, and he was more than ready to give this woman the most erotic night of her life.

"I always love this room," Cramer said, gesturing out the window. "Thanks for offering it up." He nodded to Aaron who gave him a slight smile back.

Ryan glanced outside. The nearest building of equal height was half a block down. The high-rise hotel provided a full arsenal of unintentional viewers. Curtains covered most of the windows, but many remained open, dull yellow lights glowing into the darkness.

Would anyone notice them? He didn't know or care, not really. The potential alone was enough. He could only assume that was what Cramer was referring to.

There was always a chance of getting caught. They might hold their meetings long after normal working hours, and every room used was provided by a member, but nothing was guaranteed. As the Boardroom lawyer, he knew that too damn well.

Jacob popped his head in the doorway. "I'm getting her now." He glanced around. "Any questions?"

Three silent head shakes were his answer.

"Good." He turned away before he quickly spun back. "It's her birthday present. Let's make it good for her." He winked, a devious smile appearing before he left.

Ryan crossed his arms, inhaled. He closed his eyes

and focused inward. The slow beat of his pulse came through to provide the consistency he sought. Another inhale and he released the residual irritation that lingered.

The low hum of the air conditioner filtered into his awareness. In some ways, it amplified the silence, but he found solace in it. Gone was the stress of the day. Dismissed were the troubles that waited for him at his desk. Nothing mattered but this moment.

Which was all he had to give.

A soft gasp from the hallway yanked his eyes open. Everything froze as he waited for the woman to step through the door. Anticipation buzzed on a low note to tighten his chest and entice his dick. Four on one was always an interesting tango between observing and participating.

He'd be content to watch tonight, if the scene played out that way, let the erotic show be a teaser until he got home and relieved the tension with his own hand. Controlling the build was just another part of the game.

Jacob appeared first, his focus on the leggy brunette slightly behind him. He ushered her through the doorway, a hand on her back to guide her. A black blindfold covered her eyes and most of her upper face, which only highlighted the dark red stain of her lipstick.

This was ultimate trust given by her—to a group of men she didn't know.

The power of that surged up to pick at the multitude of possibilities. She was at their mercy. Theirs to tempt and pleasure until she begged for relief…or more.

Wavy curls draped over her shoulders, the ends grazing the mounds of her breasts pushed high by the lilac bra. Her lean form curved at the hips and enticed his gaze down to the tiny silk panties, which shimmered softly in the low light.

He swallowed, pulse increasing when a tentative smile teased her lips. He sucked in a quiet breath, thoughts spinning.

There was something familiar about her. Too familiar.

Brie. That was the name Jacob had provided, and it was probably a scene name.

His eyes narrowed, doubts forming as logic kicked in. The odds were astronomical given the number of people populating the San Francisco Bay area.

Brie.

Like the cheese he detested but consumed when social situations dictated he should. Like the possible shortened name of the paralegal who worked with his law partner. Same brown hair. Same general height and build. Same nervous tap of her fingers in a run against her thumb that she failed to contain when presenting her case research.

Brighton Wakeford. *Damn it.*

Even if it was her, did it matter? She couldn't see him.

But he could see all of her. Every small dip and freckle that dotted her pale skin. Like the mole at the edge of her collarbone. And the one on her hip, just above her panty line.

Were there more? Would he find them all?

One night of lust and sex. That was all he was there for.

And so was she.

Chapter Two

Cold air rushed over Brighton Wakeford in a sudden burst as she passed beneath an air vent. She sucked in a breath, abdomen contracting as a wave of goose bumps raced down her chest to pebble her nipples into hard, tingling points. Her grip tightened around the hand holding hers.

"Are you okay?" the man asked. His voice was pitched low, concern whispering over his words. His steps slowed. Stopped.

She barely suppressed a flinch when he touched the small of her back. Her pulse thudded loud and persistent in her head in time with the racing beat in her chest.

What am I doing?

Darkness engulfed everything behind the blindfold covering her eyes. She was completely reliant upon the man leading her. Jacob. He'd never given her his last name, and she hadn't asked.

Her swallow was forced and thick. "Yes." She gave a firm nod to reassure him. She wasn't backing down. Not now.

Nerves fluttered nonstop in her stomach and prickled over every inch of her bared skin. The skimpy lingerie she'd purchased specifically for tonight suddenly felt nonexistent. The half-shell cups lifted her breasts in a blatantly sexual display. One look in the dressing room mirror and she'd known the lilac set was perfect.

Now, she wasn't so sure.

"You can stop this at any time," he reminded her. He'd gone over all the rules and answered her questions when they'd met for coffee last week.

"I know." She did. Lori had reassured her of that before she'd agreed to this insane gift. This secret group her friend belonged to was so exclusive she didn't even know if it had a name or who was involved. "I..." She blew out a calming breath. "I'm good. Really."

She wasn't running away from this opportunity. Nope. It didn't matter how nervous she was.

"We're here," he said a few steps later.

This was it. She lifted her chin, sucked in her stomach and let Jacob guide her into a room. The boardroom. That's what she'd been told.

She was going to have sex in a corporate boardroom. With...she didn't know who. Or how many. Two? Three? Did she care?

Her secret truth grew in small increments that strengthened her smile. She didn't. Not tonight. Not when she'd been promised it was safe and they wouldn't get caught or arrested for public indecency.

Awareness sprung up in an onslaught of sensory input. To her right, someone let out a low breath. The soft brush of material alerted her to a second person across the room. Another rush of goose bumps chased down her spine when the door clicked shut behind her.

"As you know," Jacob started, a note of command leveling his tone, "Brie is my guest tonight. It's her first time here." He ran his hand down her back in a caress that was both soothing and thrilling. "No pain. No toys. Kissing, fingering and oral are okay. Intercourse only at her consent. Her blindfold stays on at all times."

"Got it."

She turned toward the clipped words that came from her right, excitement creeping in to twine with her nerves.

"Agreed" came across low and firm from a man on the other side of the room.

"Understood." She whipped her head around at the last unexpected voice. Sexy, deep and somehow handsome. Could a voice be classified as such?

Wait. There were four men?

Her heart did a skip and clutch before she got her breath back. She didn't have to fuck any of them, let alone all of them. It was her choice, and Lori had sworn that they'd listen to her. Jacob had too.

"Brie?" She forced a small smile at Jacob's prodding. "Do you agree to those terms?"

"Yes," she said on a breathy whisper. Fortunately, she kept her wince from showing. She didn't want to appear timid or scared even if she was. That was not who she wanted to be in this room. She cleared her throat and shifted toward Jacob. "I agree."

"Excellent."

She could picture his smile, which had been charming over coffee and slightly devious when he'd left her to undress in the small conference room. He brushed her hair aside before he trailed his fingers down her jaw. A light touch, almost ticklish, yet tender too.

"Shall we begin?" He lifted her chin up.

Her lips parted. Every nerve ending buzzed with excitement fueled by the fear that came with the unknown. But this was her chance to be the bad girl, the one who didn't fold to the expectations of her mother or the restrictive rules of social norms.

"Yes," she said, reaching out. Her hands ran over bare skin as she slid them down to rest on the edge of his pants. She stretched up, hoping he'd take the hint. "Please."

He cupped her jaw in a gentle hold. His breath hit her lips. A spicy, sultry cologne surrounded her. She held on tighter, lifted a little more despite the nerves trembling through her limbs.

"Yes," he said, his lips so close to hers. "We can start."

Anticipation flared. Her muscles tightened. A tiny shudder raked her.

Then arms encircled her from behind.

She flinched, breath hitching. Her senses zoomed to the sudden press of heat at her back, the searing touch emphasizing exactly what she was doing.

I'm having a wild sexual encounter with multiple men. Oh. My. God.

"You're so beautiful," the clipped voice said from behind her.

A nervous laugh choked out before she snapped her mouth shut. She swallowed hard. She could do this—would do this.

With a force of will, she tried to relax into the firm support at her back. She hummed her approval, hoping it sounded real, before she reached back to grab the second guy by his nape. This was good, yet the conviction in her head didn't transfer past the wall of anxiety holding her stiff.

Jacob dipped to nuzzle a line of kisses down her throat, forcing her chin higher. Her weight shifted back, but the man behind her kept her from tumbling to the ground. His slow caresses over her abdomen tickled more than excited. Each pass had her stomach contracting until she struggled to breathe.

She was failing.

The signals blared loud and condemning behind her blindfold. Where was the wild woman? The one who wanted to explore and let go? The crazy daring one dying to break free?

The entire night would be ruined if she didn't find that woman—fast.

Relax. Breathe. Let go.

The mantra helped a little. She swiveled her hips in a lascivious circle meant to entice. Would it work? His erection slid over her lower back in a declaration of his desire. At least her bumbling hadn't killed it.

Her smile spread at the low growl that rumbled at her back. Power and lust bloomed in a tentative streak that raced from her nipples to her pussy. She inhaled, taking a moment to savor the sensation.

The darkness provided the freedom she'd longed for. No judgments. No frowns. No expectations glaring from disapproving eyes.

Her attention fluttered between the kisses trailing over the curve of her breasts and the hands easing beneath her panties. She clutched the second guy tighter, arching into the dual touch. Her brain scrambled to keep up with the sensory overload that was only just beginning.

Her pussy contracted. The scent of spice and lust infused her with the wish to be totally debauched. There was so much she had never dared to do. So many acts she'd never had a *chance* to do.

Good girls didn't do these kinds of things.

Warm breaths ghosted over her ear. Lips closed over her nipple. The wetness soaked through the silky material of her bra. A soft squeak leaked from her parted lips.

A low sound of approval from across the room shot through her self-absorption to remind her of the third and fourth guy. They were watching everything.

Her knees dipped, her breath caught yet again. She tried to suck air into her lungs only to find little.

The clang of failure increased when Jacob stepped away. "To the table." His brusque order struck as another mark on her failure.

Her head spun as she struggled to find the strength that'd brought her to this room. The guy behind her urged her forward. Her steps faltered, but she caught her footing before she fell and made a complete fool of herself.

Insecurities swarmed in to incite her doubts. *No!* She gave herself a mental shake. She needed to stop thinking. She was here to feel and experience, not think. Not doubt.

She would not get lost in her fears.

A couple of deep breaths allowed the smallest of details to race in. The soft tread of footsteps. The dull hum of the air conditioner. The heated touch that branded her back. The distinct awareness of being watched. Each step she took. Every movement she made.

They were here to seduce her.

The tabletop was cool beneath her legs when she was helped onto it. Her knees spread around the guy, and the material of his slacks teased her skin. Would they all get naked? Would this be classified as an orgy?

Her bra was removed without fanfare, the material eased down her arms and taken away as the man left her alone on the table. The air swept in to declare her naked state. Her nipples pebbled. A spray of prickles raced over her chest before they slithered to her pussy. The urge to cover herself sprang up on a condemning note of modesty.

No. This is my show.

I want this.

She rolled her shoulders back on the same plank of determination that lifted her chin. That heightened sense of over-awareness rushed up to check off another round of insights.

Her breasts were heavy and full. Each breath lifted them higher in an exposed way she'd never experienced before. Not with any of her boyfriends or the few one-nighters.

And she'd never felt as sexy as she did right then.

She couldn't see the men. Not their expressions. Not their thoughts or expectations—which gave her the freedom to be the woman she so desperately wanted to be.

She embraced that knowledge and let it flow into her sagging confidence. She leaned back on her hands, head tipping, spine arching to thrust her breasts higher. Her hair danced over her skin to tease her shoulder blades. A throaty sigh rumbled out of her parted lips as she absorbed the brazen sensation.

"Fuck."

The rough curse powered her better than a kiss. She wet her lips, uncaring if the move was obvious.

A knot of anticipation twisted in her stomach. Low murmurs reached out from behind her to taunt her with plans she wasn't privy to. But that was what she'd asked for. To be surprised and dominated in ways a woman wasn't supposed to want.

In another wave of boldness, she raised her legs up to rest her heels on the table. The spread position placed a wicked visual of herself in her mind. Her pussy ached with the need to be touched. The air teased her nipples and she longed for someone to do something—anything—before her bravery fled.

"Please." Her voice came out on a sultry note she barely recognized. It flowed from the sensuality pulsing through her.

A chair was rolled to the end of the table by her feet. Tension wound through her chest and dug into the courage she'd only just reclaimed.

Hands smoothed up her inner thighs without warning. She flinched, inhaled. Her pulse escalated to a defined beat that mocked her show of confidence.

"We've got you," the sexy voice said to her right. "Trust us."

Her stomach clenched in time with her pussy. A soft laugh bubbled out as she tried to force herself to relax. "Easy for you to say."

His chuckle trembled over her skin in a warm gust of normalcy. "We won't hurt you."

"I…" She took a breath, exhaled. "I know." Intellectually, at least.

"What are you afraid of?"

She was basically naked on a table in a room with four men she didn't know and couldn't see, and he wondered what she was afraid of?

Her dismay choked out on a sad flash of naivety. "You," she rasped. "This." She gestured blindly to encompass the room. “Of what I want,” she finished softly, the admission gutting her.

That sexy voice was closer, lower when he asked, “And what do you want?”

She squeezed her eyes closed behind the blindfold, her wants slamming against her embarrassment. A lifetime of being told the right way to be good, of being admonished for dressing too sexy or laughing too boldly or behaving in a disgraceful way, laced her jaw closed.

Shame attempted to condemn her further, but she shook her head. She wouldn’t let the false proclamation smother her, yet words still refused to come out.

The table shook as she sensed the man climbing onto it. Her legs flexed to close, but the hands were back to hold them open. Her emotions made a mad scramble between panic and want. Yes and No. Please and…

Her breath locked in her chest as she became distinctly aware of the man sliding in behind her. The energy seemed to arc from him to dance down her back, igniting a small tremble. The hairs on her arms stood on end. Her pulse raced.

The first touch on her arm jolted through her chest. The one to her shoulder vibrated up her neck. Her breaths came in quick hitches that echoed in her head. His pants grazed her outer thighs and hugged her hips as he scooted in to cradle her between his legs.

“You’re gorgeous.” The low murmur sent another shudder down her chest. Her nipples tweaked even tighter. Anticipation did a jittery dance in her stomach that chased away some of the fear that’d been lodged there.

“I feel foolish,” she admitted. Her voice was barely

audible, yet the truth snapped at the restrictions holding her captive.

He ran his hands down her arms, back up. The gentleness swept over her. "Don't."

"How?"

"By letting go."

She almost snorted at that. Almost. But he brushed his lips over her cheek in the softest of touches. *Oh.*

Her heart did a little stutter-step that made zero sense. Yet it fluttered through her chest to tease her with longing.

She inhaled and let the lighter, fresher scent of his cologne flow through her. Its subtleness was heavenly, much like the security radiating from him. *This. God, this.* She savored the sense of protection that surrounded her.

A wave of tension slid from her muscles as she slowly melted into him. His shirt surprised her. The barrier was at once reassuring and obtrusive, yet it declared that he'd made no assumptions about her or how the night would go.

She smoothed a hand down his bare forearm, the hair tickling her palms until she ran into his watch. Solid, round, with a leather wristband. His forearm was muscled and firm, strong. The description fit all of him.

He slid his other hand around her side to splay his palm just below her breasts, yet he didn't move it up to cup one. He simply held her. Soothed her with slow caresses until the knot in her stomach eased, and her reservations bled away.

"I've got you," he whispered in her ear. The heat of his breath rushed down her neck in a calming flow that matched his voice. "You can trust that."

Her low hum of want rumbled in her throat. Understanding vibrated on a chord all its own. This man had her. He'd watch over her, protect her if needed, ensure she was safe.

Jacob had told her she was, but this man behind her made her feel it.

"I do," she finally whispered. She did trust that low sexy voice. Him—whoever he was.

The truth slid in to release the last of her fears. She'd have no regrets over tonight. None.

Not within his arms.

No, with him, she was safe to let go.

Chapter Three

Ryan sucked in a breath, held it until the tightness in his chest loosened enough to allow him to exhale. The ache remained, though. Right next to his heart that he'd sworn was incapable of feeling anything.

The second she'd spoken, he'd known for sure. This was Brighton Wakeford. His subordinate and employee, even if she did report to another partner.

She was forbidden.

Exactly like the Boardroom itself.

Yet he couldn't stay away, not when he could help her. Touch her. Be there for her without her ever knowing.

He ran his palm over her abdomen, inhaled long and slow to savor her scent. Naughty yet light, it somehow matched her understated but sexy-as-hell lingerie. This woman spread out before him was not the one from his memory. The professional, polite, dedicated worker who presented every finding without opinion or judgment.

This woman was a surprise.

A wonderful, interesting, erotic one.

Her honesty had been backed by courage meant to camouflage her nerves. The ones that tightened her muscles beneath his palm and lined her words, which were spoken in that low voice coated with defiance yet still so vulnerable.

Where had *this* woman been hiding?

He caught Aaron's eye, flicked his brow up. The other man gave a quick smile from the chair he'd moved between Brie's spread legs. He wet his lips, hauled her hips to the edge of the table and dipped his head.

Brie flinched, a tight squeak escaping.

"Just feel," Ryan whispered. "Let go." *Trust me.* There was no way he'd let anything bad happen to her.

She relaxed with a low moan, her weight returning to his chest in a slow roll of acceptance. *Yes.* His abdomen contracted as he sucked in a breath. The excitement built in his chest in layers of want backed by need.

This was easily turning out to be his best decision of the day.

He ran his hand up to cup her full breast in slow increments that let him savor the weight. It filled his palm in a tempting mound that molded to his touch. He squeezed it lightly, enticed by the dark nipple that was aroused to a hard tip waiting to be teased. Tasted. Sucked.

Her breaths increased to short pants that lifted her chest with each inhalation. Her legs had fallen open, all signs of tension gone.

"You are our only priority tonight," he told her, meaning every word. "Our sole goal is to pleasure you." And what an easy task that was turning out to be. That had been Jacob's description of the scene, and they'd all signed up agreeing to it.

"Why?" she asked on a breathy whisper before a low moan eased out. Her back arched, breath hitching. Her grip on his wrist fell away in a trail of fingers when she exhaled, hips twisting. The seductive dip and roll sent his imagination into overdrive and taunted the lust simmering in his groin.

"Does it matter?" He dragged his teeth down the side of her neck, absorbing every little shift and twitch. He bit the sensitive junction of her neck and shoulder, soaked up her soft sigh as she gripped his thighs. Her head tilted in an offering he couldn't reject. "Tonight is about you." He slid his tongue up to nip her earlobe. "Only you."

There was nothing else to explain.

Aaron lifted his head to exhale a trail of warm breath over her damp panties. The tease was still on. The build would only make the end so much better. The other men stood to Aaron's left and right, their gazes filled with lust and want.

On his nod, Jacob and Cramer stepped up to remove her heels. As sexy as they were in their silver simplicity, they'd only get in the way.

Her hold on his thighs tightened. The pressure shot down his legs to incite the languid passion building in his groin. He released a low groan of his own. How could this be the demure woman from his office?

He smiled against her neck. He imagined there were numerous people who'd wonder the same thing about him.

"What do you want, Brie?" He let her name roll off his tongue in a slow beat of sex. He'd never say her name again without thinking of this night. "Were you expecting four of us?"

Her head swiveled in a negative response as the other men straightened her legs, massaging her calves as they did. He eased his hand down her abdomen, pausing to circle a finger over the dark little mole on her hip. Flat to the touch, it marked the last boundary that stood between her and full nudity.

Her stomach contracted, breath holding.

He caught Aaron's attention again. At some point they'd become the leads to this part of the scene. Jacob had stepped back without a hint of irritation, and thankfully, Cramer had as well.

Her tongue slipped over her full bottom lip in a tempting show of want and expectation. One he didn't wish to disappoint.

He studied her face as he slid his hand beneath her panties, grazed his fingers through her soft down of curls. Nice. Full bare had its advantages, but he enjoyed natural too. The added texture gave him more to tease her with.

She bit her lip, hips rocking what little they could with Jacob and Cramer holding her legs. This was how he wanted her. On the edge. Anticipating.

Aaron's lids were heavy with the lust filling his expression. He lifted a brow, hand poised to move at Ryan's nod.

Ryan eased one hand down and the other up to pinch her nipple as he stroked a finger over her clit. Just once. Slow and firm. Her flinch was quick, her sharp intake of breath soft. He rested his finger there, not moving. Her folds surrounded it in a heat that was uniquely erotic.

Her grip tightened on his thighs, those little breaths of hers getting faster. He tried to remember her eyes, were they brown or blue? Green maybe? There'd been no need to notice them before.

And there wouldn't be when he saw her again.

This was a single night of pleasure. What happened

in the Boardroom stayed in the Boardroom. That alone had drawn his interest when Trevor James had first approached him about this group years ago.

He flicked his chin at the others.

Aaron leaned in to trail another swath of hot breath over Brie's pussy. The heat passed over his fingers in a wave as the other men trailed their hands down Brie's inner thighs to tease her around the crease of her legs.

"Oh…my…" Brie groaned, her frustration taking her tone lower. She tried to lift her hips, but he wouldn't allow it.

Her pussy pulsed in two quick contractions that begged him to sink his finger in and feel the clench. *Fuck.* He let his own frustration rumble in his throat before he flicked her nipple. Back and forth. Back and forth. Not hard. Not mean.

"God," she whined. Her nails dug into his thighs in crescent-shaped bites that raced to his balls and shot up his dick. His chest tightened, need simmering over his skin on a rush of heat. "Please." Her hips bucked against his hold before she shifted back to grind into his erection.

His chuckle tumbled out before he could check it. "Is there something you want?" he taunted.

Jacob and Cramer continued to caress the sensitive skin at the edge of her panties, and Aaron released another heated breath before he needled his tongue over her hole. The material blocked any actual touch, but the wet impression remained.

They'd drive her mad and then give her whatever she asked for.

And tomorrow he'd act like he never saw her squirm in suppressed passion. Never tasted her skin or inhaled the deep current of arousal that broke over her perfume to darken the scent into something naughty.

Never imagined sinking into her heat and feeling her clench around him.

Those were only for tonight.

Brie struggled for air, her mind spinning with the barrage of sensations overwhelming her senses. She pressed into the solid chest supporting her, so damn thankful he was there. At least she knew which touch was his. She could focus on that.

Ground herself to it.

"Brie," he prodded, his low sexy voice purring so close to her ear. Her name rumbled in his throat in a distinctively seductive note all its own.

Another gust of warm air penetrated the now wet barrier of her panties to tease her with what they were withholding. Her pussy clenched in a silent cry to be filled. Or simply touched for that matter.

"What are you waiting for?" she tossed back, boldness rising when she was in no position to be. Yet she could be here.

She could be anything she wanted to be in this room.

Every part of her pussy was being teased without a full touch until she could think of nothing *but* being touched there. The slow, madding flick of her nipple should've been inconsequential, but her breast was alive with a craving for something more. Anything more. A hard pinch. A wet suck.

God. Please.

"You," he said.

It took a moment for his answer to penetrate the riot in her mind. They were waiting for her? A whimper fell out on a desperate slide that yanked at the devil burning to be free. The one that'd brought her to this room in the first place.

They were waiting for her.

In a sudden flash of daring, she grabbed the nape of the man behind her and urged his head down until his breath hit her face. Adrenaline raced at her nerves, but with it came a rush of power. It flew over her desire to unpin the passion she'd never fully released—until now.

"I want to come."

Chapter Four

Everything froze in an instant.

Her breath caught. Blood roared in her ears.

The brush of warm air over her lips taunted and drove her at once. The power was hers to own.

"Make me come." Her demand was heightened by the throaty rumble that accompanied the words. The wild seductress blazed to life, and Brie had no will to suppress her.

And she didn't have to.

A chorus of groans penetrated the silence to tangle with the energy buzzing within her. Those breaths hit her lips in a choppy clip that told their own story.

"Fuck."

The barely there whisper ghosted over her mouth in a final confirmation of his want. This man wanted her.

Just as she was.

Wild. Naughty. Bold.

She yanked him down in a desperate need to feel that want. To claim it as hers.

His mouth closed over hers in a rush of heat and passion. She opened without thought, frantic to feel the heat of his tongue, the crush of his strength.

He took everything she was offering and pushed for

more. His tongue thrust in to tangle with hers in a heady bolt of connection. This man owned her right now.

And she wanted to claim him.

He shifted, changing their angle to deepen the kiss even more. She fell back a little, welcoming the control. She gripped the back of his head, not caring if her lungs ached for air, only distantly aware of the other men slipping her panties off.

She didn't need to worry about anything. Not with him in the lead, and he had been since the moment he slid in behind her on the table. She couldn't see a damn thing, yet she could sense it. The authority hummed off him.

She gave herself over to him. The hot caresses of his tongue as it played with hers. The little nips he snuck in to sting her lip before he dove back into her mouth. The hard pinch and twist on her nipple that jolted her focus to the crazy burning sensation racing over her chest on a rush of tingles.

He caught her soft cry and swallowed it before overriding it with a deep groan of his own. The note held the frustration building within her along with the recklessness pushing her to do more. Take more.

Have more.

The hot slick of a tongue through her pussy jolted into her core, igniting a wave of heat that engulfed her with its carnal caress. She squirmed in his arms, seeking more and relief at once. A tongue circled her opening, teasing but not entering. Would it? His finger still pressed on her clit, the pressure building without offering relief.

All she needed was a flick. A little movement.

Please.

Desperation clawed at her skin and pummeled her brain with its frantic anguish.

She ripped her mouth away to suck in air, her breaths too clipped to get that deep, filling gust she needed. But she didn't care.

"Please," she whispered. She tracked her other hand down his arm until she reached his watch. She pushed on his wrist, but it didn't budge. Not even a slight shift on her clit. That tongue, the devious, glorious one circling her vagina, was beyond intense.

Evil almost.

In the best possible way.

Another tortured moan fell from her parted lips. Hands rubbed every part of her legs, from the sensitive crease near her pussy to the space behind her knee and down to the soles of her feet. And then there was him. Surrounding her. Supporting her.

"Anything you want," he said, his lips brushing hers as he spoke. "You're so passionate. Trusting. Open." Each word was emphasized by a slow circle on her clit.

Oh, my God. Lights exploded behind her eyes as the craving blew into overdrive. This man, this insanely wonderful man, knew exactly what to say and do. And she didn't want to lose it. Not his touch or his words.

His confirming, accepting words.

"More," she begged softly. "Tell me more." She could ask here without fear. She'd never know who these men were. And the one she did know, she'd never see again.

Her head fell back even more as he pressed a line of kisses down her throat. She never doubted that he had her. He wouldn't let her fall.

"I can't take my eyes off you," the clipped voice said by her foot. The hard press of a thumb massaged her arch in a mind-numbing caress. "Of how receptive you are."

"You're stunning." That was Jacob. At her other foot. "Unbelievable."

A deep rumble of consent tickled over her pussy before that man dipped his tongue into her. Finally. Fuck. Yes. But then it was gone, that silky, wet heat withdrawn before she could truly appreciate it.

She squirmed in his arms, mind overloaded with the sensual praise and touch. She had no clue what she looked like, but right now the only thing that mattered was that she *felt* exactly as they'd described.

Here, with these men, she was all those things.

"You're ours tonight," he said right before his mouth closed over her nipple.

She cried out, the gentle warmth sinking to her core. The over-sensitized nub suddenly became the focus of everything. He bathed it in wet licks and light sucks that turned deep until she arched into the maddening pull. Men had sucked her nipples before, but never like this. Never with such slow, sensual grazes of his teeth that teased at the damage he could do.

Her head spun until she was lost. "I'm yours," she said, fully believing it.

Rumbled growls of agreement filled the air to feed the wanton freedom she longed to revel in. This was… everything.

Freedom and joy. Bliss and acceptance.

The moist, wet slick of a tongue around her toes had her reflexes attempting to tug her foot from the man's hold.

She stilled. *What the... Oh...my...* The soft caress of hot wetness where it shouldn't be—where it'd never been before—was intensely confusing. One of them pulled her big toe into his mouth, sucking deeply, slowly. The sensation rippled through every part of her. Jacob joined in on her other foot to provide a dual pull like nothing she'd ever experienced. The intimate suggestion of the act was overwhelming.

Her initial rejection gave way to stunned wonder in increments of disbelief. Her muscles relaxed, the tension fleeing beneath the carnal assault.

"Wow." The word didn't come close to communicating the emotions storming through her.

"It's the simplest things sometimes," he said as he nuzzled that tender spot beneath her chin. It forced her head back, and she only wished she could bend more. Give him more room. Give these men everything they wanted.

The slow, steady swirl of his finger over her clit was precisely what she needed in that moment. The pent-up energy burst free on a wave of languid heat that quickly turned to an inferno. Her entire body became a conduit of erotic sensation. There was nothing but the wet and warmth and touch and…

"Do you want to come?" He nipped her chin before he forced her head up and claimed her mouth again. He took with this kiss. Stole her reservations and incriminations. Her smallest doubts and biggest fears. He took them all and gave her his strength. His power.

Him.

The connection wound around her until she wanted to crawl within him and never leave. Not this safe place or this reckless feeling that left her both grounded and freed.

He released her mouth, and "yes" burst out of her

without thought. "Please. Yes." The tendons on his wrist moved beneath her fingers where she still gripped him, the contact yet another oddly intimate point that brought the moment deeper.

This was just sex. Yet it was more.

Everything condensed into a tight ball of want, need, desire and lust right below his finger. That damn perfect finger. He rubbed harder. The tongue on her pussy plunged deep within her, followed by the jab of a finger—or two.

Her cry pierced the room. She curled up with the jolt of fulfillment that only increased the longing pulsing from her.

"Beautiful." The word stroked past her ear. "Stunning." She clung to the praise, letting it feed her. "So free."

Yes. I am.

"Show us." The command swept over her before it snuggled in beside her desire to please. "Let go. Give it to us."

Her release broke open on a hard clash of finally. "Yes!" The rejoicing exclamation shot out to punctuate the wave of heat and energy blazing from her pussy to her fingers.

She clung to him, grounding herself to the moment, when it'd be so easy to slip into the unknown. She dug her fingers into his hair and rode her orgasm until she couldn't breathe. Until she shattered.

The pressure finally eased. The mouths moved away. His finger slowed.

Brie sucked in a long breath. Exhaled. Floated in the glow of boneless euphoria. There were no words to describe how light she felt right then.

There was no tomorrow. No stress. No fears or worries.

His hand smoothed up her abdomen. Her feet were set back on the table. The mouth on her pussy was gone.

They were winding down.

And she wasn't ready for this to end.

He kissed her jaw in that soft confirmation of goodbye or maybe thank you. Gentle. Lingering.

Her heart wept in that instant. *Not yet*, her mind screamed. Or was that her soul?

She tensed, tightened her grip on his hair to hold him there. Right there. He stiffened. The room went still and the energy condensed, waiting for her.

Her heart pounded out a beat of fear, but it was negated by a sudden surge of determination. This was her chance, probably her one and only, to have everything. Be everything.

And she wasn't backing down.

She brushed her lips against his. The grazing stroke blazed a path to her chest to loosen the constraints clenched around it. This man. Who was he? What did he look like? Would she ever know?

Did she want to?

She couldn't answer that, but she did know one thing. She laid her lips against his, ran her tongue over the soft rise of his. Her voice was low and seductive when she finally told him what she really, truly longed for.

"I want to fuck you."

At least once. Before this glorious night ended.

Chapter Five

The rush of want stormed through Ryan in a flash of freed hunger. He crushed his mouth to Brie's, mind reeling with possibilities. Ones he could only execute here.

I want to fuck you.

Denying her wasn't even a thought.

The Boardroom let him be this guy, the one who could give a woman everything she wanted. And Brie wanted to fuck him.

His pulse beat a frantic pace in his throat that marked exactly how much he liked that thought. Her soft purrs and throaty cries plucked at his base instinct to claim and take.

He ripped his mouth from hers, breaths gusting. This was reckless—and he didn't care.

Her cheeks were flushed below the mask, lips plump and parted. Her lipstick dulled to show the dark red state he'd left them in. Her hair fell in waves down her back to tease his arm and pool on the table in a silky disarray.

The hard, unforgiving wood of the table bit into his hip where he'd shifted, and ground into his elbow where he braced his weight. His leg was going numb where Brie lay over it, but the discomforts were all part of the play.

The very public play.

He found Aaron by the window, his intent solidified and telegraphed. The lights of the nearby high-rise shone behind him in an unneeded reminder of how exposed they were. The low glow of the lamp within the room would provide more shadows than clear images, but Brie didn't know that.

Cramer stood a few feet away, a stoic facade hiding the hyped-up man from before. Ryan could sense Jacob at his back. He hadn't objected to the control shift, and Ryan assumed he wouldn't now.

In truth, he couldn't be worried about it. He was within the scene requirements, and that was the only code he had to follow.

He smoothed his fingers through the downy curls on Brie's mound, anticipation spreading once again. He'd get to watch her come for a second time.

Her hips undulated, a rumbled moan flowing from her parted lips. Her nipples had darkened to deep rose tips that begged him to suck them. Brie Wakeford was so much more than she displayed at the office.

He dropped down, rolling her until she was above him as he scooted up the table.

"What..."

Her forehead wrinkled, her limbs going stiff, but then her legs parted, and she slowly sat up. Her smile grew in a slow spread that held a glimmer of deviousness. Her shoulders rolled back as she rotated her hips in a seductive tease over his straining erection.

"Fuck." His breathy affirmation came without thought, his grip tightening on her hips. "I can't believe how sexy you are." Would he ever get this image out of his head?

Her throaty laugh tumbled over him in the taunt that it was. His nipples tightened, balls drawing up with the desire she stoked.

She tucked her chin in, her hair falling forward to cloak her face before she brushed it back. The slow rock of her pussy over his erection did exactly as she most likely intended. His dick ached to be in her. To feel that heat tempting him through his clothing. To thrust into her until he was lost in the clench of muscles and slick of arousal.

She rose up on her knees when he moved to undo his pants. His own movements were quick and succinct as he freed his erection and rolled a condom on, grateful he had one in his pocket.

He couldn't remember a time when his skin had ever felt this tight. Every nerve ending was poised in anticipation. The other men were forgotten in that moment. This was only about Brie.

He urged her lower, just enough for him to run the tip of his dick through her hot, wet pussy. His groan tore free on a flash of primal appreciation. His chest contracted, abdomen clenching with the raging need to claim her.

Her short gasp clipped the air. Her head dropped forward, pelvis rocking. The tease was both seductive and maddening. Yet…

"I love seeing you this way." He winced. *Fuck.* Would she catch his slip? "Wanton and sensual," he rushed on. "Owning all of it."

A low purr rumbled from her throat. She braced her hands on his chest. That seductive smile was back when she rotated her hips to place the head of his cock in her opening.

Heat flared over his cock head and burned down his shaft to inflame his groin. Everything tensed with her slow descent. Inch by inch she lowered herself onto him until she rested on his hips, his dick fully engulfed in her heat.

"Fucking amazing." He held her hips, eyes closing to savor the pulsing warmth surrounding him.

"You feel so good," she mumbled.

"That is so fucking hot," Cramer said. His bold statement snapped Ryan back to the reality of the moment.

This was sex. It was supposed to feel good. Be good.

And he'd make it better than good for Brie.

He gripped her hips and thrust up, unable to wait for her. Her cry urged him on. Drove him harder.

"Do you feel them watching you?" he taunted her. "The windows are wide open too. Can you feel the admiration? The desire? The craving to have you?" He grunted with his next thrust, need boiling. "But I'm the one who gets you. Only me." He drilled that home with another hard drive.

"Yes." The soft pant was lush with passion. "Yours."

She was his—for this scene.

She was riding him on a table in front of other men. The reality of that barely penetrated her mind. *She* didn't do things like that.

Yet she was.

And she loved it.

The truth burned through her chest and broke free on a wicked laugh. She rose up, swiveled her hips, waited. She only sank back down when he finally relaxed. "Mmm." He was perfect in her. Thick. Firm.

She lifted, lowered. A moan rolled out.

"Beyond hot." The agreement came from her left and she turned her head to shoot the guy a smile.

This entire experience was crazier than she'd dared to dream, and her imagination had run wild since Lori had dropped the opportunity in her lap. But this…

She let the power fill every good-girl crevasse until there was only this woman. This heady, sexy woman who owned this erotic display.

He was fully clothed beneath her. The soft cloth of his pants tickled her bottom on every descent. Somehow that was even more erotic. The imagined visual pinged every fantasy she'd never admit having.

Yet she could do it here. Live it.

She lost herself then, in the deep thrusts that filled her completely and the hot flush overtaking every limb. He caressed her thighs, ran his palms up to cup her breasts. Kneaded them before pinching her nipples in a delicious sting that raced to the tension collecting in her groin. There were no thoughts other than hitting that spot, finding that rush, creating the build that would send her flying.

He ran his thumb over her clit, shooting off a burst of pleasure. She arched back, hands braced on his thighs. The muscles contracted and bulged beneath her grip in the most delicious way. He was strength and power.

And he was feeding it to her.

The distinctive slick and smack of their movements swam in her ears in a sexual rhythm of lust. Of increasing need.

He took over once again, planting his feet on the table to pound into her in a series of relentless drives that tossed her over the edge into the blind oblivion.

Her muscles tensed, held, then released in an explosion of ultimate ecstasy. Heat washed over her, wave after wave as he pushed her further, thrusting harder until she couldn't think. Couldn't respond.

His rough, harsh grunt seemed to rip from his gut. His hold on her hips tightened to almost unbearable with one last grinding drive that lifted her knees from the table and shattered everything within her.

And then she was falling, forward, into his arms. Exhausted, sated, numb.

So very numb.

Quiet.

The hard, persistent drum of his heart rang with her own beneath her ear. Soothing caresses drifted over her back to lull her further.

Beautiful. The entire night had been beautiful.

She was being shifted before she was ready to move, before she could on her own. Her limbs were heavy weights that refused to function when she tried to assist.

"You're an amazing woman." He kissed her forehead in the lingering goodbye she'd dreaded earlier. But this was the end.

The night was over. It rang in her conscious and dug at her heart.

How could it be over already?

She was moved again, lifted and then lowered until she was cradled in a lap. Jacob's. His cologne hit her as totally wrong. Overwhelming when she longed for that subtler scent. Indistinct yet uniquely *his* now.

Rustling indicated the other men were leaving. A buckle clicked, material slithered together. She started to shake, a chill consuming her in a swift drop of reality. She didn't understand her reaction, yet she also couldn't get herself to care.

A blanket was draped over her. Jacob shifted to tuck it in. And still she couldn't move. Couldn't get herself to speak. What would she say?

She sensed him before he ran a finger down her jaw. The air hummed with his presence, whispering his power without words. There was no need for them.

She understood everything he said.

Goodbye. Thank you.

She squeezed her eyes closed, another chill raking her as he left the room. That was it.

Her heart cracked open to expose the anguish she'd never dared to acknowledge. Every deviant desire and counter that'd held them in check. The pressure of being exactly as everyone expected her to be. Of being who she never wanted to be.

The ache to finally have the real her be seen and treasured for who she was.

"Thank you, Brie." The voice was wrong but sincere. Whoever he was, he'd treated her with respect, and she'd cherish that. She managed a small nod when her voice refused to work.

"It was a pleasure, Brie." The fourth guy.

Four guys. She'd had four men focused on pleasuring her tonight. How? Why? Shouldn't she be reveling in it right now? Laughing even? Maybe?

"Come on," Jacob said before he stood, lifting her in his arms as he did. The urge to protest was swallowed by her inability to speak. This was absurd.

She couldn't be this weak.

They moved out of the room and down the hall. She tracked their progress, aware of the hushed quiet that surrounded them. He stepped into another room, which she assumed was the one she'd left her clothes in.

"How are you doing?" he asked as he settled her into a chair.

She cleared her throat, drew the blanket tighter around her. "Fine. Thanks."

"There's water on the table." He ran his fingers down the line of her arm. "I'm going to let you get dressed." He stepped away. "You were stunning tonight, Brie. Thank you. And Happy Birthday."

The door clicked shut before his last words sunk in. *Happy Birthday.*

She slipped the blindfold off, blinked. The room was lit by the pale glow of the surrounding buildings. Tall ones that matched the office building and displayed their activities in every lighted square of glass.

Did anyone really watch her? Could they see into that boardroom?

Another shiver trembled through every part of her. She was completely incapable of defining if it held dread or excitement.

She tensed at the soft knock on the door. Had it been that long? Was Jacob tired of waiting for her? What time was it?

It cracked open, Lori's head popped in. "Hey."

Brie frowned. She couldn't process the appearance of her friend. Not here. Now. "What are you doing here?"

Lori's sympathetic smile sent off more warning bells. "Aftercare." She picked up Brie's lingerie that now sat on the table. Brought there by whom? "Here." She held the items out, the lilac material seeming to taunt Brie with what she'd done.

She took them on autopilot. "I don't understand."

Lori opened a bottle of water and handed it to her.

"Drink." Brie took a long gulp, then went back for a second. Heaven. Wow. When had she gotten so thirsty?

"I'm here to make sure you're okay and see that you get home." Lori sat back on the table. "That's my job."

"What about Jacob?"

"You don't need to worry about him."

She finished off the water, determined to get her thoughts back together. This was absurd—yet she couldn't seem to shake the sense of rawness that left her exposed.

She just had to get home. Crawl into bed and leave this night in her past.

As if that was even remotely possible. Not when there was only one clear thought hammering through her head.

I have to do this again.

Chapter Six

"Yes, Mother," Brie sighed into the phone. "I'll be at brunch tomorrow." Like it was a rare occurrence instead of a weekly event. One she'd stuck to even last Sunday when she'd secretly clung to her night of deviance in the face of the country club superiority.

Her mother's crowd lived to believe they were better than everyone else, and Joanne Wakeford was the head cheerleader. Brie had been raised to fall right in line and she had—until last Friday night.

Her facade of perfection had never felt so heavy.

"Good." The pleased note grated on Brie's frayed nerves. "Rose Jacobson's son is going to be at brunch too. You remember him, right? He graduated a few years ahead of you," she went on before Brie could respond. "He's recently divorced and—"

"Mother," Brie cut her off, her teeth clenched against her frustration. "Please," she rushed on, forcing lightness into her voice. "Do you really want me to be the rebound girl?" She winced at the callousness, but the sentiment aligned to her mother's way of thinking.

A sharp intake of air snapped through the phone on an offended note. "Of course not." Brie could picture her mother, her lips pursed, sculpted brows dipping as she scrambled to salvage her plan. "But he's a doctor. In Seattle, which isn't that far from here. And—"

"The last thing he probably wants is to be set up by his mother when he's on vacation." She bit her tongue to hold back her own distaste at having yet another "eligible" man thrust upon her by *her* mother. "I have to go," she said before the conversation spiraled further. "I'll see you tomorrow."

"Goodbye, Brighton. Wear something nice," her mother added before she hung up.

Brie's nails dug into her palm in a painful bite before she forced her hand to relax. When had she ever set foot in the country club not looking nice? Never. That's when.

Her exhausted sigh dragged her shoulders down along with her floundering strength. She braced her head against the wall and stared unseeing out her bedroom window. The shallow alley that counted as the backyard between the line of attached homes in the Inner Sunset provided little to look at anyway, even when the fog wasn't present.

Her mother's last comment rang in her head in a persistent cycle that picked at every little dig her mother had snuck into their short conversation. Her stomach contracted around the burning resentment she'd harbored for so long it'd become a part of her. The one built on her inability to tell her well-meaning mother to go to hell.

At least she tried to believe her mother's constant nitpicking and gibes were done with the desire to help. Joanne had shoved her expectations and beliefs onto her two daughters, and as the oldest, Brie had taken the brunt of it. A burden she'd carried to spare her sister, who was two years younger.

Her sister had fled the area for college over ten years ago and had never looked back—unlike Brie.

She turned away from the window, her gaze catching and holding on the mirror over her dresser. Her reflection showed the straitlaced, well-mannered woman her mother had groomed, and Brie had never rebelled against.

Until last Friday.

A sly grin stole over her face to flash back at her from the mirror. The rush of her secret hummed through her chest, setting off a chain reaction of want. Memories swooped in to flush her with the sensation of being touched, protected, even cherished for accepting what those men had willingly given her: debauched pleasure.

She clamped her lips shut, stifling the groan that rumbled in her throat. It'd been a one-time deal. That was it.

A knock echoed through the apartment from the front door to yank Brie out of her thoughts.

"I'll get it," she called to her roommate as she hurried down the hallway. She glanced into the living room to catch Amy's eye. "It's for me."

Her roommate nodded around her boyfriend, who was snuggled into the couch beside her. A small douse of envy tried to sneak its way beneath Brie's lowered resistance before she slammed the empty emotion down. Boyfriends weren't required for happiness.

She swung her door open, her purse tucked over her shoulder, jacket in her hand. "I'm ready," she told Lori as she stepped outside. She plastered on a smile and forced back the wave of weariness that'd almost had her begging off.

Lori's brows winged up, question meshing with surprise. "Okay."

Brie took off down the sidewalk before she could be grilled. Lori was way too insightful, and Brie's emotions were too close to the surface for a frontal attack. The last week had been an undulating cycle of charge forward and retreat as she'd processed the shocking amount of emotional garbage her one night of wild passion had dislodged.

Her usually talkative friend stayed quiet as they walked the few blocks to the Irish pub, which was either a testament to Lori's intuition or a nod to the obvious vibes Brie was throwing off.

She snagged an open booth by the front widow and slid onto the wooden bench seat. She rested her head against the high back of the bench and closed her eyes for one long beat that didn't end.

"Are things that bad?" Lori asked, concern lacing through her voice.

"No," Brie answered, her response automatic. "I'm just tired." Drained would be a better word, maybe. She forced her eyes open and added a smile as reassurance. "It was a long week."

A splash of sun darted through the window to highlight the subtle strands of blond in Lori's auburn hair. "How so?"

Brie gave a dismissive shrug. How did she explain the lethargy that'd hit her on Tuesday, which had had her dragging ass the rest of the week and put her mind in a scattered mess? And that didn't touch on the shifting tide of delight and ridicule that slammed home whenever she thought of that night.

"You crashed, didn't you?" Lori stated more than asked. "Is that what this is?"

"Yeah." Her nod was backed with a grim smile. "It's fairly common after an intense scene like you had."

Brie's eyes bugged out at that piece of information. "And you didn't think to warn me about this?"

"First, I wasn't sure if you'd go through with the night." Lori dismissed her grievance with a wave of her hand. "And second, why would I give you more ammunition to reject what you obviously really wanted?"

Lori's counterargument had a wealth of flaws and an equal number of truths that Brie couldn't debate. Well, she could—if she'd had the will to do so. The reality was, she'd gone into that night of her own free will.

She'd been expecting the usual array of sex toys her more adventurous friend loved to shock her with for her birthday gift. Instead, to welcome her into her thirties, she'd received a wild, intense, eye-opening sexual experience.

One she couldn't stop thinking about no matter how hard she tried.

"Why was it so important to you that I went?" she asked. Lori hadn't pushed her, but she'd talked Brie through every scenario and step until completing the prerequisite NDA and medical test had felt almost normal.

"Because I thought you'd like it."

"Why would you think that?" It wasn't like Brie had ever divulged any of her deepest desires to her.

A slow grin spread in a devious slide over Lori's face. "Because you're still friends with me." She winked.

The laugh shot from Brie on a quick beat. She

dropped her head back, sighing with the acceptance flowing through her.

"And," Lori added, voice softening, "because a part of you is dying to be that wild girl your mother warned you to stay away from."

Brie snorted. "You mean like you?" she quipped. Lori was so opposite of everything Brie was, but they'd somehow clicked almost immediately. Her mother's disapproval had only solidified her determination to keep Lori in her life.

"Exactly like me." The triumph in her voice matched her pleased expression. "I'm not ashamed of anything I've done."

"Which is why I admire you." In so many ways. Lori took what she wanted from life and never showed an ounce of shame or regret.

Lori tucked a lock of hair behind her ear, the curls escaping almost immediately. Brie smiled at the habitual action. Her friend had a love-hate relationship with her hair that showed in the rotating styles and color.

"You did enjoy it, right?" Lori's confident tone was underscored by a heavy shot of concerned doubt.

There was zero point in denying it. "Yes." Heat bled over her cheeks at the memory of how much she'd enjoyed it. "I did."

"Good."

She waited for her to say more, maybe dig for details, but Lori remained silent. "That's it?" she asked, brows raising. Lori hadn't asked a single probing question, not even that night when she'd driven Brie home.

"Yup." Lori nodded. "Unless there's something you *want* to talk about."

Right. She had no idea how to voice the jumble of

want that continued to simmer within her. That night had exposed a passionate desire she couldn't seem to contain, but she had to. Unless she was willing to let that wild side of herself free. And then what?

They ordered drinks from the waitress when she stopped by their table along with a basket of fries to snack on despite her appetite having been nonexistent all week.

She glanced out the window, thoughts drifting over her life. When had she ever done what she shouldn't? There'd been no teenage rebellion or wild college years for her.

"I'm thirty years old," she mumbled. That number rang like the dark bearer of spinsterhood. Most of her high school friends were already married, some with kids. A detail her mother reminded her of frequently.

That tight, restricted sensation born of expectation wrapped around her, pressing and contracting until she struggled to sit still. The urge to burst up and run away crawled over her skin in an all-too-familiar rush of bitterness.

Her throat ached with everything she was holding in. The unspoken anger and frustration. The self-inflicted position she couldn't break free of. The obligations that'd ruled her life since the day she was born. The ones she both loved and loathed.

She ran her hand through her hair, letting the strands slide through her fingers. She caught the eye of a man wearing a dark jacket and jeans on the corner. Brown hair, strong jaw, handsome. Her slow smile spread in time with his. Could she go home with him? Fuck him until they were both sated and then leave? Probably.

She'd had one-night stands before. But that had been the extent of her wild side—until last Friday.

The guy shot her a wink before merging with the crowd as he crossed the street and headed away from them. Did he have a wife? A girlfriend? Boyfriend?

She didn't. So what was stopping her from returning to that den of indulgence?

Nothing—except her damn restrictive morals. And the secret little fear that it wouldn't be the same without *him* there.

Could she really be that sexual free woman without him behind her, supporting her, reassuring her?

And there was the big stinking crux of her problem: She'd have to go back to find out. And if she did, she'd have to deal with the outcome—whatever it was—when she was still managing the fallout from her first visit.

She wasn't prepared for that. Not yet. Maybe she never would be.

That admission pulled her skin tighter and muzzled that voice inside of her shouting for more. Tears prickled up her throat, but she swallowed them back. They were pointless. She'd be fine. No, she *was* fine. This was just a brief phase she'd get over soon. That was all.

It was just a phase.

Maybe if she repeated it enough, it'd become true.

Chapter Seven

"Burns!"

Ryan whipped his head around, scowl in place. "What?" The defensive response snapped out before he could contain it.

Charles Cummings glowered right back, thick brows drawn low over sunken eyes ringed with dark circles. "Where's your head?"

The soft whisper of *boy* floated unsaid at the end of that sentence to taunt Ryan with the man's superiority. One implied but rarely displayed—except in Ryan's head.

His stomach soured, the sick swirl of shame coating him before he could curb it. "Sorry." He sat forward, straightened his glasses. "I apologize." He picked up his pen, focus intent. "You were saying?"

Charles swiveled his head, his disappointment clear. "What part did you last hear?"

A wince kicked at his chest, but he managed to keep his expression flat. This was his job. His thoughts never wandered at work. Never.

He cleared his throat, mind blank. Which case were they talking about? His gaze drifted down the long table to land on the dark-haired minx sitting at the end.

Laptop out, gaze locked on the screen, hair curling over her black blouse.

"Ms. Wakeford," Charles barked. She whipped her head up, brows raised. "Can you enlighten Mr. Burns?"

The paralegal smiled politely. "Of course."

She proceeded to provide a rundown of the Oakman case that Charles was currently litigating, regarding land rights and lease agreements. Ryan understood the details of the case even though it wasn't his. He made a point of knowing the major components of every active case in the event he was called to assist. That was what a partner did—in his opinion at least.

The low note of Brie's—Brighton's—voice floated across the room to encircle him. More clipped than the night in the Boardroom. Professional now. Yet he couldn't miss the smoky undertones that wrapped around his chest and dug up the images of her riding him, head tossed back, breasts full and glorious as she came.

A visual that easily transferred to the table stretched between them.

Damn it. He swung his seat around to focus on Charles.

"I've got it," he said, cutting Brie—Brighton—off without looking at her. "I believe you're in the right," he told Charles before he expanded his conclusion. He firmly locked her out of his awareness and kept his attention on the other partners.

Cummings, Lang and Burns was a long-established San Francisco law firm that Ryan had dedicated his adult life to. Literally. He'd set his sights on being exactly in this position when he'd first stepped into Berkeley Law school, and nothing had deterred his focus.

He'd done everything required of him to be offered this coveted seat next to Cummings and Lang before he'd hit forty. That included the sixteen-hour days and marrying a suitable woman, one who'd been the perfect society wife until she'd realized his social aspirations differed greatly from hers. As in he had none.

He refused to screw it up now—or to tarnish his own reputation by daydreaming about a woman. A random woman he'd fucked in the Boardroom.

One of many since he'd joined the exclusive group.

His attention didn't waver through each of the reports provided by the team of lawyers seated around the table. The weekly briefing kept everyone abreast of issues and workload and allowed them to assign new cases as they came in.

And he'd been caught daydreaming in the middle of this one.

The ridicule crawled up his nape to dig into his skull. Respect was earned, not given, and he'd worked too damn hard to get his. Thankfully in-office sightings of Brie—Brighton—Ms. Wakeford—were few.

Not that it'd matter.

Keeping his dick in his pants had never been his problem. Sex had one purpose and it wasn't to ensnare him in thorny scandals or messy entanglements. Hence, the beauty of the Boardroom.

"The Marlow contracts are finalized, correct?" Charles posed the question to Ryan knowing they were.

"Yes," he confirmed. He didn't expand when there was no need to.

"Good." Charles nodded, his balding head catching the glare of the fluorescent lights. Vanity obviously wasn't high on his list of worries, yet he carried his power with a dignity that negated his physical flaws. He returned his focus to the table at large. "Are there any other items that need to be addressed?"

The array of swiveling heads and mumbled negatives meant the meeting was adjourned. Ryan stayed seated as the others gathered their stuff and filed from the boardroom. Charles hadn't asked that last question of him without having a purpose. Nothing the man did was without purpose.

He'd assessed that within weeks of starting his first internship with the firm.

Ryan scanned the parade of dark tailored suits and stylish business dress that leaned heavily to the conservative side. Exactly the image the firm wanted to present and one he endorsed.

Brighton Wakeford was a perfect representation of that image. Her blouse and skirt were both sleek and sedate while still being feminine. Her makeup was minimal yet accentuated her eyes. Big, beautiful eyes that revealed little in the office.

But how would they be in the Boardroom? Expressive? Knowing? Lust-filled?

She tucked a lock of hair behind her ear, placed her computer on top of a stack of folders after grabbing one. Her strides were confident, shoulders back as she approached their end of the table.

"Here's the information you requested." Brie handed a legal-sized manila folder to Charles. "Do you need anything else?"

Did she have any clue who Ryan was? That he'd been in that room with her just two weeks back? That he'd kissed that mole at the edge of her collarbone? That he'd held her hips and driven into her as she'd begged to come?

Now he *was* being the damn pervert who lusted after subordinates. Disgust swirled in his stomach to stir up the sick muck of loathing from earlier. He'd never sink that low. Be that low.

"That'll be all," Charles told her. "Thank you."

Ryan forced his gaze to remain on Charles, but the rest of his senses homed in on Brie as she collected her belongings and left the room. A long inhalation found only stale coffee and the underlying scent of ammonia, not her light yet sultry fragrance.

The one he couldn't place yet couldn't forget.

"Are you sure about this one?" Victor Lang asked, motioning to the documents in Charles's hand. The other partner was portly in the aged way that somehow kept him from being classified as overweight. Or more likely, the respect he'd earned and still worked to hold kept tongues from wagging negatively.

Charles lifted his shoulder in dismissal. "That's why I'm having Burns look at it." He shoved the folder across the table to him. "The request comes from a friend of my wife," he went on, brows drawing low. "Barbara asked me to consider it, and I have." He motioned to the folder. "But it's in your court if we take it on."

Meaning, it'd be his if he agreed.

Ryan flipped the folder open and scanned the summary document neatly placed on top. Succinct, organized and laid out with pros, cons and open items, he scanned the information in a matter of minutes, admiration for Brie's skills increasing with every paragraph.

"Mutual relationships prevent me from touching it as well," Victor added, sitting back. His shirt was too well tailored for the buttons to give even a hint of being stretched. He tapped his pen on the table, the habit one he used to both intimidate and distract.

Ryan ignored it but noted it all the same.

His name might be on the door and scripted in gold across the company letterhead, but he was still the junior partner.

The one who had to prove himself every damn day—without appearing to do so.

He flipped the file closed and folded his hands over it, leaning in. "I'll take a deeper look at it later." His stomach settled as he found his comfort zone. "What aren't you telling me?"

The men shared a look, the silence tempered with indecision before Charles cracked a smile. His deep, rolling chuckle held the hearty note of an amused grandfather. Yet another thing Ryan ignored.

Playing into their hands wasn't how he'd earned his position. There were plenty of yes-men in the firm who took care of stroking their egos—and his own.

He kept his expression neutral and waited them out. He'd get the information he wanted, or he'd leave the folder on the table, his decision made. And they both knew that.

Charles sat forward, his laugh dying away. He cleared his throat, checked the open doorway. "Barbara's family is intertwined with this company." He let that rest for a moment, the implications sinking deeper.

"How intertwined?" And how much was Charles himself involved?

Charles brushed it off. "Just longtime friends. You know how connections work in the Valley." He glanced at Victor who nodded in confirmation. "I wouldn't have looked at the case if it was more than that."

Ryan studied him, doubts alive. There was no success in this business without them. "I hope Bri—Ms. Wakeford has documented every connection and association within the firm, so I understand the political dynamics."

"I told her to," he said, an edge to his voice. "I have nothing to hide. Lang and I simply have connections on both sides of this property issue, and from a firm standpoint, it'd be better if you took the case, or we'll pass."

"Good." Ryan scooped up the folder along with his notepad and other items as he stood. "I have a meeting in thirty." He nodded at the men. "I'll let you know if I have questions." He lifted the folder to indicate the case.

They tracked his departure, their steady stares hitting him in the back as he exited. He didn't need eyes on the back of his head to know that. He might be the only other current partner, but he wasn't the first to have his name listed next to theirs.

Cummings and Lang had started the firm when Ryan was still learning to read. They'd fought and worked for the reputation they now maintained. He'd understood exactly what that meant before he'd signed the paperwork and taken out the massive loan required to buy into the firm.

That was also why he wasn't too concerned about the mystery case handed off to him. Both men would rather die than see their lifeblood tarnished.

That alone had driven his desire to be a part of the company.

"I'll have my usual for lunch," he told Carla, his executive assistant, as he passed by her desk. "At one, please."

"Yes, sir." Her polite smile matched her voice. "Will you need anything from me for your meeting?"

"No. Thank you."

"Should I send—" She glanced at her computer screen, clicking her mouse as her brows dipped and then lifted. "Mr. Crawford in when he arrives?"

"That'd be great."

He left his smiling assistant, a faint grin ghosting over his own lips. Carla was competent in an old-fashioned way. What she lacked in technical skills, she made up for with her cunning insight and honest kindness that held no ulterior motives. He didn't require much, and experience had taught him that having anyone more ambitious only resulted in a bored assistant and ruffled feathers—neither of which he had time for.

Self-reliance was the cornerstone of his success. Some leaned on family connections, others on business networks and still others on charm and personality. He had his work ethic and determination, that was it.

Charm could fade, and networks could crumble. And training someone to meet his standards took more time and oversight than if he just did it himself. Even as a partner.

He dropped the files on his desk, rolled his shoulders back. The day stretched ahead on yet another series of meetings and briefings, followed by hours of reading, research and reports. He glanced at his calendar and wrote up a list of items for the associate attorneys to handle, made another for the intern assigned to him. And still another for the paralegals he shared with Lang.

He could delegate just fine. He also had standards that left many cursing his name.

And that was their issue to resolve.

He had his own to deal with, including the new one handed to him this morning. Brie Wakeford, however, was not on that list.

She'd never know it was his fingers that'd left the imprints on her hips. Or his dick that'd filled her until she'd crumbled in ecstasy.

Or his lips that'd ghosted over her temple when they'd both been too wrung out to speak.

Chapter Eight

Brie sank into her chair, exhaustion dripping from every limb—not that she'd let it show. Not at work. A glance at the clock indicated it was closing in on six. The desks around hers had started to empty, but over half of them were still filled with diligent employees, much like herself.

There was no rest for those determined to climb the ladder. Every dedicated hour was put in with the hopes that their work would be recognized and rewarded. A word of praise, a bonus, a raise, a shot at partner for those who could earn it—all and any of those things were markers of success.

Ones defined by society and ingrained in each of them before they'd taken their first job.

Understanding and seeing the artificial designations didn't stop her from striving to achieve every one of them—except partner. She wasn't an attorney, much to her mother's disappointment.

She snatched up her office phone after one ring, voice set on competent before she spoke. "Brighton Wakeford speaking."

"Brighton. This is Carla." Her mind did a quick shuffle to place the woman. "Mr. Burns would like to meet with you regarding the case briefing you compiled about the…" The pause was brief, but dragged on Brie's tired nerves. "… Palmaro case."

Brie swallowed hard before she responded brightly. "Of course. When would he like to meet?"

"Now?"

Was that a question? She almost laughed aloud at that. "No problem. I'll be right there." Mr. Cummings would've strangled his assistant if she'd posed the request as a question.

She disconnected the call and paused for one brief moment to rub at the ache growing in her temple.

Two weeks later and she was still cycling through the emotional remains of her night of passion. Sleepless nights, coupled with long days put in with the hopes of inducing dreamless slumber only added to her annoying sense of disconnect.

It was beyond time she got over herself and moved on. The night hadn't been *that* amazing or life-changing. Not really.

If only she could stop thinking about it…

She brushed the wrinkles from her blouse, straightened her skirt when she stood. She didn't have time to lament about her own faults and unsettled thoughts. Not when Mr. Burns was waiting for her.

She grabbed her copy of the briefing, tucked her notepad beneath, popped a mint into her mouth and headed to his office.

Ryan Burns was the dark shark of the firm. Precise, dedicated and over two decades younger than the other partners. He had a trail of admirers that spanned both sexes. Brie had no problem admitting she was one of them.

He was drop-dead gorgeous in that well-mannered, collected way her mother would flutter over. That alone should've repelled her, but it didn't. The icy chill that surrounded him added an air of…not bad boy, but assassin or spy—007 style—that placed him miles from the country club airs.

And this was the first time he'd ever called her to his office.

She primarily worked for Mr. Cummings. The other paralegals shifted between the attorneys based on need, but she'd been tucked under Mr. Cummings's authority within weeks of her employment. He was good to work for and treated her with respect even as he passed more and more of his duties to her. She took each new task as a compliment to her skills and then added ten hours to her work week.

Her stomach did a small flip when she reached Mr. Burns's outer office. Her chest tightened with a flash of nerves she didn't want.

He was just a man. One of her bosses. There'd been zero reports of him actually biting anyone's head off, although his quiet reprimands were said to be far more painful.

"He's waiting for you," Carla said when she looked up. "I have to leave, but he usually works pretty late."

Brie smiled at the inane statement. The entire office knew that Mr. Burns was the first to arrive and the last to leave every single day. There'd been young blowhards determined to outdo him, only to fail in less than a month.

"Thank you," she said. "Have a good night."

"You too." The sincerity in Carla's voice stole a bit

of Brie's annoyance, which was mostly focused on herself anyway.

Carla draped her coat over her arm and picked up her purse as she stepped around her desk. Lodged somewhere in her sixties, if her gray hair and wrinkles were any indication, Carla had the intentions of a saint and the absentmindedness of a scattered artist. The juxtaposition baffled Brie, who made it her job to never forget a detail.

One mistake on a briefing could cost the company thousands in legal fees.

Brie hesitated, unsure if she should speak up, but company policy raged in her head when the other woman started to walk away.

"Ah, Carla," she called, mystified and amused at once. "Shouldn't you shut down your computer before you leave?"

"Oh. Yes." Carla spun around, her expression focused as she returned to her desk. "Thank you. I must've forgotten when you walked up."

Brie frowned. Had the dig been intentional or another distracted mistake? Whichever it was, she didn't have time to stress over it.

Mr. Burns was waiting.

She stepped up to the doorway, heart fluttering with nervous energy. Her soft knock rippled through the room to drag his attention from his computer. The dark-framed glasses he wore shifted his appearance from sleuth to professor. A very handsome professor.

"Mr. Burns?" She stepped through the doorway, chin lifted. "You asked to see me?"

"Yes." He removed his glasses as he shifted his chair around. "Please. Come in."

Her feet stalled for some foreign reason as her brain hitched over the subtle drop in his tone. A sexy baritone note that pinged at a night she couldn't seem to forget.

No. Way.

A hard mental shake had her moving forward despite the churning in her stomach. "You have questions regarding the Palmaro briefing?" Her courteous tone was ingrained in her to the point that she didn't have to think about using it, thankfully, because her insides had suddenly turned to goo.

"Yes." He motioned to the visitor's chair. "Please. Have a seat."

Thank God. She didn't know how much longer her legs would've kept her upright. This was sheer lunacy. She'd heard his voice hundreds of times before and not once had it ever done this to her.

Flashes of that night blazed into her mind without warning or desire. She could almost feel the hard surface of the table beneath her knees as she lifted herself over *him*, her head tossed back, his hands digging into her hips as he met each descent with a hard thrust of his own.

"Ms. Wakeford."

The reprimand in his voice had her head shooting up, spine stiff against the accusation. "I'm sorry," she quickly said. "You were saying?" That was the second time that day she'd been caught daydreaming about sex.

And that didn't account for the times she hadn't been caught.

The edge of his mouth quirked up in what could almost be classified as a smirk. Did he smirk? She'd never witnessed it before. It was devastating, whatever it was.

The hair on her arms lifted in a dance of awareness

she didn't fully comprehend. Her stomach performed a dip and dive that flooded her pussy with desire. Hot, naughty want sizzled to life where it had no business sparking.

No. Just no.

He cleared his throat, the rumble completely innocuous. Yet her nipples tightened to sharp buds that said it was anything but. How?

He snagged a folder from his desk and opened it with a brisk efficiency that should've triggered her to do the same, but her eyes remained fixed on his movements. Long fingers graced otherwise normal hands and flipped through the papers with precision. Would his touch be gentle or firm?

Her gaze tracked to his wrists, first one, then the other, in a hunt that held no logic. His shirt cuffs were cinched tight where they peeked out from beneath his black suit jacket. Disappointment whipped in to jerk her back to the moment.

This moment. Not one two weeks ago.

She dropped her head and opened the briefing, pulse pounding in her ears. Her throat ached for liquid she didn't have.

"Can you clarify the information on page two, item six B one, please?"

Could she? "Certainly." She had this.

She flipped through the pages and proceeded to answer his question, along with the rest that he fired off as he dug through the document. His concentration forced her own and brought the roaring lust down to a dull simmer.

But it shouldn't be there at all.

She flicked her gaze up, caught him staring at her.

The deep brown of his eyes hypnotized her with their quiet assessment. Her chest contracted around the want raging unchecked.

This was so wrong—on every front.

"Is something wrong, Ms. Wakeford?"

She snapped back, gaze dropping. "No, sir." Her heart attempted to pound its way out of her chest. Could he see that? Did it show through her shirt? It felt like it should. "Could you clarify your confusion on that last paragraph?" she asked, voice remarkably steady. She owed that to years of dealing with her mother's expectations.

Emotions aren't for display.

A long pause forced her to look up, her smile that simple pleasant one she'd worn through most of her life. *Be nice. Be good. Don't rock the boat or lower yourself to someone else's standards.*

She could handle this and any situation thrown at her—as long as her libido didn't suffer a catastrophic meltdown.

And that was something she'd have to tackle. Soon.

"Is there anything else?" she asked when they reached the last page of the document. Her blouse clung to the sweat that'd accumulated on her back for no obvious reason. The air-conditioning kept the office in an over-chilled state that would've been a blessing now, only it didn't seem to be on.

He flipped the folder closed, clasping his hands on top. Was that a watch poking out beneath his shirt? One with a dark leather band?

"That's all for now," he said, jolting her from her illogical thoughts. "But I may have more later."

"Not a problem," she answered, standing. "Let me

know if I can assist you further." Did that sound suggestive?

"I will. Thank you."

She made her exit as smoothly and quickly as possible. Her breath flew from her lungs the second she was down the hall, around the corner and so far from his office there was no chance he'd see her.

Her pulse still raced, and heat radiated from her skin. There was no way she could continue like this. Her mind scattered, her thoughts consumed by lust, desire flaring at totally inappropriate times.

But how did she shake it? Did she really want to?

She dropped the files on her desk and plopped into her chair. The office had emptied out, leaving her free to show every damn emotion blazing within her. She rubbed her hands over her face and tried to collect herself. But how?

She grabbed her phone and dialed up the friend who'd gotten her into this mess.

Lori answered on a cheery "Hey, Brie! What's up?"

"We need to talk." There was no preamble or humor in her voice. She could only think of one solution to her problem, and now that she'd locked on to it, her mind was set.

"Okaaay." The drawn-out word communicated Lori's caution. "About what?"

She waited a beat, pulse skipping before it sped off again. She'd been denying it to herself since she'd left that room weeks ago, but the truth rang true and clear once she'd set it free.

"I want to go back."

No. She *had* to go back.

Chapter Nine

The sun baked down on Brie the second she exited the car. She squinted up at the cloudless sky, appreciating the warmth and clear blue expanse before turning back to thank the driver. She watched the little compact whiz out of the circular drop-off area in front of the country club, smirking at how out of place it looked next to the luxury vehicles.

Hiring a car from the Walnut Creek BART station was easier than trying to arrange a ride with her parents. One missed departure time had taught her that valuable lesson. Standing contritely beside her mother as she repeatedly apologized for being late was enough to ensure Brie never did it again.

She braced a hand on her abdomen and sucked in a deep breath. This was just brunch. She did it every damn week. Yet each time was getting harder and harder to survive. The facade she'd erected so long ago had suffered severe cracks since her night of wild sex.

And she was going to be blindfolded in a room full of men, again. Soon.

An excited thrill fluttered in her stomach. She just had to make it through the coming week. Six days and she'd be back in the room acting out the naughty thoughts that'd plagued her since she'd blasted a hole through her lust dam. Or was it a kink dam? Maybe it was just a freaky wild freedom dam?

But first she had to get through brunch.

She tucked her sweater into her bag and ducked into the bathroom to check her hair and makeup. The commute from the city wasn't long, but her mother would find every flaw—and comment on it.

Hair brushed, lipstick reapplied, she took another long breath and settled into Brighton mode. She found the calm patience needed for her mother and added the sniper shield required to fend off any unsuspecting attacks.

She greeted the hostess with a smile. "Hi, Kayla. How's it going today?"

The young woman gave her a pleasant grin filled with a bit of wincing truth. "Good." She leaned in. "Mrs. Kaminski had a run-in with Mrs. Adams about twenty minutes ago," she said softly, shooting a darting glance around them.

"Oh, no," Brie sympathized. The feud between the two women had been going on for years. From what she understood, it'd all started over a parking spot, which had morphed into an ongoing battle of one-upmanship on everything from seating spots to golf carts. "What was it about this time?"

"The flowers on the table." Kayla rolled her eyes. "Apparently Mrs. Adams thought her arrangement was smaller."

Brie stifled a snicker. "Of course she did."

She waved her goodbye, her smile still locked into place as she wove through the tables set up on the patio.

The unfortunate truth was just about everyone at the club had some kind of rivalry going on with someone else.

And she was failing her mother in the "my daughter snagged her MRS degree with the eligible doctor, lawyer, tech guru—fill in the blank as seen fit—and is popping out adorable grandbabies" race. Like that was the only goal Brie had in life.

"Brighton," her mother chimed when she was still two tables away. "You look lovely."

Brie kept her smile in place despite the sharp pang in her stomach when every person in the surrounding area turned to look at her. She kept her focus on her parents and ignored the urge to glance around to see exactly how close Rose Jacobson was seated with her "eligible" son.

"Morning, Mother." Brie dipped to brush a kiss on her cheek. "You look nice, like always." Joanne Wakeford never looked anything but nice.

"Thank you," her mother preened. The precise cut of her hair framed her face with its pale blond ends. The gray had long been tastefully blended to create natural highlights instead of bold statements of age. Just like the small creases at the corners of her eyes that mimicked laugh lines, and the soft shades of makeup that brightened her eyes and added a glow to her cheeks. "Is that dress new?"

Her mother pointedly scanned Brie's navy cap-sleeve dress. The scoop neck landed broad on her shoulders but sat high on her chest. No cleavage. Not for brunch. The dress hugged her curves to end a respectable two inches above her knee.

Brie glanced down, resentment flicking to life to twist in her chest. Years of interpreting her mother's questions—which were actually comments—left little doubt to her disapproval. She didn't even try to guess why.

She forced a breezy smile. "Not really." She fisted her hand to keep from smoothing it down her side. Any hint of discomfort would be a win for her mother. Yet the expected compliment for her mother's designer yellow dress dried up on her tongue when it would've been easier just to spit the platitude out.

Her dad rose from his seat as her mother opened her mouth. "You look beautiful, honey," he said, successfully cutting off whatever comment her mother had been about to make. He wrapped her in a hug. "Like always," he added near her ear.

"Thank you," she whispered as he pulled out her chair. Her stomach settled a little at the reminder that the harsh judgments didn't run through her entire family.

Her father managed to pull off that older GQ model vibe that meshed with her mother's sophisticated appearance. His gray hair went perfectly with the age lines that creased his high forehead and spread in tiny cracks around his eyes behind the silver frames of his glasses.

"Are you golfing after this?" she asked him. His polo shirt and khaki slacks were the standard dress code for men in the club, especially on the weekends.

He glanced at his watch. "Tee time is at noon." His grin was quick, his wink even faster.

Brie's laugh released an honest burst of affection. She reached over to squeeze his arm. "Good luck."

His scoff was full of bluster. "I don't need luck."

"He's playing with Stephano," her mother said, her gaze pointed above her smile. "He knows how to handle that." Meaning, her dad would let the other man win because Stephano was a notoriously poor loser who held a lot of clout.

"Anyway," Brie said, pitching her tone into a lighter octave. "How are you doing, Mother? What happened with your charity event? Did everything go well?"

The divergent topic worked exactly as planned. Her mother dove into a long-winded story of the event that included every detail of failures by others and what went wrong instead of right. But the appropriate sympathetic notes and affirmations from Brie got them through most of the meal.

"I can't believe she did that," Brie said after wiping her mouth with the napkin, when she actually sympathized with the woman her mother was complaining about.

"Neither can I," her mother huffed, her chin lifting in a show of indignation. "I'll think twice before volunteering with her again."

"I understand," Brie agreed, knowing her mother was most likely already on another committee with every woman she'd just complained about.

Her mother had spent countless hours dedicating her time and efforts to charitable causes. Her generosity may have been induced by the desire to appear giving, but that didn't diminish the good work she'd done and continued to do.

Her mother wasn't evil, not by any definition of the term.

A faint breeze drifted over the patio to bring the scent of fresh-cut lawn. It blended with the more tempting aromas from the excellent food being served, triggering memories that dated back to her childhood. Of family meals here and the activities and social groups they'd been a part of because of the club.

A membership that'd stretched the family budget, but one her mother had insisted was necessary.

"How's work been?" her father asked.

"Good." She took a drink of her coffee. "Charles keeps me busy."

Her dad's low chuckle swept her up in its warmth. His eyes sparkled just a bit when he said, "I bet he does. I hope he's not working you too hard."

"No." She loved every second of it. "He's good." Her father's loose connection with Charles Cummings had helped her land the job at the law firm. But she'd ensured that everything she'd achieved since then had been based on her own merit. "And yours?"

"The same," her father brushed off. He never talked about his job or the specifics of what he did at the tech company. He was a company man whose own dedication and hard work had risen him through the ranks to his current VP position.

"Have you met any nice men at work?" her mother asked Brie, bringing the conversation back to one of her mother's favorite topics. Her smile held a fake innocence that Brie had stopped falling for before she'd hit middle school.

"There are a lot of nice men there." She waited a beat. "And women too."

"Maybe, but you're not going to marry one of the women."

A sharp laugh burst free before she could hold it back. She quickly morphed it into an agreeing note before her mother caught the bitterness in the tone.

"You never know..." she teased, to cover her slip. A

part of her wanted to do exactly that if only to spite her mother, but she really didn't swing that way.

"That's not funny, Brighton." Her mother sat forward, glancing around. "You're thirty years old. I know women are having children later, but the risks increase too. Don't you want a husband and family to take care of?"

The earnest honesty in the question was a firm reminder of her mother's priorities, ones that were so different from Brie's. Yes, she wanted a husband and family, but not so she could take care of them.

"What about all those lawyers you interact with every day?" her mother went on. "You could've snatched one of them up years ago. The good ones will all be attached soon if you wait much longer."

"Joanne," her father warned, his tone one of patience.

"What?" Her mother let out a huff, sitting back. "It's true."

The topic wound its way into their conversation on a regular basis, but it didn't stop the irritation from prickling down Brie's neck and digging into her stomach. Pleasing her mother had once been the sole goal of her young life—until she'd figured out there was no pleasing her. There would always be something wrong, some negative that'd override every positive.

"So you want me to sleep my way to the top?" Brie asked, the snark slipping into her tone when she was usually so careful to hold it back.

Her mother bristled, her scowl pulling deep. "Don't be crass."

"What?" Brie shoved the fake innocence back at her. "That's exactly what a workplace romance would insinuate." Especially when she wasn't a lawyer herself.

The slight narrowing of her mother's eyes was yet another clue to her rising irritation. "You interact with plenty of lawyers who don't work at your firm."

The circular discussion always came back to Brie's lack of effort. Was it true? Maybe. Bringing a man to meet her mother was one of her worst nightmares. Especially one who fit the idealized mold her mother had formed for Brie's perfect husband.

Rich. Connected. Handsome. Respected.

Her thoughts raced to Ryan Burns, the epitome of that very list. The ding, ding, ding of the checklist rang in her head and soured her stomach. Bringing a man like Ryan home would only prove her mother right and have Brie once again falling into line just like expected.

How pathetic was it that that was the last thing she wanted to do, when meeting her mother's expectations had been the foundation of her life? Thankfully, she wasn't embittered enough to bring home the antithesis of that "perfect" man just to piss her mother off.

"Rose," her mother boomed, the higher note in her voice ringing like a warning bell to Brie. "How lovely to see you." Her mother stood to airbrush kisses over the woman's cheeks in the European fashion many within her mother's circle had adopted. "How's Michael's visit going?"

The mystery man had a name. Great. The burn returned, her chest tightening against the resentment rising in her throat. But she kept her smile pleasant even as her hand fisted in her lap.

"Brighton, honey," her mother said, touching her shoulder in a subtle indication that Brie should stand, which she did on cue. "You remember Mrs. Jacobson, right?"

"Of course," Brie answered, leaning down to give the smaller woman the expected air-kiss greeting. "How are you doing?" She had the pleasantries down. It didn't matter that she had only vague memories of the dark-haired woman with the perfect bob and pale pink summer suit.

"I'm good, thank you." Rose glanced at Brie's mother, a conspiratorial gleam in her eye. "Your mother's been telling me all about you," she went on. "You're working in the city now? At a law firm?"

Brie let out a light laugh to cover her annoyance. "Yes. I'm a paralegal." And it wasn't a new event.

Rose's eyes grew wide in a show of impressed speculation that could've been faked or real. "That sounds so exciting."

"I like it." It was best to keep it simple sweet.

"I was really hoping to introduce you to my son, but he had to leave." Her frown came close to a pout. "He had an urgent call he had to take from the hospital. He's a doctor. An orthopedic surgeon." She added the last bit with a note of pride.

"Oh, darn," Brie's mother said, her lips twisting down. "I hope everything's okay," she added, her manners kicking in.

"I'm sure it is. He's supposed to be back this afternoon," Rose said, speculation displayed in her raised brows. "He has a three o'clock tee time if you're around."

Relief flooded in at the ready excuse. "Unfortunately I have a commitment this afternoon." Specifics weren't required when both women would be too polite to dig for details.

"I'm sure you could resched—"

"I can't," Brie cut her mother off, adding a deep

layer of regret to her voice. "I'm sorry." She included a sad frown to sell her tale. "Maybe next week? Will he still be here?"

"No." Rose released a disappointed sigh. "He's leaving tomorrow."

A small cheer went up in Brie's head for the dodge that wasn't her fault. Michael's well-timed call, whether it was real or faked, let her avoid a setup she was too old for.

Rose said her goodbyes and Brie did the same shortly after.

"You don't have to rush off," her mother admonished as she checked her watch.

"I'm sure you already have your afternoon planned," she said, knowing she was right. Her mother preferred to stay busy, a trait she'd given to Brie. "And it's almost Dad's tee time."

"I've got a few minutes, yet," her dad said, but he'd already flagged down their server for their tab.

"We'll see you next week, right?" Her mother waited with raised expectations even though Brie's attendance was basically mandatory.

"Like clockwork." She smiled through the glib response and grabbed her bag. "I love you." She gave both parents a quick kiss and made her exit before Rose's son made an early reappearance.

And what would he think of her upcoming sex plans? What would these prim women with their stifled views and proper images think? She snorted at her own delusions. She'd obviously drunk the Kool-Aid if she believed that a single person in this place was what they appeared to be.

People hid so much, including herself. It was past

time she had something good to hide. Like another night of wild, hedonistic sex with multiple men she didn't know.

What were the chances that *he'd* be there again? The one man that still haunted her dreams and incited her fantasies even though she had no idea who he was?

Probably little to none, but she could still hope. After all, he was the primary reason she was going back. He and his warm touch and concerned voice. His strength and devious fingers. His sense of calm that countered the passion.

If it hadn't been for him, she probably would've failed out of that night. But she hadn't. Not by a long shot. And she wouldn't the next time.

Chapter Ten

The darkness cloaking the building enhanced the deadly silences as Ryan strode down the hallway, senses pinging out for any sign of life. The solitude sunk into his awareness, honed by years of being the sole person working late in his office.

But this wasn't his office.

And he wasn't alone.

He stopped outside the boardroom, one he'd been in multiple times before, both for business and private reasons. He could still turn around, but then he'd prove nothing.

Brighton Wakeford wasn't an issue.

He stepped into the room, stopped. Every sense zeroed in on the woman sitting in the chair at the end of the table.

Brie.

A red piece of cloth covered her eyes and trapped her hair beneath its ties. The skimpy cover provided by her lacy black lingerie was more enticing than concealing. The outline of her nipples begged him to seek them out. And that thin piece of cloth between her legs did little to hide the secrets beneath.

The dark ends of her hair curled around her shoulders in sharp contrast to the pale tone of her skin. Skin he knew to be soft as silk beneath his fingertips.

His breath caught, need bursting free to wipe out every thought of leaving. He was here to fuck her. To drive her from his thoughts and burn her from his mind.

She was just a Boardroom fuck.

Her breasts rose and fell with each slow breath she took, their fullness enhanced by the subtle uplift of the bra. Did she wear that under her office clothes? Had she been wearing it last week when she'd sat on the other side of his desk?

This morning when they'd passed in the hallway?

His stomach clenched with an image he didn't need. Not when he was trying to banish every sinful one of them.

He dragged his gaze over the room, flicked his brow up at Jacob, who stood with his arms crossed in the far corner. The man lifted his chin toward Brie, a slow smile spreading.

There was just the three of them so far.

He shot Jacob a half-grin, anticipation switching to excitement. The moon was out, the fog nonexistent further down the peninsula. The glow lit the room just enough to shove back the dark. The office building rose above the surrounding area to provide a view of the bay and the long line of the San Mateo Bridge. Car lights glimmered white, yellow and red against the black of the water and night.

A lamp sat unlit on the credenza behind her. A part of him wanted to turn it on and tempt others to see. But it wasn't his scene or call.

Jacob had organized it again. Another scene for his birthday-girl guest. Only it wasn't her birthday this time.

Brie had asked to come back. The stunning, surprising Brie.

One night of excess could be excused by anyone. A second, deliberate return was completely different.

He could've—should've—ignored the post. But how could he miss this?

He dragged his gaze down to her spread legs, finally noting the loose pull of her arms behind the chair. Bound?

Fuck.

The knot in his stomach sunk lower to untangle in his groin. Was this a gift or a punishment?

Neither.

It was just a scene.

He stripped off his suit jacket and slung it over the back of a chair along with his tie. Her slow breaths quickened. Did she sense him? Had she guessed who he was?

Had Jacob told her who was coming?

He rolled his cuffs up as he approached her. Her head tilted back, lips parting when he stopped before her. The fabric over her eyes didn't hide her beauty, yet his fingers itched to lift it off.

Blue. Her eyes were blue.

A basic blue.

And he could still picture them. Studying him. Confused. Shaken, maybe? Her own intuition taking hold? Their meeting had been totally professional, despite the overriding desire he'd had to bend her over his desk and hear her passionate cries as he drilled her from behind.

He ran a finger down her jaw in a single stroke of introduction. Her breath hitched, lips parting further.

"Brie," he said, dragging her name out, voice deepened to mask his identity. He probably shouldn't speak, yet he couldn't hold that back. Not in this room.

The Boardroom was the one place he could truly speak freely.

"You," she whispered, so much hope and relief layered into that single word.

His heart stopped, stomach dropping.

"You came back," she finished.

For one moment he thought he'd been identified. But he hadn't. At least not back to their office. To being her boss.

"I did." She tilted her head back as he drew his hand around the side of her neck and traced his thumb down the line of her throat. "Why the bonds?"

Her lip curled in to be trapped by her teeth before she let it slip out. "Jacob did it," she finally answered.

He slid his fingers down, skimmed them over that teasing little mole on the edge of her collarbone. The one that played a game of hide-and-seek depending on the blouse she wore. The one that reminded him of the passion she hid and the secrets they shared.

He continued down, tracing a line beneath her bra strap, teasing, yet savoring the soft heat of her skin. "Do you like it?"

"Maybe." The word was mouthed more than spoken.

Her chest lifted beneath his touch, those dark areolas tempting him beneath the lace. "Any new rules?"

Jacob had listed her limits, which remained the same as last time, but he had to check. Things could change once a scene began.

She pushed her breasts up, back arching in invitation. "No."

"Any desires?"

He ran his finger beneath her bra to rub it over her nipple. She sucked in a breath, held it. He started a slow back-and-forth over the soft nub as it started to harden. Her breath released on a soft sigh.

"You." She winced. "Please."

He bit back the curse that wanted to burst free. His heart pinched but he ignored the strange pain as heat whipped through him.

"I want you to fuck me," she went on. "Please."

His dick went from interested to *hell yes* in a breath. How could this be the calm, organized woman from his office?

He ran his finger up to trail a circle around the edge of her lips. The red stain was a few shades darker than the material covering her eyes and highlighted each lush curve. They parted again, her tongue playing on the inner edge.

The slight change in her request wasn't a mistake. She didn't make those.

"Should I fuck you from behind?" he asked, teasing her bottom lip. The image of her bent over his desk hadn't faded in the days since their meeting. "Over the table?" Where he could control the pace, the depth, the entire experience.

Her breaths deepened, a low rumble filtering out. "Yes. That."

Sheer will held back the predatory growl in his chest, his dick flooding with desire. Did she know what she was doing to him? How crazy just the thought made him?

He cupped her chin, lifted it higher. She gulped, swallowed. A shiver shook her upper body, but she didn't object.

Power surged up to nip at the drive that'd dug him

out of an abusive childhood. He owned this scene and by extension her—for tonight.

"What if you don't like something?" he challenged, his hand drifting down to encircle her throat. He was testing her in a rather dickish way. Yet he loved the rapid thump of her pulse beneath his thumb, the excitement racing over his skin.

Her throat bobbed beneath his palm, her jaw flexing. "I say stop."

The firm beat of her words sent a jolt of pride humming through his chest. She wouldn't be pushed around—unless she wanted to be.

He dipped, inhaled. Right there, near her ear. That elusive fresh-yet-naughty scent wove into him, triggering the hard flutter of want eager to break free.

He straightened, glanced over his shoulder. Jacob remained in the same position, a satisfied smile on his face. He caught a movement from the corner of his eye and shifted enough to see another man in the opposite corner. Trevor James. The Boardroom founder and overseer.

When had he snuck in? Why was he here? He hadn't been on the scene list earlier today.

Trevor lifted his chin and motioned for Ryan to continue.

The quick bite of tension eased. Apparently, the two of them were going to be center stage tonight. It was a prospect he usually avoided, but tonight, with her, the rightness hummed through him.

And he didn't have the willpower to question it.

Chapter Eleven

The soft rub of his palm around her throat shouldn't have been erotic. It was.

Brie's breaths grew clipped, each hitch emphasizing the power he had over her. The knowledge buzzed in her mind and crowded next to the lust she couldn't seem to control. But she didn't have to here. Not with him.

Him.

After weeks of dreaming and days of imagining this very scenario, he was here.

The thrill of that alone ignited a frantic beat of hunger and longing she couldn't contain. And she didn't have to. That's why she'd come back. Not seeking him, yet seeking him.

Yes, she'd hoped he'd be here, but Lori had warned her it might not happen. That each scene was unique, the participants random.

And he was still here. Did it mean something?

No. Not above having amazing sex.

Wild. Debauched. Totally naughty sex.

He dipped low, his presence snapping over her nerves as he hovered near her ear. Again. She tensed, waited. For a kiss? A whispered word? A command?

That wonderful scent that was only his flowed into

her on a slow inhalation. She scrambled to identify the fragrance without success. It was just him.

"There are two other men here," he told her, his breath pooling on her neck. She shivered as the heat spread over her chest, teasing her more. Her nipples ached for attention, like her lips. Would he kiss her again? Claim her with his strength?

"They're going to watch us." He reached behind her, the hand on her throat tightening incrementally. Not threateningly, but enough to make her pulse race harder. Faster.

There was a tug on the cloth binding her wrists before they were freed. A wave of relief collided with confusion as her arms lowered.

"I have other plans for you."

Goose bumps sprang up on every exposed part of her flesh. How was that possible when she was anything but chilled? But the softer tone of his words managed to wrap their way around her heart. She still trusted him.

Trusted everything.

How could a location she didn't know with a group of men she'd barely, if ever, met be a safe zone? She didn't know the answer, but it was. And it was heaven.

The gentle urging on her arm had her standing, his hand still on her throat. She swayed, forced a hard swallow through the impossible arch of her neck. Her mind seemed to float in a sea of detached awareness.

This was freedom.

From expectations. From being in control.

From the fears that'd lined every action, every thought, every deliberate step she'd taken.

Here, in this room, she was simply his.

His thumb edged her jaw in a firm rub over her chin.

She rolled her head, savoring the slow drift that was tender yet not. A soft purr vibrated in her throat as she sank into his power.

"I can't believe you came back," he murmured, the words brushing over her cheek. He was so close, yet she didn't touch him. No, her hands were clasped behind her back, her chest thrusting up to him. There was strength in that too. In giving everything to him.

He skimmed his fingers down her abdomen as he slowly withdrew his grip on her neck. She swallowed on reflex, part of her mourning the loss of that possessive hold. He eased that hand around to her nape, the other hand slipping beneath the scrap of material claiming to be a thong.

She inhaled, stomach contracting. He teased the soft down of hair on her mound, that taunting awareness zinging down her pussy.

"I'm going to taste you tonight." The promise held strong even though his tone was low. She nearly screamed yes, only her voice was gone.

"Lick you." He slid a single finger between her folds, flicked it over her clit. Her knees bent, desire snaking out to churn with the building heat.

"Suck you." That naughty finger of his dipped into her. Her breath caught, trapped until he drew his hand back up.

He leaned down, his presence wrapping around her. Her breaths bounced off his to warm her lips and confirm she was still breathing. Expectation crawled over her skin, sunk into her chest, embraced her hope until she could think of nothing but the touch of his lips on hers.

The kiss she'd been longing for since his last soft goodbye.

"Then I'm going to fuck you," he whispered, each syllable peppering her lips with his promise.

"Yes," she finally managed to say. "Please."

His deep growl was cut off by the seal of his lips over hers. She moaned in response, mouth opening to take him in. God, yes. This. This and so much more.

He swept his tongue in, his hand on her nape holding her steady as he overpowered her. And she let him, her back dipping, muscles relaxing to melt into him. Every hard swipe was countered by a softer brush until it meshed into a wild crush of longing.

She gripped his shoulders, needing to be closer, wanting more. The freedom sang in her head and hummed in her blood. *This. This. This.*

Her control was forgotten as she pushed back, her tongue dueling with his. Each attack was met with a counter until a harmony was found. The rightness screamed over her senses when he gentled, slowed, frantic bleeding to savoring on a soft glide.

A hand on the small of her back urged her closer. Her hips met his on a cry of yes. His erection ran hard and firm up her lower abdomen to declare his passion. She'd been the cause of it. Her.

How could she not fall farther? Sink deeper?

She ran a hand up the back of his head, his hair tickling her palms, the strands soft yet coarse. Short. Professional. A little longer on top. Was it black? Blond? Brown?

He drew away, and her lips pulsed with each beat of her heart. Her chest heaved with the breath she couldn't seem to catch. Words were gone, thoughts scattered as he urged her forward three steps.

He came around behind her, his hands skimming

over her ribs and stomach before settling on her hips, drawing her back. She went willingly, resting into him. His shirt was almost abrasive against her skin, yet the cloth was soft. He rocked his hips, ran the length of his erection up the curve of her ass.

Her moan tore out on a rush of hunger. Want burned in her groin, the ache to be filled throbbing a demanding cadence.

"You're stunning," he said by her ear. He cupped her breasts, lifted them. "Every inch of you." He ran his palms down to her pussy.

Her legs dipped, a cry escaping. She reached back, gripping his ass for support. She squeezed, torn between awe at the firm muscles that clenched beneath her hands and the slow rub on her pussy.

"Can you feel them watching you?" He drew his tongue up the side of her neck, a finger sliding beneath her thong.

Need built in cresting waves that pummeled her reservations and lifted her higher. Her skin prickled with heat, over-sensitized by the thought of being watched. Of being on display like this.

She tilted her head, hips rolling into his touch. "I like it," she admitted. She'd analyze the implications later, but right now—it was amazing. Behind the mask, she could be this woman.

"She's beautiful."

The new voice put her on alert. She stilled, head turning to the sound. Jacob was still in the room somewhere. Or at least she thought he was.

"I told you."

There. In the other corner. His image floated into her head, but she quickly shoved it out. He was nice. He'd made her laugh on the way here. He never questioned her wants or made her feel badly about them.

But Jacob wasn't *him*.

She shifted her weight back, leaning fully on him. A long slow breath brought the scent of him. God. Another inhalation set her desire ablaze. He had her—again. The security wrapped around her like a gentle hug.

She could be anything with him. Even wickedly dirty.

Kinky.

This was heaven wrapped in the conception of hell. Her mother would croak in her designer pastel suit if she could see Brie now. A wicked little laugh bubbled out at the thought. She dug her fingers into his butt cheeks, rode the line of his erection.

She never imagined being naughty could be so fun.

His chuckle vibrated through her back and buzzed on her neck. "You're loving this."

"I am." She didn't have to lie.

He smoothed his hands up her sides as he straightened. He nudged her shoulder. "Bend over."

Her chest constricted for the moment it took his command to register. He eased her forward, and she brought her hands around to find the table. The cold surface soaked into her palms and then her chest as she slowly came to rest on its surface. A series of doubts shoved their way into her head in an attempt to dislodge the high she was floating on.

Good girls didn't do this. Good girls didn't ask for sex. Good girls didn't fuck.

Another deep giggle bubbled out as she spread her feet apart before he asked. She lifted her ass up, anticipation roaring through every nerve ending.

Her heart swelled with the freedom. Her pussy pulsed with the need to feel him in her. Thrusting hard. Sure. Owning her.

Her laughter changed to a moan when he yanked her thong down her thighs. *Yes. That.*

"Please fuck me," she begged yet again. She didn't care how it made her sound. Not when the only thing she really wanted was to feel his dick buried in her once again.

Chapter Twelve

The image before Ryan was better than the one he'd conjured of Brie over his desk. Her round ass was lifted in an offering so sweet he almost couldn't take his eyes off it. Her pussy lips glistened with her wetness, the small clenches begging him to sink into her.

He squatted, sucked in a long breath as he spread her open. The musky heat flooded him with a frantic hunger he barely contained. The heady taste hit him the second he ran his tongue through her folds. Her twitch and squeak became music to his lust.

He dipped back in, his sole purpose to give her pleasure. He wanted to hear every groan and cry, absorb each wiggle and hitch, make her feel as amazing as she was.

His gut churned with suppressed desire. Brie was beyond gorgeous like this. And she was all his to have. To tease and tempt.

He pressed his tongue over the hard nub of her clit. A low moan followed by quick pants floated down to him. The hot well of her vagina encased the tip of his tongue in coaxing invitation. His groan didn't come close to expressing the fire raging within him. It singed every restraint he lived within and threatened to burn through the walls that bound his thoughts and contained his desires.

She… Brie.

His knees protested the crouch and his thighs started to burn, but he remained focused. Brie writhed, rocking from her toes to the flats of her feet on an erratic pattern he didn't try to follow. He let her move, absorbing the energy and passion until he couldn't hold back.

Her cry of protest was a dose of lighter fluid to his control when he stood. The condom wrapper gave way with a harsh rip as he tore it open with his teeth. It took just seconds for him to free his erection from his pants. He left the fly hanging open, shoved his underwear down and rolled on the protection.

Only then did he pause, breaths ragged, blood roaring in his head.

Her back heaved with each breath, the dark lines of her bra accentuating the movement. A pang of regret nipped at his high at the sight of the blindfold. Would her eyes be darkened to a deep blue? Would the lids be heavy with lust?

But this was the only way.

He laid a hand on her back, smoothed it up as he stepped between her legs. The urge to hammer into her was squashed by the larger, bigger craving to enjoy every moment of this encounter.

It was all for her. She deserved to be cherished. Respected.

And he'd show her that.

He circled her opening with his cock head, his focus shifting between that and her profile. Her lip was clamped between her teeth in a hold he longed to soothe. He forced himself to wait for another beat, two, three until she lifted on her toes, whimpered.

Only then did he sink into the sweet heaven that was her.

His growl tore from the rush of satisfaction that raged in his groin and blinded his thoughts. His heart thundered against the barriers he'd placed around it so damn long ago he had no idea how to tear them down.

He sucked in a breath, blinked. He held her hips still as he slid out, mesmerized by the sight of his cock easing from her. This was power and connection as he rarely experienced. Why her? Why now?

His hard drive back into her heat ripped another groan from his chest. He let go then, let it all go. The ties that held him strong. The confines that set his direction. The focus that kept him steady.

He didn't need them here.

Each hard thrust pushed him deeper, and he fell willingly into the lust and ecstasy. "I can't get enough," he mumbled, lost. So damn lost.

"More," she whimpered, hands braced on the table as she pushed back.

Fuck. He'd never longed to see someone's face like he did right then. Was the passion etched into her brow? Her pupils dilated?

He shook his head, yet the thoughts wouldn't go away. The yearning only grew, spread until he wanted to scream at it, tear it out and set it aflame.

He pushed harder, feeding off her moans and cries. The hot clench of her pussy sucked at the strength he employed every damn day to simply keep going. It coiled in his groin, drew his balls tight, holding, holding, holding…

Her walls contracted around him, and he reached down to stroke her clit. Sweat collected on his nape, his muscles strung so tightly he could barely breathe.

The sharp burst of her cry timed with the hard clench around his dick unhinged the last of his restraint. He powered into her, taking everything until there was nothing but her. Brie.

The woman he should forget.

If only he knew how.

Awareness came back to Brie in small increments, penetrating the fuzzy haze she floated in. The press of his chest on her back. The braced weight holding her secure. The quick cuts of breath warming her neck and catching in her ear.

Words were elusive in the hushed peace that surrounded her. He still had her. She couldn't dismiss the sense of protectiveness that wrapped her up and kept her safe.

He was the most giving man she'd ever been with. This stranger who'd touched her as none other—both literally and emotionally.

Her breaths started to slow, the table bit into her thighs and an annoying pinch near her breast begged to be eased, yet she refused to move. Once she did, this would be over.

The glide of his dick slowly slipping from her said the seconds were ticking away. She wanted to clench him tight to hold him in, but that would only quicken the end.

She slid her hand over to find his where it rested on the table. The hard bumps of his knuckles guided her until she could lace her fingers between his. He curled his hand into a fist, trapping hers in a hold that reached down her arm to wrap around her heart.

The tenderness spread to bathe her in hope and more impossible wants. Ones that couldn't come true. Not here. Not with him.

He shifted up, pressed a long, tender kiss to her temple, a kiss that shattered the fragile wants struggling for life. His hand tightened around hers to send off a wave of churning anguish.

He slid it away, and she reluctantly let it go.

This was it.

"Thank you," he whispered. "You were stunning."

Her eyes burned, and her throat ached with the building loss. She couldn't cry, though. Not here, in front of these men. In front of *him*.

This was just sex.

Yet it wasn't.

Not for her.

And that was on her.

He lifted. His hand nudged her bottom as he slid from her, and the emptiness spread through her on a cold wave of reality. The table was suddenly hard and unyielding. The air chilled on her back and exposed ass. The gritty scent of processed wood rushed in to cover the heavier, sultry aroma of sex.

She lay there paralyzed as the soft rustle of material roared in her ears. The harsh rasp of his zipper was the final note on his pending departure.

A light touch on the small of her back nailed her with a flight of rejection. *No.*

No!

She wasn't ending it like this. Not as this weak, shattered girl.

She shot up, spinning to catch his arm before he withdrew. Her heart lurched into a frantic pace backed by the determination burning to life. Hope flared once again when he didn't withdraw. She had no idea if they were alone now and couldn't find it in her to care.

This man was all that mattered.

He was everything.

And she still had no clue who he was despite feeling as if she'd known him forever. Despite that acute awareness that he knew her, all of her, better than anyone in her real life.

The sharp cut of disappointment pierced her chest before she shoved it away. There was no room for that now. Not here.

Not when there was nothing stopping her from removing the mask—if she was only brave enough. And what would she do with the gained knowledge? A visual wouldn't change the reality of what this was.

A night of anonymous wild, passionate public sex.

She ran her hand down his arm, halting on his watch. The round surface bit into her palm, the band firm but soft beneath her fingers. A blind hunt with her other hand found the solid plane of his chest. God, how she wished for the heat of his skin instead of the barrier of his shirt.

The hard, rapid beat of his heart pounded its own statement into her palm. One that gave her something to cling to. A belief that he wasn't completely unaffected. That their connection wasn't a simple product of her imagination.

He didn't move as she skimmed her hand up to cup the side of his neck. The smooth flush of his skin along his jaw told her he'd shaven recently. Would his beard be full or sparse? Dark or possibly peppered with gray?

The amount she didn't know about him overwhelmed the little she did, yet there was no denying this tie. This…pull that tugged on her soul and screamed she *knew* him.

She lifted up as she urged him down to press her own last kiss on his jaw. She held it, eyes squeezed tight against the rush of emotion clamoring to escape. "Thank you," she managed to rasp, each word cutting lines in her parched throat. "For everything."

He remained stiff, the moment lapsing into emptiness as she lowered her heels to the ground. The urge to rip her blindfold off screamed up to defy every rule and agreement she'd signed.

Her stomach swirled with the muck of nerves, fear and want crammed into it. This was stupid. They were consenting adults. But he caught her hand as she dug her fingers beneath the edge of the material that blinded her.

"Don't."

That single syllable wiped out her courage along with her fledgling dreams. Questions screamed through her mind, but she bit her tongue to hold them in. She refused to grovel when she'd signed up for just this.

Blind, unknown sex.

Was he married? A politician? A celebrity?

She was just a random fuck. She knew that.

The truth still cut when it shouldn't.

She dropped her hands, chin lifted as she stood there fully exposed. She wouldn't cower despite the glaring awareness that she stood there in nothing but her bra—with an audience.

"All right," she said, resolute. This was the end.

He moved away, her senses tracking him as he went around the table, pausing briefly before he left the room.

The weight hit her the moment he was gone. Her bones threatened to turn to mush when she wanted nothing more than to sink through the floor and disappear. A blanket was eased around her shoulders, causing her to flinch, but she clutched it automatically, grateful for the protection.

"Are you okay to walk?" Jacob asked, concern so tender in his voice. The ice surrounding her melted a little at his kindness.

"Yes," she assured him, completely unsure if it was true. But her feet moved, and her legs held her up as he ushered her from the room.

One she left with regret and relief.

The intensity was exhilarating in the moment, but was it worth it? Now? When she wished so badly for one more kiss, one more touch from a man she'd never know?

Yes.

Her heart broke and healed in one deep inhalation.

She'd be forever grateful for what he'd released within her. For the freedom he'd given her, even if it was for two short nights.

Because this person, this wild, sexual woman, wasn't going away. She lived now, and it was up to Brie to figure out how to manage her.

Chapter Thirteen

Ryan whipped his head up, coming to a halt a few feet from his car. Tension sprang through his spine to yank his shoulders back.

"What?" he snapped at Trevor, who rested against the door of Ryan's car.

Trevor's brow hitched up in an irritating display of starched question. He didn't shift from his lax position, hands tucked into his pants pockets, one foot lazily crossed over the other.

Ryan spread his stance, arms crossing in preparation for the apparent smackdown he no doubt deserved. Guilt ate at him, and he hadn't even made it out of the parking lot. Hell, it'd started before he'd stepped from the boardroom. Brie's display of strength hadn't concealed her hurt.

"What was that?" Trevor asked, his gaze lifting to the building behind Ryan.

"A scene." The snarky response was all he had.

"Right." Trevor straightened, stepping away from the car with a casual stride. Envy reared up to snip at Ryan. He'd tried his entire life to present that exact image without success. "Care to try that again?"

Not a chance in hell. He was done with Brie. There was no way he could repeat tonight.

"What do you want to know?" he countered. Trevor was digging, and Ryan wasn't in the mood for guessing games. Not when half of him was still focused on the building looming behind him. Was Brie okay? Was Jacob taking care of her properly?

Would they be coming out soon?

The muscles hitched tighter through his shoulders and knotted in his stomach. Chitchat was a skill he'd never acquired and had no interest in taking up, especially now.

Trevor took another step closer, eyes narrowing with that predatory focus he unleashed with precision. Ryan braced but refused to look away.

"That wasn't *just* a scene. Not for you."

Fucking hell. The man could be absolutely infuriating…and deadly accurate. Rage seethed in his chest when it'd do no good. Fighting back only resulted in a harder counterattack. Yet another lesson beaten into him from childhood.

A gust of wind blew in to sweep over Ryan's nape and ruffle Trevor's hair, which was more gray than brown. The nip of chill did little to diminish the clammy sweat that clung to his back.

"It was a scene," he restated, calm warning in his voice. "I don't grill you about Danielle." He let that stand. There was no need to expand.

Trevor's glare frosted over in less than a blink. The friendly charm switched to stony anger without a muscle moving. "Tread carefully."

His counter warning was sent with dual meaning

Ryan didn't miss. Trevor strode away then, his pace clipped.

Ryan tracked his departure for a long moment before he jerked around to get into his car. A pile of nervous energy buzzed over his skin as he sped out of the parking lot, headed toward the highway. Every bit of peace he'd found in Brie's arms had been erased the second he'd pulled out of her.

The moment when he'd fully accepted just how fucked he was.

And now?

There was nothing.

He wouldn't go back to her even if she did make another appearance in the Boardroom. The risk was too high. He'd lost himself and that wasn't acceptable.

He'd worked too fucking hard to let this derail everything he'd achieved.

He cruised onto the highway, heading back to the city on autopilot. The line of taillights gave him focus when it seemed he'd lost his own.

His conscience slipped out somewhere between San Mateo and South San Francisco to add another layer to the guilt nibbling away at him. Going back to the Boardroom, knowing she'd be there, had been a deliberate action.

And she had no idea that he was her superior.

He was a fucking lawyer. He understood every consequence his actions could rain down if she ever found out. The Boardroom NDA only stretched so far. He should know. He'd created it years ago and enforced it now.

And all of that was just a distraction from the true source of his conflict.

For the first time in his life, he'd met a woman he couldn't forget. His ex-wife hadn't even held that distinction.

They'd both gone into the union with expectations. His to check off the married box and hers to change him into a more feeling person—or so he'd discovered when she'd packed her bags and walked out. An event that hadn't fazed him and had proven he really was an emotionless bastard. And nothing had changed since then.

Relationships were tangled with traps. Nasty, often blind, sinkholes that dared a person to believe in false truths. That stronghold of conviction worked its way in to support the teachings beaten into him when he'd had no understanding that things could be different. And it was too late now.

He'd walked away from his parents the second he'd turned eighteen. His brains had gotten him out of the stench, and they'd laid out the path to get him a corner office in the most respected law firm in the city.

He wasn't the silent kid in the corner anymore. The one with high-water pants and hair buzzed to his scalp under the shaky hand of an inebriated mother. But in so many ways he was still that roughed-up kid made stronger by the hours spent locked in a dark closet.

His parents hadn't defeated him no matter how hard they'd tried. But they'd taught him well. Emotional attachments only led to pain, and he refused to place that hurt on anyone. Especially someone as passionate as Brie.

Chapter Fourteen

Brie marched down the hallway, thoughts centered on the meeting ahead. She'd barred all the lascivious ones from her mind after her last trip to the land of hedonistic sex. There was no place for them in her daily life, especially at work.

She could control that much at least.

That didn't stop those same wicked thoughts from invading her dreams and penetrating her daily awareness. In too many ways, she'd awakened a beast with little knowledge of how to contain it, but she would.

She owned that bitch called her libido, and although she wasn't ready to stuff her back in a box, she also didn't get to run around willy-nilly creating havoc in her life.

There were hours and hours of work to keep her focused, and if she planned correctly, she was too exhausted to do more than dream about case points and briefings. Her libido was checked into an extended time-out. Period.

She rounded the corner and entered a small conference room close to Mr. Cummings's office. The Palmaro brief was tucked beneath her arm along with a couple of others Mr. Cummings was working on, just in case the conversation strayed to them.

She blinked and quickly dodged the late afternoon sun that pinged off an opposing building at just the right angle to create a focused laser beam of brightness. Darkness ringed her peripheral vision as she took a quick glance around the room and found it empty. Good.

She chose a chair opposite the door, clear of the death rays. Her laptop came to life with a quick tap on the touchscreen. She tucked her hair behind her ear and arranged her folders neatly beside her.

And there she sat.

The room wasn't a boardroom. There was no coffee credenza or fancy paintings, and the table was simple oak instead of gleaming cherry or dark mahogany. Would the wood smell the same? She barely resisted the urge to bend over and check.

She rubbed a distracted path over the sharp edge of the table. Five days later and she could still feel the bite of the table edge on her thighs. The bruises had faded to a faint purple with no lasting sting, but she knew they were there, just inches below her pussy.

She'd discovered the perfect line bisecting both thighs the next day. Shock had been quickly followed by wonder as she'd traced it. A swivel of her hips had revealed another matching set of prints on each side. Did he know he'd left them? Had he wanted to leave a reminder? To what purpose?

Yet the hidden bruises had gotten her through another country club brunch filled with the barrage of petty rivalries and reminders of her failures.

She shook her head, frustrated at her lack of control. Lori had assured her this wild fluctuation of emotions would fade, only she hadn't said when. A week? A month? Years?

She pressed on her upper thigh, hunting for the lingering hit of pain. *He* hadn't criticized her, not once, for what she'd wanted or who'd she'd been.

And it meant nothing when he was barely more than a figment of her imagination.

Approaching footsteps had her straightening. Mr. Burns stepped through the doorway, all put-together power and focus—until he ran into the deathly sunbeam.

He lurched back, scowled darkly as he moved down the table, head turned away.

Her smile bloomed at the simple sight of normal coming from the impeccable man. "The sun can be deadly sometimes," she quipped, unable to resist. He was still just a guy, right?

He dropped his files on the table before a chair diagonally across from her, the corner of his mouth turning up in that hint of a smile. Did it ever fully bloom?

"Ms. Wakeford." The greeting came with a nod.

"Mr. Burns," she said right back with the same formality.

Mr. Cummings stepped into the room, stopping before he encountered the death beam. "Brighton. Burns," he greeted them. "Let me know if you need anything," he went on before they could respond. "And Burns, I do appreciate you taking this on. Barbara will be pleased to know it's being handled."

Brie kept her expression neutral. She'd pulled the briefing together and knew exactly why his wife would be pleased. A win for their client would be a financial boon for members of Barbara's family, whereas a loss would mean the opposite. The land agreement had complex ties with prominent names on both sides of the dispute. It was big, messy and filled with political land mines.

Burns had grilled her on the intertwined connections when they'd reviewed the document. But for some naive reason, she hadn't realized Burns would take the case. Willful blindness maybe?

"Brighton," he said, shifting his focus to her. "Give Burns whatever time he needs. You can hand off the Chalmers and Hanson work to Casey. She has room and has agreed to take them over."

The thought of turning over the work sparked an instant jolt of rejection that dried out her throat and dug at her chest, but she gave him a smile. "Certainly." She glanced at Burns, her heart doing that strange pinch-and-drop thing it had no right doing around him. "I'll be happy to assist you as needed." Not that he was known for handing much off.

He stared back at her, his expression once again void of...anything. Yet that strange awareness vibrated over her skin and shimmied down her spine.

"Great," Mr. Cummings said, clapping his hands together in a final declaration. "I'll let you two get to work."

Brie blinked, snapping around to shoot a smile at her departing boss. Her pulse hitched up a notch for no understandable reason. She'd worked with many attorneys—most of them men—in her years as a paralegal. This was no different.

Yet her skin still heated when she turned her smile back to Burns. Why? There was no logic to it. Zero. Zip. None.

But her body was apparently completely disengaged

from her brain. Her nipples puckered in blatant awareness when he did nothing more than return her regard.

"Should we get started?" he asked, slipping his glasses on as he glanced down.

"Yes." They should get started, right now. Maybe then she'd have a chance at locking her misbehaving libido back away. With a dead bolt. Three dead bolts.

And tossing the keys.

"Let's start at the top," he went on, flipping a folder open. "I'm going to need…"

Thankfully, her mind engaged immediately. She automatically started typing every request he made into her case notes. This she could do. Just work. It didn't matter if the cadence of his voice slid over her nape to tease her with longing or if each shift of his hand drew her gaze to his fingers that had no right being sexy.

How was that even possible? Sexy fingers?

It wasn't. Full stop. End of thought process.

Work. Focus. Be the professional she was.

A long while later, he sat back, lifting his arms over his head as he did. His shirt pulled across his chest as the stretch held, a look of relief falling over his features.

Brie couldn't drag her gaze away from the stunning sight. He'd removed his suit jacket around the same time she'd officially dropped the Mr. from his name. Or maybe that'd happened when he'd scrubbed a hand through his perfect hair and left the strands sticking up in front.

He'd become human then. A simple man doing his best at a job he obviously loved. His passionate dedication spoke to her own thriving need to succeed and be seen as such.

He slid his glasses off and rubbed his eyes, elbows

propped on the table like any normal tired person. Papers were splayed in orderly stacks that tracked the work they'd defined and information they'd both printed over the last—she glanced at the clock. Five hours? Wow.

She stretched her neck and turned around to glance out the windows, finally logging the setting sun and hazy strips of fog snaking their way toward Alcatraz. The little lump of rock sat like a beacon in the middle of the bay, tempting the elusive streams closer.

"I think I've kept you long enough," he said, rolling his shoulders back. The half-smile he shot her nailed her with authenticity. And it was a smile, no matter how small it was.

Her heart did that strange tug she dismissed as utter fantasy. She was way too smart to fall for her boss. She was, right? But she could still admire him from afar.

"Did you want to continue tomorrow?" she asked.

She double-checked that her work was saved before closing the windows on her computer. Burns had retrieved his own laptop not long after they'd started dissecting the personal entanglements between the plaintiff and their new client. The action had stunned, impressed and irritated her at once.

Mr. Cummings had never done his own research—at least not since she'd been working for him. Did Burns not trust her? Did he doubt her competence? He'd obliterated those doubts not long after they'd divided the tasks, removed their jackets and gotten to work.

"What's your schedule like?" he asked, moving his mouse and clicking, his focus on his screen.

She tracked the line of his forearm, bared beneath his rolled-up sleeve. His wrist flexed only slightly but it mesmerized her. The power was controlled, exactly like him.

Her gaze jumped to the slick watch strapped to his other wrist. The black leather band emphasized the strength beneath it while the sleek silver timepiece declared the reserved class he exuded but never flaunted.

Her fingers itched to wrap around it and let all that power sink into her. To feel the bite of it in her palm and the rush of hunger that'd come with it.

She was fully aware she was overlaying her fantasy experiences onto him. It didn't stop her imagination from going wild. In fact, it fed it now. The thought of being fucked over the table until she couldn't breathe raised the temperature in her crazy-ass libido. The damn bitch refused to stay quiet.

Burns wasn't married, that much she knew from office gossip. Was he dating someone? Gay? No. That rumor had fluttered around for a brief period before it'd been squashed by the openly gay men in the office who swore by their gaydar. Did he—

"Brie?"

Her eyes jerked to his, heart lurching into her throat. He stared back at her, expression cloaked. He didn't move a muscle and neither could she.

Had she imagined the tone? The low rumble that'd swooped in to caress her lust.

Could it be? *No! God, no!*

The silence stretched on the insistent beat of her heart. It roared between the tension that'd sprung so tightly between them she swore it was going to snap and crush her on the spot.

How did he know her nickname? She never used it at work. Never.

Her gaze dropped to his watch, dragged up his forearm covered with a light down of hair to the rolled-up cuff, over his chest to the smooth line of his neck and jaw, his beard stubble nonexistent even now.

Blood rushed in her ears. Panic skated beside the counter-logic she tried to apply. It couldn't be him. *Please, please no. But...*

She met his gaze again, heart still locked in her throat where it made a frantic attempt to escape. A clammy sweat broke over her chest and nape the longer he sat there. Not moving. Not speaking. Not questioning her obvious freak-out.

The silence became a physical thing as it wrapped around them, shoved them closer. Her stomach swirled in sick understanding she refused to accept. *No. No way.*

He gave away nothing. Not a hint of emotion showed, when she was pretty damn certain every one of hers was blaring across her face.

Another long moment passed before he slowly closed his eyes.

Her panic launched into a full-on attack.

She thrust up, her chair wheeling back unchecked. Her legs shook. Her stomach heaved in the sick soup of embarrassment and anger. Her head was swiveling as she inched away, denial holding strong despite the intuitive knowledge that it was him.

Him.

He slowly stood, his movements cautious yet sure. His focus remained on her, his stone-cold facade still locked in place.

"How—you—no!" She shook her head harder, still

refusing to accept what her instincts had known all along.

She was moving before she consciously thought about it. She flew around the end of the table, focused on escape. She had to get out so she could think and process the impossible. Denial still rang a loud *no, no, no* in her head when she knew it to be a lie.

But he beat her to the door.

She came up short, breaths chugging out on a panicked wind as he deliberately closed it, his eyes never leaving hers.

What? Why? What did he want? Or should she be asking what did he expect?

"Brie—"

"No!" she cut him off, hand held out in firm refusal. "I am not Brie here. I'm Brighton or Ms. Wakeford. Not Brie. Never Brie."

Brie was for her closest friends. Brie was the woman who let herself be fondled, sucked and fucked while she hid behind a blindfold. Brie didn't exist in this space.

He gave a single slow nod that could've been acknowledgment or a passive-aggressive knock to her fleeing sanity. The urge to yell at him was squelched by her inability to form a coherent rant. What could she say? She'd gone into that room willingly.

And he'd been there too.

The denial didn't rear this time. Nope. There was nothing left but dread and burning humiliation.

"I apologize."

He what? Apologized? "For what?"

The meaning didn't log in her scrambled thoughts. Was he apologizing for fucking her—twice—or for letting his secret out?

His deep inhalation sent a wave of apprehension through her. Her mother did the exact same thing whenever she sought patience for some perceived misdeed Brie had done.

"For—" He cut himself off this time, lips pinching tight. "I'm sorry you found out this way."

Her shoulders went back, spine stiffening in rejection. The ache in her throat turned hollow as she tried to process that. Oh, no. He wasn't getting off that easy. She might not be an attorney, but she wasn't stupid—or that gullible.

She cocked her head, frowning. Her show of cunning was one of her best performances. "Found out what, exactly?"

Her stomach gave another sick heave, but she refused to let him off. Maybe she was wrong. And maybe unicorns farted sparkling pink rainbows.

His soft chuckle held a hint of admiration she refused to read into. He tucked his hands into his pockets, nodding as the corner of his mouth turned up. It fell a moment later, taking the hint of emotion with it.

Her stomach contracted with the last nugget of wishful hope.

"I was in the boardroom." He paused. "Both times."

The floor dropped out from beneath her. Her head spun, so many of her dreams sinking into the abyss. Was this the end of her job? Would he demand something in return for keeping her secret? Would the harassment begin along with the undermining of her position?

But…wait.

Her head snapped up, the big picture coming into focus. The swashing in her stomach diminished to soft swells as logic finally kicked in. Her eyes narrowed with each piece of the puzzle that fell into place.

This wasn't just about her.

"You were in the boardroom. Both times," she repeated, voice clear and even. And that meant he had even more to lose than she did.

Chapter Fifteen

For the first time in years, fear curled in Ryan's chest. It snuck up his throat, choked his thoughts and paralyzed his muscles.

He'd fucked up. Bad.

His future and all he'd worked to obtain sat on the precipice of her discretion. The Boardroom had always been a calculated risk. It'd been the one and only dalliance he'd ever let himself have in his forty-one years of life.

And now it could sink him.

"I was," he stated, despite the screaming urge to deny his own admission. He'd been in the Boardroom with her. He'd fucked her twice. Inhaled her scent, tasted her skin, her mouth, her pussy until he'd drowned in the decadent flavors.

He couldn't deny those things even if it cost him everything.

She sucked in a breath, acceptance passing over her features in incremental shifts from understanding to resolute. And she'd never been more beautiful.

Brie Wakeford didn't cower or crumble or preen under the weight of her newfound knowledge and subsequent power. Her initial fiery reaction had given way to this cool control he could only admire.

She'd pulled her hair into a low pony about an hour into their working session, but thin wisps fell free now to frame her face in tempting softness. Her cheeks were flushed an alluring shade of red that'd risen with her anger. Resentment spewed from her glare to darken those normal blue eyes to a deeper, richer hue.

The power she held over him extended far beyond her knowledge of his sexual activities.

Her firm swallow hitched her throat and dragged memories of that same action beneath his palm. The feel of the muscles working. The power that'd hummed through him at her blind trust.

Would she ever trust him like that again?

No. She had no reason to.

"So where do we go from here?" Her voice had dropped to the focused business tone she'd employed in all her professional interactions with him. He never thought he'd miss that huskier, playful one. Or the softer one that could beg so beautifully.

Where was his head?

Emotions such as loss were something he'd purged long before he'd reached middle school. Attachment to anything, even his favorite stuffed animal, only resulted in its accelerated demise.

He checked his rambling thoughts behind his wall of useless items and shifted through the available tactical strategies. Every battle had a weakness along with a possible settlement.

"In many ways, I believe that is up to you," he finally said. "But I should remind you of the NDA you signed prior to entering that room."

Her nod was slow and cunning. "As did you—I presume." The slight lift of her brow brought another wave of brash respect for her. She'd earned a heavy dose of that over the last hours of work, but to see that same calm intelligence applied now hitched it up another level.

"I did. As does everyone who chooses to play."

"The details and clauses left little room for litigation."

He ignored the shot of pride that could lead to arrogance at her unintentional compliment. "As all solid NDAs should."

Her soft humph held only a small dose of mirth. "Nicely done."

He didn't deny or affirm her assumption when there was no point in it. "Your private activities will remain as such within the group."

"The group?" There was no way to miss the dose of sarcasm attached to the question.

Years of practice kept his frustration from escaping. "If you have a question, ask it. Fishing will get you nothing."

A long moment ticked by on the wavering line of her mouth. It lifted, fell, pinched slightly before a disbelieving smile broke free. She shook her head, arms falling from their crossed position over her chest. Her fingers started that quick running tap against her thumb before she spoke.

"How much will you honestly tell me?"

"How much do you want to know?" He could answer open-ended questions with questions all day.

"God." She clamped her mouth shut, eyes closing briefly before her shoulders fell from their stiff hold.

"I can't do this now." She shook her head in a defeated motion before she moved back to her computer and proceeded to shut it down.

Ryan had no words. Nothing, when he should be laying down promises and platitudes. Yet the contract they'd both signed didn't need clarification. She understood the law and the terms of the agreement. What happened in the Boardroom was completely separate from the office. She should understand that without him needing to explain.

He bent over his computer, pointedly rejecting the notion of disappointment that tried to wedge its way into his chest. "I have a meeting first thing tomorrow, but I can meet you in here at nine," he told her as he checked his calendar.

Her stunned stare caught him off guard when he glanced up. He lifted a brow. Was she going to refuse to work with him now? And there was nothing he could do or say if she did.

"I have a dentist appointment in the morning," she finally said.

Regret snuck in to settle deep in the pit of his stomach. She was by far the best employee he'd worked with since joining the firm. He understood why Charles had laid exclusive claim to her almost as soon as she'd been hired. Her attention to detail and intuitive understanding of both the law and the information required to defend the case had been refreshing.

He straightened, debate clashing between calling her on the apparent lie or letting it go. She slipped her suit jacket on, scooped up her personal items and headed toward the door. He'd reserved the room indefinitely, so the files could remain in their organized stacks, but would she be back?

Her skirt swished softly in the silence that seemed to deepen the closer she got to the door. An errant thought hammered that he should be doing more to stop her. That he hadn't secured her assurance of secrecy or any real understanding of their current professional footing.

Her hand was on the doorknob before he finally found his voice.

"Brighton." Her name flowed out on the deeper tone he reserved for the Boardroom. He hadn't consciously thought to use it, but there it was.

She froze, visibly tensing. Her scowl could've cut him if he'd had thinner skin. As it was, it left a grazing slash somewhere near that empty space in his chest. The burn warned of trouble he'd avoided his entire adult life.

"Yes?" The flat note left another cut that he dismissed. There were far deeper and worse ones that could be inflicted with a simple tone or selection of words.

The last glow of the sun cast soft shades of orange and pink into the room in a final battle against the harsh cast of the fluorescent lights. She was stunning even in her guarded anger—or was that disappointment? Her suit was tailored to accentuate every curve that shifted the basic black from sedate to alluring.

"Brie is safe with me." *Always.* He shoved the truth out before he could check the statement against the long list of possible consequences. She deserved to know that bit and he wouldn't keep it from her.

Her eyes fell closed in a slow descent that lasted through a long inhalation. They gave away nothing when she reopened them. "And what about Brighton?"

"She's safe too." Probably more than any person in the office, including himself. "I respect them both equally." How could he not?

Her shoulders lifted with another deep intake of air. Did she believe him, or did she doubt everything he said? Did it matter?

For his career, yes.

For himself, no.

The lie ripped open to release the remnants of his father's cackling laugh that he'd thought he'd banished long ago. It bounced around in his head, mocking him.

She left without another word. Her departure sucked the air from the room and took his volleying thoughts with it. There was nothing he could do about her or the knowledge she now had.

No, there was a lot he *could* do. There was nothing he was *willing* to do—yet.

The outer office echoed with the deserted emptiness that was his comfort zone. The lights would dim automatically before long, but hours remained before the cleaning crew appeared.

He pulled his chair in and sat back down. He blinked at his computer screen, mind blank.

Do you even have emotions? The accusation tossed out by his ex-wife had bounced off him back then. There'd been no need to respond when she'd already formed a conclusion. But now, he found himself pondering the question.

He snatched up a notepad littered with scribbled to-dos for the case and homed in on the top one. It was pointless to waste time or energy on anything else. And he had even more work to finish now that Brie was off his team.

Brighton.

Ms. Wakeford.

Brie was a part of his past, and after tonight, he'd be lucky if he ever caught a glimpse of her again.

Chapter Sixteen

"Brie. What's—"

Brie stormed past Lori and into her friend's apartment without a hint of guilt. Her controlled calm had spun between empty acceptance and outright rejection on the bus ride across town. She turned on her now, frustration overriding heartbreak.

"Did you know?" She pointed her finger at Lori in accusation that she hoped wasn't just.

Lori shut her door, a confused frown in place when she faced Brie. "Did I know what?"

"About Burns?"

"Burns?" Her brows winged up to declare how lost she was. Did she really not know? Or was she playing Brie for the naïve fool she wasn't?

"Burns," she stated again, like that would clear up everything. She tried one more time when the blank stare remained. "Ryan Burns."

Her eyes went wide then, her lips forming an O. She moved into the room, ushering Brie with her as she did. "Have a seat."

Brie spun out of her hold. "I don't want to sit." With the amount of compressed energy buzzing within her, she didn't know if it was even possible for her to sit.

She strode to the window, turned back to glare at her so-called friend. "And don't placate me."

Lori raised her palms in a show of defeat. "I wasn't trying to. Honest." She waited a beat in which Brie didn't respond.

She didn't know what to think anymore, let alone what to believe.

Her friend eased a bar stool out from under the small breakfast counter and sat, her gaze only shifting from Brie in brief increments as she did.

The combination kitchen, eating area and family room was short on space in typical San Francisco fashion. The one bedroom offered little in the way of luxuries, but Lori had the proud distinction of claiming sole occupation of the unit. Her status in the legal community was higher than Brie's, whose salary, although nice, trapped her into roommate status if she wanted to stay in the city.

Brie braced her back against the wall, her purse and bag sliding to the floor as she locked into the stare-down her friend had engaged. She wasn't backing down. Not on this.

Not on Ryan Burns.

"How'd you find out?" Lori finally asked.

"So you did know!" She thrust away from the wall, the betrayal slamming into her heart. "Why didn't you tell me? No." She looked away, jaw aching with the emotions sealed behind her will. "Forget that." She refocused on her friend, her pain leaking out. "Why did you let it happen in the first place?"

"I didn't *let it* happen," Lori defended herself. "It just happened. That's the way the group works."

It just happened.

The stunning connection that'd melted her insides and woven false dreams into her heart. Ones of her own doing with no encouragement from anyone.

Yeah, that *just happened.*

She dropped into the cushioned armchair as the huge mountain of hurt swooped in to replace the fight that'd brought her there. Resignation sucked away the energy that'd kept her moving since Burns had ripped her world apart with one simple word. *Brie.*

"I trusted you."

Lori had taken Brie under her wing way back when she'd been a TA, and Brie had been drowning in legal case studies her junior year in college. Their friendship had only grown stronger in the ten years since.

"Okay." Lori accepted the cutting remark without so much as a flinch. "But I don't see what I did wrong." The comfy lounge pants and baggy cotton top didn't diminish the authority Lori tended to wield without thought. Even with the messy topknot, her regal confidence reigned.

Brie barked out a harsh laugh. "Right." She rubbed her brow in an attempt to ease the throbbing behind it. "The blame is all mine. Got it." After all, she'd been the one who'd stepped into those rooms of her own free will.

And no matter how many times she repeated that truth, she couldn't reconcile this outcome with her own actions. This was what she got for daring to be a little naughty. For breaking out of the mold her mother had stuffed her into before she could walk.

She ended up in a compromising position with the exact type of man her mother would love for her to snag. And he was her boss. Her. Boss. How humiliating was that? God, what he must think of her now... "How did I not know?" she reprimanded herself. "His voice. How'd I not recognize it?" But she had, right? At least her subconscious had.

"You weren't expecting to know anyone."

"But still—"

"How often do you work with him?" Lori cut in.

Brie tensed, recognizing her friend's debate intro. "Not very."

"You were in a foreign environment *way* outside your comfort zone. You weren't expecting to know anyone. In fact, you didn't *want* to know anyone." Lori's shrug was the final note on her simple argument.

She hadn't, Lori was right on that point. No one was supposed to know the intimate details of what she'd done there. No one she knew, at least.

But Ryan did. He'd had a front-row seat to every embarrassing moan and plea for more.

"But I *still* should've," she insisted. Shouldn't she have been aware enough, smart enough to place his voice to someone she worked with? If not before, then after? Unless she'd willfully chosen to *not* identify him? Which, apparently, she had.

"So it *is* my fault," she concluded, sinking deeper into the chair.

"I don't see why you're intent on placing blame on anyone." Lori moved from the bar stool to enter the kitchen. Her turned back allowed her to miss the childish face Brie made at her. She pulled a bottle of wine from her cupboard along with two wineglasses. "Can you please state what, exactly, is upsetting you so badly?"

Brie could only stare at her as she set the items on

the coffee table. Did she really not understand? "He's. My. Boss."

Lori lifted a brow in a clearly unspoken "So what?" She twisted the cap off the bottle, grinning. "I truly love screw-caps on wine."

Really? That's where her thoughts were?

Brie gaped at her, lost and too exhausted to even attempt to understand her friend's thinking. She accepted the glass Lori held out to her. The generous portion of red liquid sloshed in the oversized glass as she sat back.

She didn't wait for a toast before taking a long hit of the liquid. The flavor sat on her tongue like a dry crumb of burnt wood, but she swallowed it down and took another. The magical sense of relief floated through her muscles to loosen every tightly clenched one that lined her neck and dug into the base of her skull.

The wine might suck, but the effects were wonderful, even if they were only a temporary illusion.

"He's your boss," Lori stated with a shrug. "Nothing that happened in the Boardroom will impact your job."

"Easy for you to say." She wasn't the one who had to face him in the office every day.

Lori curled her legs up to tuck her feet beneath her as she settled into the corner of the couch. She eyed Brie with the same look she'd wielded back in college. The one that said think before you jump off the cliff of insanity. That plea only worked once, and it was best to save it for emergencies.

"What?" Brie snapped before giving in. "Okay. Fine. Just lay it out for me. What am I missing or misconstruing?"

Lori tossed her head back, a hardy laugh flowing out to tug a reluctant smile from Brie. Lori raised her glass in silent salute before taking a drink. The college déjà vu continued to soothe her. Those years spent living at home but stretching her freedom at school had provided the basis for her eventual flight from her mother's tentacles. Granted, they still stretched across the bay, but they were easier to evade now.

"Sex can exist without ties," Lori said. "Separating the expected emotional bullshit from the physical act is just one of the benefits of the Boardroom."

The boardroom. The NDA flashed in her mind, the term jumping out to signal its significance. She'd dismissed it before as a loose term for the entity, but got it now. "That's cute."

"What?"

"The name. The Boardroom." She waited for Lori to respond but got nothing. "It's a play on words, right? Because the sex takes place in the boardroom." The wine was apparently going to her head faster than normal because it all seemed funny now. Hysterical actually.

Only she wasn't laughing.

Lori wasn't laughing either.

"The name of the group is irrelevant." Lori swirled the liquid in her glass in an act of casualness Brie wasn't buying. "You're upset because you now know the identity of a man you performed sexual acts with. But it's only a big deal to you."

She'd only performed "sexual acts" with her boss. Great. That made it feel better—not.

"Have you?" she asked, both wanting to know and hating the thought of it. "Performed sexual acts with my boss?"

Lori gave away nothing as she eyed her. That blank mask was essentially a prerequisite for anyone involved in law, but it irritated her to no end now. Didn't anyone show their emotions anymore? When had everyone lost their heart?

Thank God her dad had swung the pendulum of icy superiority wielded by her mother to show her how love was supposed to work. The man had dedicated his life to providing for them, his gentle kindness often overshadowed beneath the louder demands of her mother's. But he'd never shied from showing his love in each hug, kind word and gentle encouragement that'd bolstered her courage and assisted in landing her the job at Cummings, Lang and Burns.

Burns.

She was so screwed.

"One." Lori raised a finger. "I can't disclose that. And two," she lifted a second finger, "you know that. You read and signed the NDA and I know you're not a dumb cookie."

"So what?" she challenged. "Are you going to turn me in for violating the terms? After all, I just told you who I performed *sexual acts* with." The heavy dose of sarcasm hung on those two words to show her disdain for them and everything they represented. But wait. Her frown deepened as she slotted another piece into the picture. "How did you know about Burns before I told you?"

"There's an app for that." Lori shot her a cheeky smile before taking a drink of her wine.

An app. Of course there was. There was an app for everything. Why wouldn't there be an app for arranging group sex in public boardrooms?

Brie slumped further into the chair, utter defeat sucking the last dregs of resistance from her bones. She was in over her head and it was apparent her only friend in the area wasn't tossing out a life preserver.

She closed her eyes and found a small dose of solace in the darkness. Could she simply stay there? With her head in the sand and heart numbed to the vicious swirl of hurt, disappointment and rebuke compressing it tight?

"This is personal because you're making it so."

Lori's voice floated into her quiet to shatter her small moment of attempted peace. "So fucking my boss isn't personal?" Because it sure as hell felt like it to her. Every fiber of her was screaming with how personal it'd been. His gentle caresses ghosting over her skin. The throaty rumble of her name as he'd filled her. The tender possession that'd kept her safe.

Yeah. Those classified as personal—to her.

"Would you feel this way if you didn't work with him?"

"Yes."

The truth was out before she'd thought about it. Every moment in those rooms had been personal—with him. Just him. And that was the real issue. If it'd been just sex, then maybe she wouldn't care so much. But she'd made the encounters into way more than they'd been, and that just added another layer to her embarrassment.

"Then I suggest you figure out how to deal with that."

"No shit."

"Without sacrificing your job."

Brie raised her hand and flipped her friend off, her eyes still closed. Lori's soft chuckle quirked her own lips up. The action had been received exactly as she'd intended—with unspoken sarcasm. And Lori was probably her only friend who would've taken it that way.

This was exactly why she was here. To hear the brutal truth when she'd rather hear how wronged she'd been. The latter would justify the anger and hurt burning a hole in her stomach. The former would show her reality and make her face it.

"Can I *really* continue to work with him?" The silence stretched until Brie was forced to open her eyes. She studied Lori below half-opened lids, not entirely prepared to face her or the truth.

Her friend leveled that interrogation glare and laid into her. "Did he threaten you in any way?"

Her reluctant "no" came out after a long moment of internal debate between telling the truth and justifying her own reaction.

"Did he make an unwanted advance?"

Another "no" was pulled out against her will.

"Did he imply that—"

"No!" she cut her off, too deflated to continue the detailed breakdown of exactly how irrational she was being. "No. Okay? No. He didn't do any of those things."

A smile that could only be descried as smug landed on Lori's face as she patted herself on the back. Brie didn't even have the energy to flip her off again.

"So what *did* he do?" Lori asked.

Brie is safe with me.

She squeezed her eyes closed against the shot of pain that laced her heart. The sense of protection had wrapped around her and shredded her at once. She'd understood exactly what he'd meant. He hadn't been talking about just her secrets or her physical actions in those rooms, but who she'd become.

Who she'd let herself be.

That Brie was one only he knew. Not even the other

men in the room could understand what his touch had done to her. Did he have a clue to the havoc he'd set free?

Brie is safe with me.

Was she though? Truly?

"Tell me something," Lori said, breaking into Brie's thoughts. She opened her eyes and lifted the corner of her mouth in assent. Lori cocked her head, brows lowering a tad. "Would you or did you do any of those things to him?"

Brie jerked up, scowl set. "No." Her indignation raised the hair on her arms and sparked the fire that'd burned out after her first sip of wine. "I would never do those things—to *any*one."

Lori's slow nod was one of quiet victory. "Then don't expect less from him."

Brie sputtered, rebuttals dying in quick succession until only one was left. "But that's our job. We're trained to expect and prepare for the worst."

"While ensuring the best possible outcome," Lori finished. "And in most cases, the worst never happens."

"We don't win every case."

"True. But that doesn't mean we're going to lose them all. Or that we should stop trying."

Brie squinted at her, lost in the sea of innuendo and veiled analogies. "What are we talking about again?" Her brain was fuzzy from the wine and the overload of thoughts that'd been flying in and out of it. Processing any of the hidden meanings in Lori's words was impossible.

Lori's laugh filled the room with much-needed lightness. "We're talking about how you're going to go to work tomorrow and act as if nothing happened." Brie's eyes widened, and Lori nodded, her expression firm. "You are. Your little hitch of unnecessary conscience will not be the cause of you quitting a job you love."

"Who said I was going to quit?" But the thought had crossed her mind multiple times since she'd fled the building. There were plenty of other law offices where she could work. And none that she'd be able to walk into and have the power and position she did at C, L and B. She was well aware of her elevated status on the paralegal totem pole within their office.

"Excellent." Lori sat forward and motioned to Brie as she lifted the wine bottle. "At least we have that down." She refilled Brie's glass and sat back. Her own was still half-full. "Now what else is there to cover?"

Brie blinked, her mind empty for the first time in hours. Was there more? Yes, but nothing she was willing to share with her friend. Not when Lori clearly had no ties to anything or anyone she interacted with in the *Boardroom*.

There was a clear line of delineation between the two of them. Brie apparently couldn't be that detached even when she'd tried to be.

"Nothing," she deflected. The weight settled over her to press her further into the cushions. "I'm fine."

Lori's sharp bark of laughter said how much she believed the bullshit Brie had just fed her.

"Really." Brie forced a smile and willed her words to be true. "I am. I'll go to work. Do my job and pretend I'm not daydreaming about every 'sexual act' he did to me."

"Oh, you're free to daydream," Lori said with a wicked grin. "Daydream all you want. Just don't act on any of them—until you're in the Boardroom. Then it's game on." Her glorious cackle set off a wave of dread within Brie.

There was no way she'd ever return to the Boardroom. Not when she had to face her fantasy every damn day for the foreseeable future. There, that was another decision made. She wasn't backing out of the Palmaro case either.

They were both adults. If he could pretend those two wild, erotic, wonderful encounters never happened between them, then so could she.

Damn her lusty Libido Bitch and every obnoxious thought she'd generated. She'd never thought with her pussy, and she wasn't about to start now.

Even if the vision of being spread across that conference room table and fucked senseless by him eventually drove her insane.

Chapter Seventeen

Ryan looked up from his computer, stretched his shoulders back.

"Did you find the property codes and regulations from nineteen eighty?" he asked the room at large.

"Donaldson did," Brie answered.

A scowl tugged on Ryan's forehead, his distaste for the schmoozer associate attorney coating his throat.

"They're printed in that stack over there," Brie went on, pointing to a pile of papers beneath a file labeled in black marker as City Regulations. "The information is summarized in file CR one nine eight zero A," she went on before he could ask. "The findings support the plaintiff, so I placed it in your To Read folder."

He clicked on the electronic folder. Brie had set up the file structure for the case with a precise logic that was organized and easy to follow. The office had some basic standards, but Brie had taken it a step further, making the critical info easier for him to find.

His back ached from the hours spent hunched over his computer doing research and assembling briefings and filings. Thankfully, Brie had started most of them or pulled in the ones they needed.

The Palmaro case had become as much hers as his,

and that hadn't happened since he'd taken his first case years ago.

He slid his glasses off, rubbed the grit from them before sitting back. Only then did he realize they were alone in the room. His gaze landed on her like it had so often over the last two weeks. She'd been sitting in that very spot when he'd arrived the day after he'd blown every boundary he placed on both himself and his work.

She'd come back.

He'd stalled in the doorway for a fraction of a second before taking his seat and getting to work. Their relationship had proceeded in the professional manner he extended to everyone he worked with, which he was grateful for.

He refused to acknowledge the swipe of regret that tried to take hold. This was the best possible outcome of a situation that could've been disastrous for him.

"I had Carla move your ten o'clock meeting tomorrow back to two," she told him, glancing up. "We should have the supporting evidence in place for the collusion theory by then, so you can better present it to our clients."

"Thank you." The platitude came out automatically when he would've bristled at the overstep under any other circumstances. But this was Brie.

She'd swooped into his awareness on a gasped breath and whispered "please" only to sneak into his life on a wave of efficiency, brains and decorum. The very things he longed to wipe away with one long thrust into her clenching heat.

The memory of her cries and moans wove their way behind the walls he rebuilt daily to withstand her nonexistent assault. Not literally anyway. It was his own damn head that continued to create havoc where none should be.

She brushed her hair back, a smile gracing her face before she looked to her computer. Her profile displayed the straight line of her nose that drew his eyes to her lips. Her mouth flexed with each thought that entered her head while she worked. Frustration was a slight pinch. Annoyance a compressed line. Excitement a slight uptick at the corner.

The light poured in from the window behind her to highlight the varying shades of brown, red and blond in her hair. She rarely wore it up even though it spread over her shoulders and down her back in a wave that'd been declared unprofessional by some outdated standard. She defied that and so many other rules defined by those who wanted to stake out their superiority.

Whoever raised her had done right on that aspect, or had she grown into that strength on her own?

"Where are you from?" he asked before his brain engaged to halt the intrusive question.

She squinted at him, confusion drawing her brows together. "What?"

Did he retreat or proceed? Desire to know conflicted with the more clearly established desire to not care. He reached for his coffee cup, caught in an awkward position of his own making. Yet another thing he wasn't used to.

He glanced at his empty mug, annoyance increasing.

"I was born and raised in Walnut Creek." Her frown deepened. "Why?"

He wasn't surprised. The affluent commuter-burb west of the city offered an illusion of superiority, of distance from the peninsula. But the peninsula, crammed with people as it was, held a quiet power Walnut Creek would never penetrate.

"Just curious." He set his cup back down. "Is your family still there?" He dug in when he could've dismissed the subject.

She sat back in her chair, a half-smile forming. "Yes. My dad works in the city."

"And your mom?"

Amusement flashed before her smile fell, the light dimming from her features. "She does charity work."

Ah. The secret code words for the country club elite who were privileged enough to spend their time raising funds for all the poor suckers who need two incomes just to get by—and then only barely.

And his resentment was showing.

"What about you?" she asked.

He kicked himself for opening the topic in the first place. "In Oakland." He left it purposely vague. The city was large, with plenty of both good and not-so-good areas. He sat forward. "I haven't spoken to my parents since high school."

His stomach clenched, heart contracting in a hard wince of *what the fuck?* He kept all of that from showing, though. The fact was nothing more than that, despite how little he shared it.

Her brows lifted higher, and he prepared to dismiss her condolences or apology or whatever other platitude people felt compelled to offer. Another reason why he didn't divulge the information.

She didn't move or lower her gaze at all. Her study of him dragged on until it crawled over his nape and dug into the very part of him he refused to let others see.

"You've done well without them." Her voice had lowered to those whispered notes of intimacy he habitually avoided. "Did you have other family to support you?"

He shook his head when everything urged him to shut this discussion down. The more she knew, the more power she had. "No." He answered anyway.

"That must've been hard. Doing all of this on your own." Empathy flowed from her voice, but absent was the pity he'd heard from his college counselors, who were the last people he'd allowed to dissect his upbringing.

He shrugged, neither confirming nor denying her claim. "It just was." And every painful step had brought him to where he was now. "You can't change the past."

"No," she agreed. "But it follows you nonetheless."

His bark of laughter burst free to shock them both. He shook his head, the sound dying to a low hitch as her surprise shifted to a soft laugh of her own.

"You speak the truth," he finally said. That empty space in his chest filled with a tad bit of warmth.

"I know from experience." She lifted her shoulder in dismissal. "Everyone has something that dogs them."

"And those somethings all vary." He rested his elbows on the table, enjoying the morphing conversation. "Some are far darker and more gut-wrenching than others."

"By whose standard?" She sat back, arms crossing as she dug into the discussion.

"Maslow's hierarchy, to begin with."

"Needs do not equate to individual experiences and impact."

"No," he agreed, a smile tugging on his lips. "But the hierarchy sets the foundation for assuming impact."

She frowned. "Explain."

He leaned back, his debate forming as he went. "If a

person has no food and no home but is given both, the subsequent loss of one or both would be disappointing but not catastrophic. However, for someone who's always lived in a grand house with more food than they can eat, losing both would be devastating."

"The same could be said for love and social standing, if you apply it like that."

"Exactly."

"So that's *probable* impact," she said, nodding. "How do you assess *actual*?"

"How would you?" he challenged right back.

Her eyes narrowed, a smile edging her lips at his turnaround. "You first have to understand their background and their current situation. Much like your example, only deeper. Such as, if in example A, the loss of food and shelter was due to the death of a loved one, then that could be catastrophic, especially if the child has no one else to care for them." Her triumphant smile begged him to counter.

How could he resist? "And what if that child is finally able to escape the one person who was supposed to love them, but only showed them contempt and abuse?" He raised a brow as her smile fell. "Then the same event could invoke relief and be seen as an opportunity."

"And the woman who gets hospitalized after being abused by her husband?" she asked, her frown back in place.

"That would depend on how she responds. Does she report it? Go back to her abuser? Seek shelter?" Was Brie speaking from personal experience or knowledge? Was that the cause of the scowl that formed when she answered some of her texts? The thought of any man abusing her sent a rage boiling through him. He cleared his throat, reined his thoughts back in. "No matter how crushing an event may be, the actual depth of the pain is often dependent on how that individual responds."

"I disagree." Her head was shaking before he'd finished. "Pain can be camouflaged. People can move forward, make decisions and go on with their life while the pain is ripping them apart inside. Everyone doesn't *show* pain in the same way."

He only had to look at his own experience to see the validity in her statement. No one ever knew how hard his parents had struck him, both verbally and physically. Showing his pain had only gotten him more.

"And what about the longevity?" he tossed out, if only to stop his memory trail. "Can actions or steps shorten the length of the pain?"

She propped her chin on her thumb, a finger curling over her lips as she contemplated his question. "Yes and no." She sat back. "And again, that depends on the person. A funeral service can help put closure in place for one person, but it's an expected motion for another. Just like buying lumber to rebuild a destroyed home or applying for a job to restart a career brought down by a random mistake. Those steps can be seen as moving forward, while the individual is still mourning what they've lost."

"So it's about the state of mind and the individual point of view?"

"Of course."

"Then the conclusion based on that theory is that actual impact can only be determined by the individual." He paused before circling back to the original statement. "Which means the standards applied to exactly how much, and to what extent, our pasts impact our current lives—no matter how gut-wrenching or dark they may be—is completely dependent on each individual."

She studied him, another of those cryptic smiles creeping over her lips. No, there was amusement in this one, along with something he construed as respect. "That's pretty deep, Burns."

He shrugged that off. "It's all part of the job, Wakeford." They'd shifted to the use of last names without fanfare. He liked it though, when he normally didn't care for the implied camaraderie. But it'd already been there with her, even without the shift in names.

"Not necessarily," she countered, her smile softening. "But it's nice to see that you believe it is."

His scowl yanked at the offended hurt he often didn't acknowledge. "Why wouldn't I?"

The dismissive lift of her shoulder didn't match the penetrating heat of her gaze. It smoothed over him on a slow shift that plucked at that damn awareness he'd tried to bank where she was concerned.

"You don't always come across as a warm and compassionate person," she told him, the honesty refreshing and harsh at once.

"I'm fully aware of that." He'd been told so often he'd have to be stupid or in complete denial if he didn't recognize that about himself. "But that doesn't mean I don't understand how to be."

"I know."

The soft agreement floated between them on a wave of memories he couldn't repel. Of the passion she'd unleashed in him. Of the roar of possessiveness that'd raced forward at her first lust-filled whimper. Of the need to see her cry out in pure abandonment.

The sun was making its descent through the fog

that'd rolled in yet again. The diminished light didn't hide the understanding that rushed between them, or the questions that came with it. Had the Boardroom really been just a moment? Could there be something more?

How?

"How much of your debate was based on actual experience?" she questioned, true concern and warmth in every word.

He could shut that intrusion down with a single clipped remark. Yet within this room, with the door half-closed and the outer office drifting into a different world, his truth was safe.

"Enough." He could expand, but her small wince told him he didn't have to. "You?"

Her slow inhalation lifted her breast and softened her expression even more. There was a true sadness there when she answered. "Not nearly enough."

"Why do you say that?" He frowned. "Actual knowledge isn't required for empathy." Another fact he knew from personal experience.

"True." She wet her lips with that same slow glide that'd driven him mad in the Boardroom. He tracked the movement, his breath hitching against the urge to follow its retreat and rediscover every sweet, heated corner of her mouth. "But there are times when I have to step back and see that my own past and problems are so incredibly minor when compared to others."

"Yet we just concluded that the only one who can judge the impact of each event is the person who experienced it." He let that stand for a long moment, curiosity bursting to learn more. What was her pain? Her history? Where did she want to go? What had she overcome to be here? "What may be perceived as minor by others could be devastating to you."

She swallowed. The silence stretched as she stared at him. Understanding buzzed over his skin on the energy that flowed between them and never seemed to go away.

The distant ring of a telephone filtered into the room to remind him of where they were. The interruption was innocuous, yet highlighted the lines he'd crossed once again.

They were at work. She was his subordinate.

And he still wanted to sink into her until he was lost in her sweet passion once again.

Brie cleared her throat, jerked her focus to her computer, lips compressing as she squinted at the screen.

"Donaldson and Jackman are working through the state files to untangle the property rights," she said, all professionalism now. Gone was the note of remembrance and the easy banter between friends.

Ryan stared at her for another long moment, that damn regret hardening into a permanent ball in his stomach. Regrets were useless when they couldn't be changed. Actions stood as deeds that didn't morph with time, and he owned every one of his.

They'd fucked in the Boardroom under the agreement of detachment, and in her case, anonymity. He'd already blown one of those terms. He refused to do so with the other.

"Good." The crisp snap of the word cut through the last of his useless longing. "Have them go back as far as the records provide. I don't want a loophole being missed." One that could benefit either side.

"Done."

They worked in silence for a long while before he

arched back, stretching his arms once again. The persistent pinch along his neck and shoulders rarely went away anymore. Except in the Boardroom, and he hadn't been back since Brie.

He was staring at her again, his gaze traveling to her without conscious thought. Her hair fell in a soft fan where she'd brushed it to one side as she read through a document. A low blush highlighted her cheeks and countered the deeper rose of her lipstick.

It was lighter than the Boardroom shade she'd worn. More subtle. Yet it still highlighted each arch and curve to perfection.

The outer office had gone quiet and faint shadows ran long and thin over the table from the surrounding buildings. He glanced at the time, winced.

"You can go," he said into the quiet.

She straightened, blinking before she frowned. "What?"

"It's after seven." He pointed to his watch. "You should go home."

"Oh." She looked around, brow furrowing. "I had no idea."

He chuckled softly. "I understand." He lost track of time more than he kept it when he was buried in research.

The wrinkles disappeared from her forehead as she let a hushed laugh roll out. "I bet you do." She started clicking away on her computer and he assumed she was shutting things down. He should do the same, or at least get back to his own work, but he didn't. Not when each little movement she made fascinated him. There was a concise grace to everything she did. She was always so engaged in what she was doing.

Just like in the Boardroom. Only there, every movement had been layered in passion.

"You should go home too," she said as she tucked her laptop into her bag and stood.

"I will." At some point.

"When?" Her raised brow said she knew the answer wouldn't be soon.

He motioned to his computer. "After I finish this."

Her light chuckle should've irritated him. It normally would've—from anyone else. But she left it at that. Missing was the reprimand for not having a personal life. Yet no one complained when he won his cases or brought in a high-profile client based on his work ethic and record.

He tracked her departure as she moved to the door. She'd worn black slacks today and paired them with a gray summer sweater that hugged her breasts. A string of pearls capped off the professional look.

She paused at the door, her hand braced on the frame. She scanned the outer office before looking back to him. That softness was back in her expression. The one that reached beneath his defenses and warmed him when it shouldn't.

Her hand tightened around her bag strap, and her tongue snuck out to wet her lips. The action had become a tease that almost had him groaning with the want it stirred. He doubted it was intentional, yet the effect was the same.

"In case you didn't know," she said, the throaty rumble of her words reaching out to spread the warmth through his chest, "Ryan is safe with me."

His heart fell to his stomach while his pulse raced in

the long moment it took for him to process her words. *Ryan is safe with me.*

She cracked a half-smile and left before he could respond. But what would he have said?

He slumped forward, head braced in his hands. His heart declared its presence with every hard beat that nailed his ribs. He squeezed his eyes closed in a useless attempt to block the full meaning of her words.

Ryan is safe with me.

She'd turned his words on him with a deftness he had to admire. Which also made it impossible to misinterpret her intent, and fucked up every good intention he had when it came to Brie.

Chapter Eighteen

The energy of the city hit Brie the second she shoved through the revolving door and stepped onto the sidewalk. The sun was out, and the street was crowded with people hustling to their own destinations.

She turned back to wait for Burns as he followed her outside. He adjusted his suit jacket, squinted as he glanced up, but a smile was on his face when he caught her eye. A real one.

Her heart did that useless dip-and-flip routine she couldn't seem to stop no matter how hard she tried. It'd been weeks, and his smile still devastated her. It changed his entire appearance and set off a wave of wild thoughts and fantasies that had zero chance of becoming reality.

"That went well," he said, glancing up the street.

"Yes. It did." His mild optimism was just one of the things she'd come to expect with him. He wasn't a man of wide-ranging emotions, at least that he let show. "The new information will benefit our latest property findings."

"It does." He nodded to her as they headed toward his car. He'd driven them across town for the deposition at the opposing counsel's office.

His clipped words put another smile on her face. The efficiency of his speech was a direct reflection of the man himself. Nothing was ever wasted. Not his time, thoughts or actions. And that simple fact alone irritated more people than appeased, but she liked it. It meshed with her own productive tendencies.

She automatically slowed as he did. Her thoughts were racing ahead to the documents she needed to pull and the additional research to be done. The billable hours on this case were well beyond any she'd had under Mr. Cummings.

Her focus jerked back to the present when Burns opened a door. He waited, brow raised.

A quick glance at the building had her frowning. "What?"

"Come on, Wakeford." He motioned with his head toward the restaurant. "I'll buy you dinner and a drink."

His words wouldn't penetrate her brain. "Why?" She glanced at her watch. There were still two to three hours left of work they could get done that night.

He stared at her, his head slowly swiveling. "It's dinner time. I'm hungry. And there is nothing that *has* to be finished tonight."

"Oh." That was the extent of her brilliant comeback. She stepped forward, stopped. "You don't have to buy me dinner." The idea of sharing a quiet meal with him bordered too close to personal territory when she was barely controlling her emotions as it was.

Her Libido Bitch was not backing down.

And that was creating more havoc than she wanted to admit. Because in truth, she was falling harder for him every damn day, and most of that had nothing to do with her libido. Her mother would've cheered if she'd known, but only if Brie “snagged” him too. That term alone gave her a gigantic reason to slap her longing down.

He released a heavy sigh, his lips compressing in a sure sign of suppressed frustration. She’d become very familiar with that look over the last weeks.

She bit back a smile, nodding. “Fine.” She moved forward, a quiet “thank you” sent as she passed him. She inhaled long and slow in a move that only punished herself. That distinctive scent of his cologne filtered in to tease her with the longing that never really died.

She held both in—the air and his scent. Her stomach twisted around every promise she’d laid down for herself before she’d walked back into the office so many weeks ago.

No lustful thoughts. No dreams. No fears. No mention of those two amazing encounters. The Boardroom had no place in the office. None. Zero. Zip.

But those rules hadn’t stopped her from speculating every time she entered their corporate boardroom. Did those private sex events take place there? When? Did Ryan participate?

He followed her inside, his presence tingling over her back. The continued hyperawareness of him was slowly driving her insane. And it showed no sign of diminishing anytime soon. The awareness or the insanity.

She clutched her briefcase in her hands, nerves rattling her chest, skin stretched tight in that familiar crush of restraint. This was just a business dinner. Nothing more.

“A table for two, please.”

The lowered tone in his voice took her back to the Boardroom and every luscious, intimate thing he’d done to her. The rumbled groans and—God! She gave her thoughts a silent shake. She had to keep her shit together.

The hostess led them to a table near the back. The small booth provided a sense of privacy even though the place wasn't busy yet. More bistro than restaurant, the casual atmosphere helped set her headspace in the professional mode.

This was very *not* a date. Not even close.

She focused on the short menu, suddenly starved now that she'd stopped to notice. That usually happened, especially when she got lost in work.

"It all looks good," she remarked.

"It does."

She looked up, heart catching when she found him studying her. The heat in his gaze had to be imagined, right? But why? Why did she keep denying what he wasn't trying to hide?

She lowered her menu, mouth going dry. "Have you decided?" She lifted her chin toward his menu, eyes never leaving his. She wasn't backing down if he was issuing a challenge of some sort.

"Do you drink wine?" he asked instead.

Did she drink wine? In general, or with him? "Yes."

"Red or white?"

"I prefer reds."

The corner of his mouth turned up in that quirk of a smile he used more and more around her. The amusement danced into his eyes to shove away a bit of that sizzling heat. The rich brown color had a way of drawing her in if she let it. Especially when he let his guard down, like now. Another thing that was happening more frequently.

"You?" she asked when the silence grew.

He lifted a shoulder. "Reds. I guess."

She smiled at that. "You guess?" She loved that he admitted that given the abundance of wine snobbery that prevailed in the area.

"It's wine," he stated with a quick twist of his lips. The rare show of true emotion was yet another surprise. "I don't think it requires an opinion."

Her laughter bubbled out in a freeing release. "I think you're one of the few with that outlook." Some of the tension drained from her shoulders as she settled back in the booth.

"What's the point in being like everyone else?" he countered before shifting his attention to their waiter.

Burns was definitely not like anyone she knew. And there was so much about him she still didn't know. But she wanted to, and that was a problem.

She waited until their orders were placed and the waiter left before she questioned him on his choice of wine. "Syrah? I thought you didn't have an opinion on wine."

He tipped his head, a smile forming. "Just because I don't have an opinion doesn't mean I'm not knowledgeable."

Of course it didn't. She begrudgingly gave him that point, her own smile spreading. He could be charming when he let himself be. Kind too. Gracious and generous.

She hunted for an inkling of the resentment or hurt that'd hammered her when she'd discovered *he* was her secret fantasy man. She found none. In many ways, this man sitting across from her wasn't him. No, this man had the potential to be even more dangerous, if she wasn't careful.

"Is that true for a lot of things for you?" she asked. He was wicked smart, yet offered so few opinions about any topic, unlike a large majority of people in the world today. It seemed like everyone had a judgment of some kind that they brandished on social media without fear or thought.

"I suppose." He loosened his tie, slipping his fingers beneath the knot to undo the top button. The move had become almost familiar to her now. He could relax, some. Even in public. "But just because I don't share my opinion doesn't mean I don't have one."

She smothered a smile. "Do you ever *not* debate?"

"Yes." He waited a beat, face serious. "But it's more fun if I do."

"For you, maybe."

He nodded, smiling just a touch. "Sometimes that's the only fun I have."

"Ouch." Her reflexive thought was out before she'd thought better of it. Was he serious? How…sad. Her heart went out to him when she knew it shouldn't. But how could it not?

"Why ouch?" His brows dipped, his fingers curling into a fist.

How did she answer without sounding patronizing? "What do you like to do in your spare time?" she asked instead, hoping to dodge his question.

"What does it matter?"

"Just answer me." She leaned in, intrigued now. "What else occupies your time?"

The corner of his mouth turned up, a hint of mischief lighting his eyes. "Now you're assuming that what occupies my time is also something I like to do."

Her groan was long and tortured as she slumped

back in the booth. She leveled a glare at him. "You can be so infuriating."

"I've been told that once or twice." His serious note left her pondering the depth of his meaning once again. Did he ever really open up?

Yes. In the Boardroom.

She'd felt the depth and passion he didn't seem to show anywhere else, not even in the courtroom.

Her phone buzzed in her bag, sending a jolt of annoyance through her. She'd turned her phone back on after the deposition and now wished she hadn't.

"Sorry," she mumbled. She glanced at the text alert only long enough to see her mother's name. There'd been three waiting for her earlier, all having to do with yet another "eligible" son of so-and-so.

Her annoyance doubled down to trigger her resentment. Her mother would crow with delight if she knew who Brie was having dinner with—and then she'd start maneuvering to see how extensive his connections were, and if they could benefit her.

Brie switched her phone to silent and tucked it back in her bag.

"Is everything okay?" Ryan asked. Concern drew his brows together, which loosened her own.

"Yes." She forced a small smile as reassurance. "It was just my mother."

His chin lowered slightly, eyes narrowing. "Does she text you a lot?"

Her harsh bark of laughter contained a heavy amount of the bitterness still churning in her stomach. "Yeah," she finally said, her tone saying more than she'd intended.

His low humph was at odds with the speculation that darkened his eyes before his frown eased.

Brie took a long, steadying breath and hunted for a conversation topic far away from her mother as Ryan went through the motions of approving the wine.

"Can I ask you something?" she dared after their wine was poured. She hummed her appreciation for the Syrah he supposedly didn't care about. Even so, his taste was drastically better than Lori's when it came to wine.

He lowered his glass, caution emanating from him. "Sure. I can't promise I'll answer."

"Of course not." Her laugh blended with her sigh. She took another sip of her wine, eyeing him over the glass. Was it possible to truly understand what made him tick? Would he let anyone get that close? "Why Carla?" she finally asked.

"Why not Carla?" he returned without a blink.

She barely held back another groan. She dropped her head back instead, amused and annoyed, but a smile held when she looked to him. That reflex to deflect and debate was just…him.

"Well…" How did she word this without sounding bitchy? "She's not who I would have imagined as your ideal assistant."

It was really none of her business, but after weeks of working with both of them, she couldn't figure out why he kept her when he could succinctly cut down an associate when his standards weren't met.

"She does her best." He took a drink of his wine, his hold on the stem appearing delicate beneath his fingers.

Brie cocked a brow. "And her best is good enough for you?"

"It is." That was it. His expression gave away nothing. She'd learned to read it, though. This was the clear FU-and-I-dare-you-to-call-me-on-it look.

"All right," she said, backing off. "She's nice."

He gave a single nod that didn't expand on his thoughts at all. No surprise there. Yet she couldn't help wondering why Carla's best was okay when he was so hard on others.

"Carla is the sole guardian of her four grandchildren," Ryan said without preamble or emotion. He dipped his head, the hard line of his mouth softening. "And she has a good heart," he added. "In this field, it's nice to be reminded that not everyone is out simply to get ahead."

A rush of tenderness spread through her chest as she added compassionate to her list of Ryan descriptors.

Their dinner arrived, and Brie let the topic slide. The food smelled wonderful. She sucked in a long breath, savoring the aromas. The apparently simple dish held hints of unexpected flavors so like the man sitting across from her.

Evening had settled into night when they returned to his car. Their conversation had returned to work through their meal, and a part of her was happy about that. The other part, the sluggish, mellow, probably-shouldn't-have-had-that-last-glass-of-wine one, was sad. He'd never answered her question about what he liked to do outside of work.

Did he have any hobbies? Friends?

She studied him as he drove back to their office. His car was luxury defined. She wasn't surprised by that. It was all part of the expected partner image. Just like the tailored suits, silk ties and perfect hair. And he wore the look beautifully.

But that wasn't the only side of him. Did Ryan only

make appearances in the Boardroom? Did he trust anyone with his secrets? His dreams?

"Do you have a girlfriend?" she asked without preamble.

His gaze jerked to her, brows drawn, but she didn't look away from his icy glare. Maybe it was the wine or simple apathy, but she wasn't intimidated by him.

He refocused on the road. His jaw flexed. "No."

A soft, knowing smile spread over her lips. "Why not?" She shifted in her seat to see him better.

The little jump in his jaw went off again. Her smile grew.

"Do you have a boyfriend?" His counterattack happened right on cue. His words were clipped with impatience, and there was that cinched-lip thing he did.

Her low laugh had his knuckles whitening on the steering wheel. Poking at him was fun. "No," she answered when her laughter died out. "I wouldn't have gone to the Boardroom if I had."

His focus stayed on the road, which gave her the freedom to admire his profile. The clean-shaven look rarely disappeared on him. Would there be stubble in the morning? Did he have hair on his chest? A treasure trail?

She cursed the blindfold for all that it'd hidden. But she never would've gone to the Boardroom without it.

"Why did you?" he asked, startling her. "Go to the Boardroom?"

She should've anticipated that question given his excellent interrogation skills. Her smile spread once again. The expected shame or embarrassment didn't flood her this time. No, there was only a casual awareness of why she shouldn't answer him. Of why this entire conversation was dangerous.

She couldn't seem to care. Not right now.

"Freedom," she finally said, voice soft. "Defiance. Desire. Curiosity." The pure exhaustion of always doing what was expected of her. "Rebellion." She added the last with a coarse scoff.

His brow flicked up at that, but he didn't look at her.

"Why did you?" she asked. Turnabout was fair play. "Join the Boardroom?"

His lip quirked, his shoulders relaxing as he loosened his hold on the steering wheel. "For the sex."

She waited a beat for more. Her burst of laughter broke free when nothing came. "Of course."

He shrugged, sending a sly glance her way. There was a solid smirk on his lips now. Even that looked good on him. What didn't?

"Why else?" She wasn't letting him get off that easily.

"Why does there have to be another reason?"

"Because you can get sex anywhere." Especially a guy as good-looking and successful as him.

"Can you? Truly?" He came to a stop at a light and looked over. There was honest question in his expression, and she braced for the coming debate, that stupid smile of hers still slapped in place. "Without fear or risk of attachment and consequences?"

"And the Boardroom offers all of that? Really?" She doubted it. Nothing was a hundred percent risk-free.

The light changed, and he refocused on the road. "As close as anyone can get."

She had no comeback for that. She wouldn't have gone herself if she hadn't been guaranteed those things. "It's just the sex then. Nothing else?"

"Wakeford." The warning in his voice was lost in the hushed chuckle that followed. He shook his head, a smile breaking free. "You're trying to torture me, right?"

Her eyes sprung wide. "No. Not really." But it was definitely fun. "I'm just curious."

The quiet confines of the car seemed to insulate them from the rest of the world. This was just between them. Safe. She had no quantifiable proof of that, but it embraced her nonetheless.

"Why am I not surprised?"

"I could say the same about you," she countered. "Now answer my question."

He let out a frustrated growl that sent a rush of goose bumps down her neck and arms. Her nipples tightened, adding to the sudden flash of heat. Impressions of the Boardroom flew into her mind in the next breath. That same sound. His passionate touch, firm hold.

She swallowed.

He shoved his fingers through his hair, holding the short strands before he let his hand fall back to the steering wheel. An odd shot of resignation laced his tone when he answered. "Because it *is* a risk," he practically snarled. He pierced her with a quick dagger-eye that clearly warned her to drop it.

Yeah, no. "And that excites you." It had for her. The risk had been part of the draw.

His deep inhalation lifted his chest. "Why are you pushing this?"

She shrugged. "Just curious."

His sarcastic huff of annoyance only drove her more. Her line of questioning was getting to him, and she found that fascinating. Nothing broke through his collected shell.

But this conversation had.

A calm reserve settled over him in a wave of controlled movements. His chin ticked up, shoulders settling as he drew them back. One of his hands shifted down the steering wheel to grip it lightly from the bottom. The air of frustration was wiped away with a slow breath and long exhale.

And just like that, Ryan was gone—or the small glimpse she'd gotten of him was. Sadness wove its way in to pluck at the tender barrier around her heart. Was he afraid? Who had hurt him so badly that he couldn't let his guard down—ever?

Except in the Boardroom.

"Have you gone back?" she asked into the quiet. The road noise was nonexistent in the luxury soundproofing. The black interior added another level to the dark hush that bled into the leather seats and silver accents. Her pulse was steady, nerves silent as she softly added, "Since…me?"

Chapter Nineteen

Ryan whipped the car into the parking garage entrance. He came to an abrupt stop before the gate, his jaw clamped beyond tight when he swiped his badge before the card reader. His pulse thrummed with the resentment and annoyance—and fear—boiling in his veins.

He hit the accelerator the second the flimsy wooden arm rose. His tires squealed around the turns as they plunged into the gray depths of the garage.

Had she really asked that? *Since me?*

A large majority of the parking spots were empty with the flight of the nine-to-five crowd. He gripped the steering wheel, slowing as a car eased past them on its way out. The steam simmering within him worked its way out to cover his skin in a clammy sweat that had his shirt clinging to his back.

Brie was pushing. Hard.

For what?

His mind raced to the most unlikely yet probable reason. She wanted to go back to the Boardroom. And what the hell was he supposed to do? Ignore her? Answer? Shove her firmly back into Ms. Wakeford status?

He pulled into his reserved parking space, slammed on the brakes, shoved the gearshift into Park before twisting in his seat to nail her with a hard stare. Her quick inhalation cut through the air. Her eyes widened as she met his intensity head-on. No flinching. No backing down.

"What are you getting at?" He waited a beat. "Brie."

Her nostrils flared slightly, her lower lip curling in. "It was just a question."

"Wrong. It was more than that." Way more.

"Was it?"

She actually had the nerve to quirk a brow. At him. When he was ready to…

He bit back the thought before it could form. It'd do no good, however it ended. He burned now. Raged. It coiled in his chest and gnawed at his gut with a fierceness he didn't recognize.

His emotions never got to this level.

Ever.

Even that cold empty space in his chest was filled with heat.

He leaned in, refusing to be bested. "Then tell me. Would you go back?" Her brow lowered, and a hitch of victory laced through his anger. "To the Boardroom?"

Her eyes darkened in incremental shifts that he shouldn't notice. Shouldn't.

"Answer my question first." Her voice was hushed, yet it seemed to scream through the tension. Her steely resolve was layered into her steady stare and tugged on that damn admiration he continued to pile on her.

Admiration. Right. That's all it was.

His response wavered on the thin edge of charge or fall back. Her lips were, God, just inches away. She'd edged forward as their standoff dug in. So had he.

"No." His admission snapped out on a flat note. No.

He'd had zero desire to go back. Not even to get her out of his thoughts.

And he wasn't analyzing that.

He caught her swallow in his peripheral vision. There was no way he was tearing his eyes from hers. None. Her pupils grew bigger, the blue richer until the thought of basic blue was gone.

"With you," she whispered.

It took a moment for her admission to sink in. *With you.* Understanding slammed in with a punch to his restraint. *With you.*

A vision of her splayed on a table, engulfed in passion, eyes locked on him, burst into his mind with ease. The burn of want sunk to his groin to free the desire he'd been incapable of quenching. Not when it came to Brie.

He worked to keep his careening thoughts from showing, but he honestly had no clue if it worked. "Is that an invitation?"

She bit her lip, let it slide out. "Would you accept?"

Would wasn't in question. "I don't think *would* is the right word." Should, though? That screamed at him in an attempt to hammer home the answer—which he couldn't decipher.

"We know the answer to should." Her lids lowered. A hint of a smile lifted her lips. "That's unrelated to would."

He could've debated that. His rebuttal was already formed before it slid away. Here, in this secluded cocoon away from the world and work and every possible consequence, he had only one answer. "Yes."

Her eyes closed on a soft fall, cutting off the want that'd burned in them. He sucked in a breath. It got lodged in his chest when he tried to expel it, tried to resist the desire hauling him closer—to her.

It didn't work.

His lips found hers on a crush of yes. *Fuck. Finally.*

Her low moan cried of indecision, of longing and that same, anguished *finally.*

A burst of echoing voices penetrated the car with a slap of harsh awareness. He sat back, cursed. He tensed, gaze locking on the three women as they crossed the garage to a minivan parked down the row. He didn't recognize them.

He scanned past the empty parking spots to the glass doors that led to the elevator foyer. The threat prickled over his nape and struck up a beat in his chest.

They could've been caught.

And then what?

He looked to Brie. That same awareness blazed back at him.

Of the danger. The risk. The want that shouldn't be there.

He eased back until he was fully in his space, not crossing the center or intruding on hers. Yet his desire still raged. It clawed at his restraint and shoved his entrenched calculation to the side. This wasn't logical—whatever it was.

Neither was his intent.

His tongue slicked over his lips, the imagined remnants of her taste swarming inside his mouth. He slid his phone out of his pocket and opened the Boardroom app. Each click dismissed every reason for why this was wrong. Why he should stop.

There. He glanced at the time.

"Tell me no, Brie." He didn't lift his gaze from the

Active Scene screen. A knot twisted in his stomach and fought against the compulsion driving him forward.

He waited.

Her breath hitched. "I don't want to."

Her whispered admission was his undoing. *Hell.*

He scanned the list, found one that fit. He added their names to the players, along with their limits. His thumb hovered over the Add button. This wasn't smart.

He turned to Brie. She watched him with those big eyes of hers. There was little hint of her thoughts displayed on her face. Was her pulse racing like his? Did she ache for his touch? Would she cry out when he drove into her? Toss her head back and dig her nails into his shoulders?

Was this a wild dive into tragedy? Was he consciously throwing away everything he'd worked for? For one more night of sex?

Her single slow nod finished his irrational descent.

He let his thumb fall, the scene reposting to the active board.

He turned off his phone screen. "You can change your mind at any time."

"Okay."

That was it.

His chuckle was empty and dry. What was he doing? He honestly couldn't remember if he'd ever gone into something without knowing precisely why he was doing it. The only answer he had now was the unrelenting need to feel her again. To have that passion focused on him, surrounding him, pulling him in until he felt nothing but her.

Felt her.

He thrust the car into Reverse and backed out of his

spot on that enlightening thought. He hit the brakes, her gaze meeting his when he glanced over. Her emotions were locked down behind that professional mask he usually appreciated but now despised.

No. This was good.

The Boardroom was not connected to work. It had boundaries, rules and limitations. And she'd agreed to each one.

He took a breath, locking his own flailing emotions behind the wall of correctness. He looked back to her. That same fucking wall was erected around her, and he wanted nothing more than to kick it down.

And he would. Soon.

"Do your rules still stand?"

Her brows dipped, lifted. "I'll let you know." She looked away, chin raised, back straight. Her fingers were laced on her lap, feet crossed at the ankles, the hem of her skirt rising just above her knees in a prim facade that brought a crazy-assed smile to his face.

He was so fucked—and she could never know exactly how much.

Chapter Twenty

The office building was another basic concrete-and-glass high-rise that loomed over the surrounding area in a lopsided declaration of superiority. And Brie didn't give a rat's ass about the building. Or the plush entry and the etched lettering on the glass declaring the tech company's ownership.

Nope. None of that mattered. Not when she was following Ryan down a darkened hallway, their steps muted by the pale gray carpet.

She tugged on her shirt in an attempt to circulate some air over her back. She'd left her suit coat in the car, at his direction. Her cream blouse wasn't revealing. Nor was her suit skirt. She couldn't even remember which underwear she'd picked out that morning.

Thankfully, her mother had hounded in the decadence of matching lingerie when she'd been a teenager. She would never bitch about the expensive habit or the annoying washing requirements again.

His hand tightened around hers as he slowed. He'd left his tie in the car, but that was all. His unbuttoned suit jacket along with the three undone buttons on his shirt were his only nod to casual.

Were they truly going into a Boardroom scene? A

part of her was starting to think this was all a big joke—on her.

Until he turned his gaze to her.

Heat rose up in another rush of *oh fuck* that left the Libido Bitch cackling.

"Any changes?"

To… Her rules. The answer snapped in, and she nodded. "Just one." His brow inched up and for some unknown reason, that simple action brought a smile to her face. The tightness eased from her chest. She lifted to raise her mouth to his ear. "Only you can fuck me."

His hitch of breath sent goose bumps down her neck to pucker her nipples. She hummed her desire, eyes closing as she let the Libido Bitch go. Consequences be damned.

She stepped back only to get lost in the smoky heat of his eyes. She should ask questions. Seek information. Demand…something.

But the trust wove around her to wipe out those nagging doubts. He wouldn't betray her, nor she him. This—whatever *this* was—was outside of anything she'd ever experienced. It threaded through her heart and embraced the part of her she so rarely dared to expose.

And he wanted it. Wanted her. Every scandalous desire and lustful craving.

The corner of his mouth turned up before he dipped closer. "No one will dare to fuck you but me." He blew a line of warm air down her neck, back up. She bit her lip to keep her tremble from showing. "But they're going to watch every thrust and wish to God it was them sinking into you."

Well… Okay then. She forced a swallow, her headspace dropping into the world of decadence and lust only he stirred up.

He turned away to give two quick raps on the door. It was opened a moment later, and he led her into the room. The Boardroom.

The shadowed darkness hit her first. A lusty moan second. She blinked, inhaled. The sultry, musky scent was third.

She found the source of the last two as she followed Ryan to the side of the room. A woman was perched in the middle of the large table that ran the length of the room. The dark stain of the wood gleamed even in the low light, the gloss shiny enough to reflect the graceful line of the woman's back. Her brown skin seemed to absorb what little light there was with the sole intent of preaching its softness.

There were men too, and another woman, standing around the perimeter of the room.

Ryan leaned a shoulder on the wall and urged her to stand before him. A small desk lamp on a back cabinet was the only source of light, leaving their end of the room in the shadowy fringes.

She frowned, a pinch of disappointment seeping through her lust. She'd thought… What? That she'd be the show again? That she'd be the only woman being ravished?

Her naivety was showing.

Ryan slid his hand around her waist, tugged her back until she was crushed to him. "Our turn is coming," he said by her ear, his hand easing up to caress her ribs.

She had no idea what he meant, but her pussy clenched at the implied promise.

The woman on the table let out another erotic moan.

Her head fell back, and she braced a hand on the table. The other was moving between her bent legs, her hips rocking in a suggestive movement.

Oh. Oooohhhh.

Brie sucked in a breath, her weight falling into Ryan even more. This was…

The woman lay back, her black hair spreading over the table in a scattered spray, her dark nipples declaring her arousal. Her hand moved faster between her legs in an urgent rush.

Brie's pussy contracted yet again, a surge of desire blooming. Ryan eased his other hand up her arm, his fingers playing with her shirt collar. She tilted her head, her focus traveling over the room. The others were tuned in to the woman on the table, lust smoldering on their expressions. The men were all in suits. Some wore ties, others didn't. The dark outline of the hills, peppered with the twinkle of lights, shone behind them through the windows.

She caught the eye of one man. Her heart sped up in a burst of adrenaline. He was watching them. The awareness blew over her skin in a remembered wave. But it was a hundred times more intense now—with the blindfold off.

Her nipples pebbled into hard points that begged to be touched. She wet her lips, her neck arching further when Ryan trailed his fingers up her throat, back down. A shiver spread from the inside out to sensitize her skin and kick off a rush of longing.

"You like being watched," Ryan whispered, as he slowly cupped her throat. Heat radiated from his palm, heightening the craving she hadn't fully acknowledged.

His firm hold sent off another stream of memories

and corresponding wants. She relaxed into his touch, thoughts scattering, will fleeing. There was nothing but him now. Ryan.

Her gorgeous, reserved boss.

But he wasn't her boss in here. No. Here, he was just hers.

He eased his other hand down to skim his fingers beneath the waistband of her skirt. She sucked in her stomach, knees dipping. Her low whimper fell out to float through the room. More heads turned their way, and she noted each one.

Power rolled in to embrace her unspoken want. The lust and desire on every single face fed the Libido Bitch, who refused to back down. It kicked her bravery into high gear and triggered emotions she'd stuffed away after her last trip to the Boardroom.

The slow caress of his palm up and down her throat served as a blatant reminder of who was in control. She reveled in that too.

She let her eyes fall closed, her head dropping back to rest on Ryan's shoulder. Her hips did a dance of their own as she urged his other hand lower. The outline of his watch imprinted against her palm and ignited an array of erotic memories linked solely to Ryan.

Every part of her begged to be touched by him. Would the others be envious? Would they come watching them fuck?

The thought sent heat blazing through her groin. She ground her ass into his erection. His groan vibrated through her back to set off her own.

"I don't think I can be gentle," he murmured.

His warning hiked her need into overdrive. Weeks

of pent-up desire fueled by dream-filled nights had her begging to be fucked. Hard. "Then don't be."

He whipped her around, crushed her against the wall and claimed her mouth in the next breath. *Yes. Yes. God...* She opened instantly, meeting every demanding thrust of his tongue. This was what she'd missed. The heat and possession. The frantic longing scrambling for a foothold when there were none around.

Her mind spun. Her breath was lost. And she didn't care. Ryan was all she wanted. She clung to him, her fingers digging into his neck to draw him closer.

Her blouse was tugged from her skirt, her hands somehow maneuvered and trapped over her head. *More.* She screamed the plea in her head, her mouth consumed by his. Her verbal skills were diminished to inarticulate sounds. He tore the moans from her with every nip that stung her lips and jaw and each demanding touch.

"Fuck," he breathed near her ear. "I'm—I can't—"

"Don't," she managed around a choked exhale. "Give it to me." He dove in to plunder her mouth with the primal urgency ripping her apart. She tore her lips away, desperate. So damn desperate. "Please." *Now. Soon.*

The dark lust swirling in his eyes called to every deviant desire her Libido Bitch released. Being fucked in a room full of watchers was only one of them. Being ravished by him was the main course.

Her breasts heaved with each quick breath and the forced arch of her back. Awareness shimmered over her at the show they'd become. There'd been no handoff or signal, but she knew without looking that everyone was watching them.

He tore through her blouse with hard tugs that sprung each button and wrenched small gasps from her. A devious smirk curled his lips as he slid his hand up her abdomen in a dragged-out tease. He flicked open the front clasp on her bra. Her breasts fell free from their containment, their weight heightened by the need aching within them.

He cupped one, pinched her nipple. Pain-laced ecstasy bloomed across her chest and raced to her pussy. She tried to clench back the rapidly spreading fire, her mouth falling open to catch some air. Any would be good.

"Hold on," he whispered, dark intent communicating his coming actions.

He released his hold on her wrists, dipped and took a nipple in his mouth before she could process his movements. Her cry split the air with the hit of wet heat and sharp teeth. He sucked hard, pulled back. "Yes." She clung to his shoulders, her head falling against the wall in complete submission.

She squeezed her eyes closed, lost to him. His hands seemed to be everywhere. Clenching her ribs, digging into her ass, rubbing up her sides. His mouth did wicked, wicked things to her breasts.

Her head swirled with the dizzying rush of intoxicating lust, want and hunger. God. Hunger. She wanted him in her. Around her. Driving until she couldn't breathe.

Her skirt fell to the floor and she could only pant in approval. Then his fingers were in her folds, stroking her clit, plunging into the ache to stoke it higher.

She squirmed against the wall, struggling to get closer when he held her pinned in place. Her head fell forward, and she lifted her eyelids to scan the room over his head. The ravenous looks answered that decadent call within her. They'd driven those looks to those faces.

Erections were outlined beneath the thin suit pants and no one tried to hide them. There was no need here.

The woman who'd been on the table was now standing, her back pressed to a man, an arm slung back to grip his nape. She met Brie's gaze, erotic appreciation lifting her lips.

And there was the power. It surged forward to crash with the lust to send her reeling.

Ryan sprung up, claimed her mouth in a hard kiss that left her lips throbbing. This was raw. Wild. And so, so perfect.

She clawed at the fastening on his pants. The belt stuck. She cursed. And then his hands were there, working the buckle free. She yanked his zipper down, dove in to find his erection. Her moan blended with his when she shoved his underwear down and fisted his dick. The velvet heat warmed her palm and sent frantic signals to every desperate cell within her.

His feverish touches and quick kisses matched the hyper beat of the energy coursing through her. She managed two hard tugs on his dick before he knocked her hand away. "Fuck." The mumbled curse rasped near her ear.

She cupped her hands behind his head, dragged her nails over his scalp, urging him on with the same crazed fire he'd started. He arched his neck, his head tilting back with a strangled groan before he whipped his chin down. The sizzling heat in his eyes scorched the last of her thoughts.

He rolled a condom on, anticipation cresting to *please, please, please*. He lifted her up and her legs wrapped around him instantly. Her panties were shoved aside and then, finally, he slid into her.

Her vision darkened to Ryan. Just Ryan. And he stared right back through the descent. Her muscles contracted, her mouth fell open, her breath held until her lungs were ready to burst. She gasped for air. His jaw flexed, passion rolling through his eyes along with possession. The primal cry of *yes* tore through her to latch on to him.

There was no holding back. No walls or boundaries or proprietary rules. Not now. Not when he filled her, clung to her, cried out for her.

Her back rode the wall with each powerful drive into her. She held on, incapable of helping, trusting that he had her.

She tried to raise her eyelids, but they were too heavy to open fully. Her head rolled to the side as she observed the room in a detached way. A couple of men had their dicks in their fists. The two women were being openly fondled by the men behind them, their expressions mirroring Brie's own lost awareness.

Ryan sucked a hard, biting kiss into the juncture of her neck, dragging a cry from deep in her chest. Her focus zoomed back to him and to the flames threatening to burn her from the inside out.

She arched into him right before she was swung around. Her mind shorted out, her world disorientated until the hard plane of the table hit her back.

He rammed into her. Jarred a gasp from her. "Yes." That was it. Right there. He nailed her again and again until their frenzied wave of lust swirled with the want and need burning in her pussy. It knotted in her core, growing tighter and tighter.

He took her lips in a brief crush of tongues. His fingers dug into her hips, one hand twisted her nipple.

"Come," he groaned near her ear. "Clench my dick and show them how beautiful you are." His teeth sunk into her shoulder, he thrust hard, rubbed her clit and she fell.

The knot exploded in a blinding wave of power and sensation that ripped over her in wave after wave of ecstasy. Her cry rang in her ears and morphed with his growled grunt as he sunk into her one hard, grinding last time.

Her limbs quivered, nerves jumped and hitched in an uncontrolled state as she surfed the dark ripple of contented awe.

That—this—was Ryan. Her Ryan.

And with him she was safe to be this Brie.

Chapter Twenty-One

Sweat slid down Ryan's temple to catch on the corner of his eye. His breath still burst from his lungs in hard pants that did little to circulate the air. His heart pounded through the warmth that flooded his entire chest, her exhaled breaths matching his own.

He had zero strength or will to move. The wild, frantic sex had released a valve he had no chance of capping. At least not yet. Not when his dick was still entrapped in the warm, clenching heat of Brie. His muscles still trembled in his legs, and he could barely piece together a logical trail of thoughts.

Brie had been amazing—was amazing. Her eyes were blue. A stormy gray blue that'd crashed into his and raged alongside his own wild fall. She'd been everything he'd remembered and so much more. Free. Wild. Trusting.

So damn trusting.

The wonder of that alone humbled him. She'd submitted to his rough treatment and had begged for more.

A long, harsh groan tugged him back to the here. The now. They were still in the Boardroom.

A series of soft slaps indicated that someone else

had taken over the show, and the others were still enjoying it.

He lifted. Her limbs tightened around him before they relaxed. He eased from her protective hold, regret eating at his rules.

To achieve success. To earn respect. To be better. To deserve more.

To not feel.

Brie was a gorgeous sight to behold. Her eyes were closed, lips parted, their deep red plumpness declaring the punishment he'd given them. He slicked his tongue over his own that throbbed as he became aware of their soreness. Her blouse was spread wide, the white cups of her bra parting to leave her breasts on full display, dark rose tips still puckered. The color matched the blooming line of bites he'd left down her neck and over her shoulder.

Possessive pride raged before he could call it back. He dragged his fingers over each mark, awed and proud at once. Her panties were shoved to the side, his dick still encased in her heat.

Regret sucked at his chest when he slid free, a firm hold on the end of the condom. Her soft whimper kicked that sore spot in his chest. The one he didn't recognize and didn't know how to acknowledge.

A wet wipe lay on the table next to them, and he didn't question where it'd come from. Just like he hadn't questioned the condom that'd been handed to him. He cleaned up quickly, taking care of the condom and tucking himself away. Brie was still lifeless when he finished. Most of the room was focused on the next act, but he caught more than one guy admiring Brie.

He didn't condemn them for doing so, yet he also

didn't like it. Not now. When she was vulnerable and still so damn trusting.

He scooped her up, her arms and legs coming around him without prompting. She clung to him when he'd thought she was weak and listless. She buried her face in his neck, a soft sniff reaching his ear.

His arms tightened. His heart hitched. That soft little sound tore through his resolve and demolished every damn wall he'd spent years erecting.

He turned to the door. A guy held out her skirt and one of her heels that'd fallen off. He took them, grateful for the assist.

"That was stunning," someone said quietly as he passed.

"Fucking hot," another added.

The same guy who'd let them in held the door open as he departed. His smirk and nod had Ryan's arms cinching tighter.

The door clicked closed behind him and finally they were alone. His lungs filled with air, the tension slipping from his shoulders on his exhale.

Brie snuggled closer to him with each step he took. He hunted for an empty office but gave up when his hold started to slip.

He found a desk with a cleared surface and lowered her onto it. "Brie," he urged, easing back. "Hey." He cupped her face, concern weaving in. "Brie."

Her eyes fluttered open, a lazy smile curling her lips. She looked at him beneath heavy lids, a mellow daze still holding.

She lifted a hand, pressed it over his on her cheek. "Thank you," she whispered.

Thank you. His heart pinched, dug in, but he withheld his wince. He couldn't remember being this lost. Not since those dark days locked in the closet before his plans were laid out and set into motion.

He had no plan for this. For Brie.

He brushed a kiss over her lips, a soft touch that trembled in his chest and threatened everything. He rested his forehead on hers and floundered through the wreckage of his mind.

A shiver shuddered through her limbs and down her back, reminding him of the basics. "We need to get you dressed."

His chest contracted at the site of the tear trailing from the corner of her eye. She quickly wiped it away, looked down. "I'm fine," she mumbled. "Really." But her hands shook in her lap and goose bumps stood out on her forearms.

She was crashing. The same way she had after that first Boardroom scene. It wasn't unusual after an intense scene, and he kicked himself for not being prepared for it.

The need to care for her roared up with unexpected force. He slipped his suit jacket off and draped it over her shoulders. She shot him a weak smile as she tugged it around her.

He kneeled and eased her skirt over her feet. Her giggle had him jerking his head up. She covered her mouth, a bit of the strain leaving her expression when she lowered her hand.

"Sorry." She grabbed the waist of her skirt from his hold. "I can get it." He gave her room to stand, but stayed close. She handled the back zipper with an efficient tug and closed her bra in the next movement. She came to a halt when she grabbed the sides of her blouse.

A swarm of pride and something close to embarrassment pressed on him. Every button on her shirt was missing. She glanced up, quirked a smile.

"I'll replace it," he promised.

She didn't respond as she slid her arms into his jacket and tugged it around her. She tucked her hair behind her ear and slipped her missing heel on as another shiver raked down her torso.

He hauled her to him, tucked her head beneath his cheek, unable to stand back. She relaxed into him immediately, relief falling out on a slow exhale. This was Brie. He had no idea what he was going to do with her, but he couldn't stand there and let her struggle. Not after what she'd just shared with him.

Given him.

He kissed the top of her head, resolute on his next steps. The plan formed almost without his consent, but he wasn't backing away from it.

He kept his arm around her as he ushered her from the building and to his car. The silence held during their drive back to the city. The road hummed softly around them, the mood mellow but not tense. Brie had sunk into the seat, her head back, lids lowered. Her hands were lax in her lap except for that almost unnoticeable run of her fingers over her thumb. His hand fisted with the urge to grab hers.

He didn't.

The traffic picked up as they entered the city. He braced when he cruised past the turn that would take them to work. Her frown marked deep lines in her forehead when she glanced over. Her unspoken question was clear.

He didn't answer though, and she didn't push. He

turned the heat up a notch when he caught her shivering again. She was still deep in her drop and he wasn't leaving her alone. Not like that. Not until he was sure she was okay.

He gave in and grabbed her hand, squeezed. A wall crashed and burned with that one simple action.

She stared at him. It prickled over his side and alerted him to the danger of his path. The risks were mounting in stacks that crowded in his stomach in the sick little way he remembered from his youth. Did he make a run for the kitchen to sneak food or wait until dark? Would there be anything left to eat? Would the hunger be better than the beating if he was caught?

He reluctantly let go of her hand when he turned in to the entrance of his parking garage. The loss slithered up his arm in a cunning cry of *See? This. This is what you fear.*

"Why?" Her soft question broke through the quiet.

He caught the doubt in her expression as he pulled into his parking spot. He found her hand again after he turned off the car. "I'm not dropping you off after that. Not when you're still shaking."

She swallowed, doe-eyed. "Oh."

He drew her in for a kiss, his lips holding on hers for a long beat. His heart gave another hard thump before he exited the car. He grabbed their briefcases from the trunk and met her as she got out, his hand extended, assisting her and reassuring himself that her legs were steady. His own thirst was clawing up his throat to reprimand him for his lack of preparation.

But none of this had been planned. Not even close.

She clung to his hand, her other clutched his jacket tightly closed. A hundred thoughts swirled in his head now, but no words came out. What should he say? What was she thinking? What the fuck did this mean?

He led her into his condo, the silence stretching down the hallway into the open space beyond. He dropped their bags on a kitchen bar stool and plucked two bottles of water from his fridge. She meandered past the kitchen to the living room, her heels clicking out her path on the hardwood. Her back was to him, her gaze locked on the view outside.

He took a long drink from his bottle, finishing half of it before setting it down. The city glowed softly beyond her. He'd neglected to turn on a light, so used to finding his way without it. Late-night visitors had never occurred—until Brie.

He could say that about so many things.

She fit perfectly into the space before him as he wrapped his free hand around her waist and held the bottle of water out to her.

She took it, her weight falling into him in a way that screamed the trust she continued to give him. Would he crush it someday? Unintentionally? Purposely?

Her water was almost gone, her shivers fading before she spoke. "I don't understand."

He stared at nothing. The city landscape with its sea of multi-colored lights was lost to the gentle rock and slide of peace he was reluctant to label.

"About what?" He kept his tone hushed, fears shoved back.

Her low snort carried the sarcasm she didn't voice. "This. You. All of it."

So am I. But he couldn't say that. "Then stop trying."

She set her bottle on the table next to them before she turned in his arms, her scowl only slightly menacing. "I'm trained to understand. That's my job. Find the facts, sort out the truth and deliver a non-biased analysis."

"And this isn't work."

"But it's related." She sagged into him, her arms folded between them, her head resting on his shoulder. "It's all related," she mumbled, the misery floating out to punch him.

Was he pushing her? Forcing something she didn't want? Doubt wedged its way in for the first time since he'd decided to bring her here. "Do you want me to take you home?" The words ground against his throat and chilled the warmth that still flooded his chest.

She didn't respond for the longest time, and he prepared himself to step away. He'd broken the Boardroom rules. No, he was simply ensuring that she was okay. She'd been his guest, technically. But she'd stopped shaking, and that dazed look had retreated from her eyes.

"Do you want me to go?"

Her question floated up to him on a clear, flat tone. He could feel her withdrawing when she hadn't moved. That would be for the best, though. They still worked together. She was still his subordinate.

His arms tightened around her. "No." He spoke the truth when the denial rested on his tongue. "I'd like you to stay."

A long pause followed before she answered. "I'd like to stay." The soft response whispered of the same doubt and fear cascading through him.

He squeezed his eyes closed against the wave of nausea that rolled through his stomach. The leap into the unknown was terrifying in ways he'd never expected.

This was already so much more than anything he'd experienced with his ex-wife.

How? Why?

Fuck if he could explain it.

He led her down the hall to his bedroom. The clean lines and stylish decor had all been picked out for him, but he liked the feel of it. It reminded him daily that he was never going back to the scared kid huddled in the closet.

He flicked on the bedside lamp. "Would you like to shower?" His words came out stiff, drawing another internal wince. Could he be a bigger ass? Yet there he stood, waiting for her response.

The kid who'd never dated, never hung out, never even thought of bringing a girl home reared his scared head. How could he admit that he had no clue what to do next?

A smile gentled her expression. She brushed her fingers down his jaw, over his lips. "I'll just clean up quickly." Her steps were steady as she crossed the room to the open door of his master bath.

He sank to the bed the second he was alone, dropping his head into his hands. His heart raced on a wild flight that drew his chest in tighter and tighter. *Breathe. Breathe.*

The toilet flushed, and he laughed. The dry rasp tore at his throat to blare his insecurities when there was no room for them. She was just a woman.

His laugh cut off instantly. That lie wouldn't work anymore.

He removed his shirt, every movement concise as he stripped down to his boxer briefs. He quickly used the guest bath, dropped his laundry into the appropriate bins for his cleaning service to handle.

He slid between the bedsheets, but remained sitting, one foot still on the floor when she came out of the bathroom. Her clothes were held in one hand, the other clutched his suit jacket to her chest.

The lusty woman from the Boardroom had slid away to reveal this quieter version of Brie, one he could empathize with. The revelation spread in a soothing coat of understanding. They were both a little lost.

He came around the bed to take her clothes and set them on the chair in the corner. She tracked him, her expression as locked down as his own. The image of a soundless dance flashed in his mind as they tiptoed around the unknown.

He stood before her, questions and doubts lashing out before he cupped her cheeks and brought his lips to hers. A shiver threaded down his spine in a long sigh of *oh fuck* and *yes*.

Her eyes were bright when he eased back. He caressed her cheek with his thumb, that damn warmth holding steady in his chest.

"We'll figure this out," he promised.

Her brows lifted. "Will we?"

He nodded. They had to. There was no other choice.

Chapter Twenty-Two

Brie woke to the blinding glare of the morning light and a warm trail of kisses across her shoulder. Her low hum was hitched on the languid flow of memories weaving their way into her consciousness.

Ryan smoothed a hand down her abdomen, eased it beneath her panties. His leg slid between hers to spread them apart. She arched into his touch, moving on a wave of filtered awareness. She wouldn't let herself think, not yet.

He dipped a finger through her pussy on a slow caress that circled and teased. Her moan gave voice to the pleasure simmering to life. She floated in the hazing mellowness that lent an air of unreality to the sensual heat flooding her. The slow rub of his finger on her clit matched the dreamy brush of his lips as he nibbled her ear.

She reached back to rub his thigh. The muscles flexed beneath her palm, the power declared. He'd used that strength to thrust into her, hold her up and drive her wild. The memory alone brought a rush of longing.

She twisted her head toward him, and he covered her mouth with his. The fresh hit of toothpaste broke through her haze for a moment. Just a moment to wonder when he'd woken.

But then he swiped his tongue over hers, playing so sweetly she could only focus on the slow dip and swirl as she chased his kiss. Gone was the hot wild passion, but in its place was something that burned just as bright, just as powerful.

He shifted to slip her panties down her thighs. She kicked them off once they reached her knees, and then he rolled, bringing her under him. Her legs opened to cradle him, the hard line of his erection running hot and firm over her mound.

She arched into her moan, her eyes opening to find the same sultry passion burning back at her. Ryan.

She drew him down, the faint scruff of his beard tickling her palms. The sensation brought a smile to her lips before she claimed another kiss. Another long, slow exploration that merged to another and another. The kisses melted her worries and breathed life into her hope. Into the wishes and wonder that continued to whirl.

Time spun out until there was only his touch, down her sides, on her breasts, and the hot press of his lips, over her neck, sucking her nipples. She sought him too. The curve of his back, the line of his shoulders, the smooth plane of his chest. And finally, the hard heat of his dick.

Her moans carried that same hushed quality that melted her bones and slushed through her blood. They merged with his in a cascading volley until he rolled on a condom and slid into her.

She stared at him, devouring every dark mystery churning in his eyes. The rich brown color twisted with a haunted intensity she couldn't place, yet understood. This... This.

He stilled, his girth stretching her walls in a claim of ownership she welcomed. The rightness thrummed through her and wrapped her heart in its sweet embrace. He moved, pulling out only to descend on the same patient rhythm. The burn simmered in her core as it absorbed the slow, tantalizing build.

She found his lips again, her pulse crying her wonder. She was still Brie, and every touch, every slow glide into her proclaimed he saw her. He wanted her.

After last night, after now, there was no denying how much she wanted him.

She wrapped her legs around his hips, his pace increasing with the insistent need churning to life. The low slap of skin merged with the hushed grunts and purred moans to create its own symphony so sweetly different from the night before. Yet the tune was the same, the notes familiar.

She rode the crest to a shattering fall that left her breathless and dizzy. Ryan shuddered, groaned, drew her in until nothing separated them. The oneness hummed through her chest with a resounding ring of completeness.

She held him, her thoughts floating, mind wandering with no destination. She skimmed her palm over the short hairs on the back of his head, her other hand finding the curve of his shoulder and the long line of his spine.

His last kiss was just as long, just as full and hopeful as his first. She mumbled her complaint when he pulled out, rolling to the side to clean up.

She studied the line of his spine that ended at the

dark shadow of his butt crack. His muscles were compact and sleek, so like the man himself. She smoothed her palm down his back if only to keep her thoughts from running ahead. There was still time to savor this quiet. The storm would hit soon enough. The world still existed beyond these walls, and there was a pile of litigation they needed to attack.

But not yet. Please, not quite yet.

Her brows dipped, hand stilling over the faint line of circular burn scars on his lower back. She brushed her fingers over them, compassion flaring. Who'd done this to him? When?

He turned around, scooped an arm beneath her and pulled her in until she was nestled into his side, her head resting on his shoulder. Her heart fluttered with her sigh.

She closed her eyes and floated in the peace. This. That was it. Just…this.

He trailed his fingers through her hair, the strokes slow in an absent-minded way. Each pass released a spray of tingles over her scalp that incited a tiny flash of teasing shivers.

"I let Carla know we had an unscheduled deposition this morning."

Brie sprung up, eyes wide as she stared at him. "We do? When?" Why hadn't he told her? Did she have time to go home and change? "What time is it?" She stretched to see the nightstand, scowling at the pristine surface. "Where's your clock?" Who didn't have a clock next to their bed?

His chuckle shook his chest, his smile growing when she leveled her scowl at him. He drew her down to press a firm kiss to her lips. It shifted, smoothed and flowed into another slow, quiet exploration that shoved her concerns aside.

His smile was still in place when he eased away. Little crinkles formed at the corner of his eyes and the barest of a dimple showed near one corner of his mouth. He swiveled his head in absent wonder, which brought her frown back. "What?"

"We just conducted the meeting."

She twisted her lips, confused, until understanding dawned. "Oh." She let her head fall, embarrassment sweeping in as his laugh tumbled over her. But he hugged her to him, teasing a defeated chuckle from her. "Thanks for calling."

"My pleasure." He brushed her hair back when she looked up, that smile lingering on his lips. His hair was mussed, and a faint stubble darkened his jaw in a totally rakish way. Burns would never be seen like this.

"How long do we have?" She squinted out the window, not even fazed by the open view that included a sight line into nearby buildings. Had anyone watched them? Gotten off as they had this morning? Her Libido Bitch purred.

"I have another meeting at eleven." He drew a finger down the line of her jaw, leaving a trail of shimmering awareness behind. "I should be at that."

A ping of guilt worked its way into her glow. Blowing off work to get laid didn't fall within the good-girl code. But he'd done it too. And he was her boss.

Reality landed like a cold bomb. She dropped her gaze, doubt and questions rushing in. They wiped out the mellow contentment and stomped all over the hope that'd dared to rear its head.

"Hey." He urged her chin up, his frown confused. "What just happened?"

She searched him. Did he have no concerns? Fears? "What about this?" She motioned between them.

His chest lifted and fell in a deep breath. His expression flattened out until Ryan was masked behind Burns. "We'll figure it out."

"How," she pushed, the risks and pitfalls already spinning out before her. Her job, her reputation, her mother…her heart.

"I don't know," he said, his voice smoothing into the efficient office tone. "We'll go to work. We'll do our jobs. That won't change." His eyes closed, hand stilling on her shoulder.

Her pulse jammed in her throat as she kicked herself for forcing what he clearly didn't want forced. "Okay." She rolled away to sit on the far side of the bed. She glanced over her shoulder, smile in place. "I'm going to jump in the shower." She didn't wait for an answer as she strolled to the bathroom, heart aching, gut churning.

"Brie."

She froze, her hand on the door frame. She looked back, the internal tangle of doubts and illogical deductions locked deep in her chest. Nothing would show that she didn't want to be seen. Life with her mother had schooled her in the art of subterfuge.

"Yes?" She waited, every lengthening second highlighting her nudity until she was certain he could see the flaws she didn't dare expose.

"This won't change either." His voice had lowered into that dark sexy timbre that called to the Libido Bitch and made her squirm with lust.

She wet her lips. Nodded. "Good."

The bathroom door closed behind her with a defined click. She dropped her forehead against the door and breathed. *Just breathe.*

A shiver began deep in her chest, spreading in waves over her heart and across the longing she'd tried so hard to ignore. But she couldn't. Not anymore.

Not with Ryan.

And she had no idea how to handle that without getting hurt.

Chapter Twenty-Three

The city spread before him in a glorious interplay of man and nature, from the white-and-gray rooftops to the random pops of greenery. The metropolitan crowding was cut off by the blue expanse of the San Francisco Bay and the rolling gray-and-green hills beyond, the distance too great to expose the population crammed onto it.

The million-dollar view was partner-level perfect, and Ryan saw none of it. His mind was buried deep in the paths and obstacles that kept him from moving forward. The quiet surrounded him yet it offered no peace. Work waited, decisions called and still he sat, staring blindly.

They'd returned to work after their night of sex and morning of…sex wasn't the right word. It was too…cold. He didn't have a replacement, though. Not one that worked in his landscape.

Not his old one anyway.

A knock sounded on his office door to shatter his thoughts. Good. They were going nowhere.

Brie poked her head in. "Do you have a moment?"

His chest did that strange undefinable clench-and-release thing. How could he define what he didn't understand?

"Yes." He swiveled his chair to face her. "Come in."

Her hair was pulled into a loose tail at her nape, her pantsuit standard navy with a patterned blouse. She kept her smile to that artificially pleasant curve he'd grown to hate since their night together. The one that screamed Wakeford. Just Wakeford.

And for that, he had no choice but to respect her.

"I have these briefings for you to review." She handed him a small stack of folders, all marked with printed labels. "And you need to follow up with Morrison on filing for a court date." She clutched the rest of the folders to her chest, her stance calm. "I've spoken to his paralegal and confirmed that they're done with depositions."

"For now," he added. He'd faced the opposing counsel before. Morrison was a cagey bastard.

"For now," she agreed. "Mr. Cummings has asked about my time. I told him I'd check with you. We're winding down our discovery and our case has solidified—"

He held up a hand, cutting her off without words. Annoyance seethed in a quiet ember of self-derision. Brie had shifted back to Wakeford without further question after her one push last week. The one he'd shut down when she'd still been wrapped in his arms.

And here they were: in a stalemate of his making.

Her smile fell in a flat line that wiped her expression clean. The marble mask held the same frosty gloss that'd greeted him when she'd stepped from his bathroom that morning. He hadn't countered it then, not when they'd needed to get to work. Not when his world had been turned upside down from the...sex that morning.

And sex was what he had in the Boardroom, not his bedroom.

Not with Brie.

His moronic attitude was going to sink him if he kept it up.

He came around his desk, decision made. She tracked his path to the office door where he closed it. A small frown had formed to pull her brows in slightly, but that was it.

Everything she was showing him was a hundred percent appropriate for work. He should respect that. He did. Yet…

She stared at him as he approached, her frown fading. He let his intent show. The unleashed want and frustrated desire. The anger at himself and the driving urgency to have Brie back.

To be seen again.

"Tell me no, Brie." Her name ghosted out on a note of longing.

That dark stormy blue shifted into her eyes, her lips parting. Her breaths turned heavy, but she didn't look away. Her forced swallow telegraphed her answer before it came out. "I don't want to."

He cupped her face and dove in for the kiss he shouldn't take. Just add it to the list of many shouldn'ts. Her moan vibrated into his mouth and urged him deeper. He sought and found the sweet taste that'd locked into his memory as her. Brie.

Her hand came to his chest, eased up to cup the back of his head, urging him on. Relief spread to beat back the chill that'd encroached. Brie was still his. Still here.

When he'd given her no reason to be.

He slowed the kiss to a soft peck. A little nibble. A

last brush. He rested his forehead to hers, breaths long and full.

"Thank you," he murmured, eyes still closed, the weight on his chest gone.

"For what?" Her breath warmed his lips and tempted him back for more.

He laid one last kiss to her temple and shifted back. He used his thumb to wipe away a smear of lipstick below her lip. Gone was the distant mask. In its place was the open smile and lustful gaze that danced with secrets and promises.

"Letting me do that, to start," he said for lack of a better explanation. "I'm not very good at this." The honesty came out on a rush of trust he rarely extended.

She ran her fingers through the short hairs near his nape, inciting small shivers that chased each other to his heart. "I've noticed." Her smile matched the teasing spark in her eyes. "And I get it."

His brows dipped. "You do?"

She lifted to press her lips to his in a short but gentle kiss. "I do." Her tongue traced a quick path over her bottom lip. "It's a little new for me too."

"You?" He shook his head. "I can't see that."

Her brow lifted in staunch reprimand. "Getting fucked by my boss in a room full of watchers is *not* something I can claim experience with."

He grunted at the verbal punch, yet his smile lifted with that damn appreciation she continued to earn. She didn't cower or back down when the facts were in her favor.

He tugged her in for a hard hug that pressed into his soul and calmed the riot of protests raging there. "You—" he forced back the laugh that threatened, muffling it to a dismayed chuckle "—are so right." He covered his floundering with a quick kiss.

Brie smiled back at him. "Remember that."

"I don't know how I forgot." He stepped away before he let his base needs override all his logic.

"Don't worry. I'll keep reminding you." She waggled her brows in a completely unprofessional way as she teased him.

"I'm sure you will." And for some unknown reason, he was looking forward to it. "Do you have plans tomorrow evening?"

She secured her folders under one arm, smoothing a hand over her hair. "I can check my calendar, but I believe I'm free. Why? Do you have another deposition to conduct?" She set her folders on his desk, opening her notepad to scan the page, frowning. "I don't have a note on that."

Her expression was void of confusion or inquiry. She'd simply stated a fact without inference or assumption. The quality was so damn rare yet invaluable in this line of work.

He understood why Charles was ready to have her back. And Ryan wasn't ready to let her go. Not even the Wakeford portion.

"Good." He moved around his desk to stand by his chair, victory gracing his steps. "I'll pick you up at seven. Wear something nice."

Her jaw dropped. "What?"

He held back his humor for a long moment before his smile escaped. "I'm asking you out, Brie. I have a fundraising event at Berkeley. I was hoping you'd be my guest."

"You…" Dismay switched to amusement on a slow

shake of her head. She flipped her notepad closed, placed it on top of her folders and tucked the stack back to her chest. "You need to work on your approach."

"I need to work on a lot of things."

She smirked. "Facts can't be disputed."

He lifted a brow, but opted to skip the debate around that. "Do we have a date?"

Brie headed to his door, turning back before she opened it. "I'll see you at seven tomorrow night. And," her smile softened, "thank you for the blouse. You didn't have to."

"I told you I'd replace the one I ruined." He'd had a new one shipped to her, just like he'd promised.

Her nod was small before she opened the door, pausing again. "I'll be working on a case for Charles this afternoon. Let me know if anything comes up on Palmaro."

Her exit sucked the air from the room until he let a broken laugh burst free. *Fuck.* He scrubbed a hand over his face, but refused to answer the doubts peppering for attention.

"Is everything okay, Mr. Burns?"

Ryan whipped his head up to see his assistant wearing a concerned expression. "I'm fine, Carla."

Her wary once-over could've been applied to the crazy guy on the corner who rambled warnings about the coming apocalypse. She gave a soft humph, eyes narrowing. "You should do that more." She motioned to him.

He held in his sigh, his reserve crawling up to block out his boundaries. "Do what?"

She pulled her shoulders back. "Laugh." The kind

grandmotherly smile warmed her face and tempted one from him. "It looks good on you."

She departed before he could respond, his mouth gaping when few in his life had had the ability to draw that response. He stared at the empty doorway for another beat before another laugh tumbled out. He let it flow, the levity worming through cracks and sealing up emotional holes left open since childhood.

"Thank you," he called when he could speak again.

"You're welcome." The cheery note floated into his office on the solid tone of understanding. Carla may be absentminded and appeared incapable to many, but she saw things most missed.

He sat, his head still shaking. The landscape had changed when he hadn't asked for a remodel, yet returning to the old view held no appeal.

His humor died in a slow dawning of clarity. Had his parents really fucked him up so badly that he'd shocked his assistant by laughing?

No. They hadn't. He'd done that all on his own.

He flipped open the top folder that Brie had left for him. She was right in assessing her workload. They'd packed up the conference room two days back and were ready to move forward.

They were handling their relationship just like he'd said. A load of words and an extended discussion weren't needed to clarify things. He'd created stress where none was needed.

And that was a mistake he wouldn't make again.

Chapter Twenty-Four

Music streamed over the terrace in a pleasant flow of background noise that dampened the low hum of conversations. Brie glanced over the crowd, her social smile in place. To say she felt at home would be a stretch, yet she understood the vibe and how to navigate it. Now if only she could get a handle on the man beside her.

Was this a personal date, a social interaction for professional benefit or a combination of both? And what did that mean for her?

"Can I get you another drink?" Ryan motioned to her empty wineglass.

She hesitated, aware of the effects already mellowing her thoughts. "Sure." She could sip it.

He set their empties on a table and wove his way through the people to the bar. He cut an imposing path that had heads turning even in the affluent crowd, not that she was surprised.

The late-summer night held a gentle nip of cool that hinted at the approaching fall without tipping the temps into cold. A breeze blew over the lawn behind them, and she lifted her face into it. The scent of fresh-cut grass greeted her with unheeded memories of home. Her childhood hadn't been bad. She'd spent hours playing outside, laughing with her sister and friends before her mother's social ambitions had been thrust upon her.

"Here you go." Ryan handed her a glass, his other hand coming around to rest on the small of her back. Their spot by the concrete railing provided a quiet escape along with an advantageous viewing point. "We don't have to stay too much longer."

She closed her eyes for a moment, absorbing the comfort and sense of belonging that came with his simple touch. Out here, in the open among his peers. That was...good. It warmed her in a way far softer and more dangerous than his passionate caresses.

Yes, he was still her boss. People would talk, no matter how inconspicuous or professional they were in the office. She should care, yet she wanted to be with him more—wanted this more. It was irrational and totally against her character—for Brighton. And maybe that's why Brie was okay with it.

She studied his profile as he scanned the terrace. His serious nature kept so much hidden. His invite to this event after a week of business as usual had come as a surprise, yet not. Nothing was planned or normal with him.

"I'm fine," she informed him, softly. "We don't need to leave on my account."

He snapped his focus back to her, brows drawn. "Did I say it was on your account?"

"No." Her lips quirked. The debater was always quick to counter. "I'm just saying, I'm fine." She glanced over the terrace. "They did a nice job on the remodel." He'd given her a tour of the renovated library when they'd first arrived. "Did you spend a lot of time here?"

The giant alumni sign would've tipped her off that

he'd graduated from the university if Berkeley Law hadn't been stamped under his company profile.

He looked at the building, took a drink of his wine. "At one point in my life, yes." The note of sad whimsy caught her attention.

"When was that?"

He huffed a laugh. "Years before technology overtook paper."

"So you're ancient. Is that what you're saying?"

"Careful," he warned, a teasing light in his eyes. He leaned close, pulling her in with the gentle urging of his hand. "I'm still young enough to fuck you against a wall." She gasped, hitting him lightly on the arm, but the Libido Bitch hummed her wicked pleasure at the memory. His smile held a devious gleam. "We can repeat that, unless you're worried that I might hurt myself."

Nope. No worries on that front. Now, her own damn heart? That was already walking too close to the line of fire.

She narrowed her eyes, reaching up to flick her fingers through the edge of his hair. "I don't see any gray yet."

He gave her butt a light pat. "Behave."

The jolt wasn't close to painful, but the heat spread to warm more than her bottom. "Why would I want to do that?" she taunted when she would've punched any other man. But he was...different. Everything was different.

"Good question." His eyes danced with heated amusement.

"I've been known to have a few of them."

"Among other things," he murmured before stepping back. He made a casual gesture to the building. "I probably spent more time in there than my dorm room."

"Why was that?"

His shrug was meant to be casual, but she saw the stiffness. "I needed the grades." He took a sip of his wine, evading her eyes. "And I generally disliked my roommates."

She laughed at that. "I'm not surprised."

His glare had no heat when he directed it at her. "Do I dare ask why?"

"Like you don't already know."

He flicked his brows in the impression of a shrug. "And the geek is now the partner."

She squinted at him, shook her head. "Nope."

"What?"

"I can't see the geek." The corner of his mouth turned up. "Now, the focused asshole..." She made an exaggerated nod. "That I see."

"Even assholes have a place in society."

He fell back into debate mode without a hitch. Her heart softened, regret slipping in. He'd opened up to her and she'd...missed the opportunity.

She laid a hand on his chest. "You're not an asshole, Ryan."

He looked away, stiffening. "I can be one. I know that."

"Can I ask why?" There was no point in denying it further. But she also knew that there was so much more behind the asshole image he projected.

A distant wariness held in his eye when he looked back to her. He hadn't shut down though—or shut her out. "An asshole doesn't get teased, because he doesn't care." He winced, his lips compressing. That little movement showed more than his words. "People try, but when nothing takes hold, they move on to more vulnerable prey."

And he refused to be vulnerable. The unspoken ending defined him so clearly.

She bit her tongue to hold back the sympathy welling in her chest. Yet her heart ached for the boy who'd had to figure that out and the man who still believed it. "How old were you when you learned that?"

"Eleven." No hesitation. No emotion. Nothing.

The music kicked up, and he grabbed her hand. "Come on." He set his glass on a table and did the same with hers.

"Where are we going?" she asked, allowing him to draw her along. Their conversation was done, and she wouldn't continue to push, yet she'd still wonder. What had happened? Would he ever tell her?

She saw the man Ryan was, pitfalls, walls and all, and she still wanted him. The last week of being just Burns and Wakeford had shown that she could do this. She could remain professional at work *and* have a personal relationship with him.

He *was* her boss, but he was also just a man.

Brie smiled at a group of people tracking their path across the terrace. She'd been introduced earlier, but their names had been lost beneath the mass of introductions. Her mother would've been so disappointed in her.

And what about herself? How did she feel?

She caught the eye of an attorney she recognized from another law firm. This man didn't even attempt to crack a smile as he studied her, calculation marching over his expression. She tightened her hold on Ryan's hand, meeting the man's challenge with a strength of her own. The Bay Area might be huge, but the legal community was very intertwined.

Her inner battle sprang to life in a crash of fear and want. Her Brighton instincts urged her to push Ryan away before her mother heard about him or her professional reputation was ruined. But the stronger, awaking Brie desires had her hand tightening around his.

Tongues would wag after tonight, but one thing she would never be was a secret. Her personal pride overruled her work pride on that point.

Her career had been her priority since she'd left home, but now, with Ryan, she had a chance at something that was growing to be just as important, if not more. And it had nothing to do with her mother.

Ryan spun around at the edge of the small dance area. She gasped, smiling when he drew her into his arms. "Dance with me."

He didn't give her a choice and she didn't object. Why would she? "I didn't know you danced." He fell into an easy two-step with a grace that didn't surprise her.

"You know me better than that," he murmured. He tucked her close, his hand holding hers, the other possessive on her lower back.

Her soft laugh was one of understanding and acceptance. "I do." She really did. Knowing how to dance was an image requirement. One she was all too familiar with. She melted into him a little more, that empathy spreading until she imagined it wrapping around him in a protective embrace. "How'd you learn?"

"Classes."

Of course. Her quiet laugh soothed the hurt she'd tried to ignore for the last week. Logic hadn't stopped her doubts from dropping bombs each day. This was so right and wrong at once. And perfect in so many stunning ways.

"Me too." Before her sweet-sixteen party. It hadn't mattered to her mother that most of the boys had only known how to shuffle back and forth.

Ryan did an easy step and turn that managed to draw her closer. Any premise of a respectable space between them was now gone. She was fully aware that he was making a declaration, both to her and his peers.

This was personal.

She could object, ask more questions.

She didn't.

Worry fanned a small breeze through her chest before she let it go. He'd only push back, shut down, and she didn't want to lose this right here.

The blindfold was gone. Her eyes were open, and Brie wanted this. Him. The passion and the ice. The quiet and the frantic. The distance and the impossible closeness.

She closed her eyes and blocked the stares from reaching her. They still prickled over her nape and slithered down her spine with their intrusive power. But she was safe here, within his arms. His strength held her strong when the impropriety threatened to weaken her. He had her, both in and out of the Boardroom.

"There'll be talk," she murmured. She breathed him in. His scent eased the tension and warmed her with knowledge, of who he was and who he could be.

"There will." He squeezed her hand. "I won't let it hurt you."

His reassurance blended with her understanding to

anchor her doubts. "You have a plan." She didn't leave it as a question.

His breath warmed her temple and soothed its way to her heart. "Company policy doesn't prohibit this."

This. She squeezed her eyes against the onslaught of dreams. Nope. Not yet. Not…yet. She forced a lightness to her voice. "This? As in dancing?"

"Dancing." He made another smooth step-step-spin that freed a laugh from her. "Kissing." His lips held on her temple in a press of intent that replaced her laugh with a choking ache of longing. It melted her heart and released her hope. He nudged his lips near her ear. "Fucking." He nipped her earlobe. The sting raced to her core on a cry of want.

She sucked in a breath and locked down the express ride to love her heart was attempting to make. Dancing, kissing and fucking *could* happen without a hint of love in the mix.

The song changed. Couples departed the floor. Ryan kept dancing, and she moved with him, willing to follow where he led.

She looked up at him, her emotions swirling in a murky mix of unknown. He didn't hide from her when she'd feared he would, especially here. His eyes burned with passion and softened with a tenderness reserved just for her. The knowledge sank into her heart and breathed of a freedom she never dared dream of.

He dipped her, halted. His breath ghosted over her lips, but his eyes never left hers. "Tell me no, Brie."

Blood roared in her ears. Shivers spread from her heart to shimmer over her skin and flutter in her stomach. Her pulse jack-rabbited its doubts, but a quiet, sweet calm settled into her bones.

"I don't want to," she whispered.

Something flashed in his eyes that had her heart stuttering and her dreams singing. His lips touched hers, her eyes drifted closed and she let herself fall. Into his arms. His kiss. Him.

And he caught her. Claimed her.

The kiss was gentle, so soft she wanted to package it up and keep it with her. He made one small pass of his tongue over hers, another, before he withdrew.

She opened her eyes to find his. Understanding flowed between them on a current stronger than words. The very one that'd blazed in the Boardroom and bound them still.

She couldn't define it, but she refused to fight it. Words weren't needed when her heart spoke directly to his. The thought was foolish, reckless. Yet that was the only way she could describe it.

He led her from the dance floor, his arm wrapped around her. He nodded at everyone who met his gaze, and she let the tenderness spread into her smile. Happiness bubbled inside her to twist with an unspecified fear. At the unknown maybe? Or the risk? Or the awareness of the gigantic leap she'd just made?

They didn't talk about the change. Not on the way back to his condo. Not as they climbed into bed. Not as he stared into her eyes and filled her. Not through the multiple times they came together over the night and into the next day.

And not when he dropped her off at her home with a tender kiss and no promise to call. But he did, that night.

It didn't come up over lunch the next day or on their walk along the Embarcadero. Nope, it didn't come up the entire weekend. He held her hand, kissed her roughly and just as tenderly, laughed at her stories and shared a few of his own.

And at some point between leaving the fund-raiser and heading back to work on Monday, that fear eased.

Chapter Twenty-Five

"I'm seeing Brighton Wakeford."

Ryan met the stares Charles and Victor sent his way. He didn't flinch or waver when the frowns formed or the scowls followed. He met each one with the same cool calm with which he greeted opposing counsel. Nerves didn't sour his stomach and doubts never entered his thoughts.

Brie was a part of his life, and the weekend had confirmed that she wasn't leaving anytime soon. Not if he had any control over it. Doubts still raged right next to the fear that continued to laugh at him, but they didn't alter his determination. He'd never let them before and he wouldn't now.

Charles cleared his throat and Ryan cut him off before he could speak. "Company policy doesn't prohibit employees from dating."

"Don't quote company policy at me," Charles snapped. "Who do you think wrote it?"

Ryan hitched his brow. "HR?"

Victor barked out a laugh, pointed a finger at Ryan. "Good one."

"Shut up," Charles growled, sending Victor a glare.

"He's right," he said with a shrug. "You have to give him that."

"No, I don't."

Ryan crossed his ankle over his knee, sitting back. The table situated in the corner of Charles's office was littered with various notes and files they'd discussed, including the Palmaro case. He'd timed his bomb to land with the least possibility of prolonged fallout.

Victor eyed his longtime friend, shifted his gaze to Ryan. "Is this a new development?"

Ryan weighed his response. "Yes and no."

"That is not an answer," Charles objected. His years of litigation experience slammed down on Ryan with the vigor of a scorned lover. "Did you force her? Use your authority to manipulate her consent?"

Ryan shot forward, anger blazing. His snarl ripped over his throat to slam with force before Charles. "You will retract those insults." He seethed and didn't care if the other men saw. "I resent the implication to myself and Brie—Brighton." He corrected his slip at the last second, but didn't miss the narrowing of Victor's eyes.

"Charles," Victor said. The reprimand in his tone was one only he could give his friend. Charles jerked his glare to him, glowered for a long moment. He finally sat back with a tug on the edges of his suit jacket.

Victor turned back to Ryan. "I believe what Charles is trying to ascertain was if the reputation of this firm has been tarnished."

Ryan forced himself to sit back, but he remained primed for attack. "I would hope that you know the answer to that without having to ask." He'd followed every damn rule, overachieved every goal, and toed every fucking line they'd ever defined. And they had the gall to question him now?

"One can never be too sure."

"And would I have said something to you if any of those things were possible?" Ryan countered.

"You could be forming a defense prior to the accusation," Charles stated. Some of the anger had cooled from his tone, but his claws were still drawn.

So were Ryan's. "Or I could be acting like a professional and informing my counterparts of a relationship *instead* of sneaking around like it's a dirty secret." He would never disrespect Brie that way.

A crisp knock blew through the strain. Ryan glared at the door, biting his tongue to hold back his irritation.

"What?" Charles barked, his voice edging back to a bellow.

Ryan sat up, his stomach clenching around the sudden shot of concern when Brie stepped into the room. The tension lacing through the room increased as she shut the door behind her and approached their table, stopping between Ryan and Victor.

She clasped her hands before her in a loose hold that didn't match the sharp pull of her shoulders or the hard cut of her gaze. She scanned them, that cool professional smile in place.

"Gentlemen," she said, looking to each of them equally. She didn't linger on Ryan or show any sign of her purpose, but every instinct in him swore she wasn't here to discuss a case. Especially since he'd told her of his intent to tell the partners about them during this meeting.

"I'm assuming you've already discussed the relationship between Mr. Burns and myself," she continued. "If you haven't, then I guess this is news. In either event, I hope you'll have the courtesy to hear me out."

"Brighton..." Charles's tone held a warning that rankled Ryan's need to defend. He glared at the man who was quickly losing his respect.

"Mr. Cummings," Brie interrupted, her smile never faltering. "If I may? Please." She sent that unwavering challenge at Charles and held her ground. That controlled mask was in place, her emotions shored up behind it.

She didn't need Ryan to defend her. Nope. She clearly had this covered.

He relaxed on a slow wave of admiration he should've been used to when it came to her. He'd told her he'd handle this, but here she was, confronting the issue with grace.

"Yes, Ms. Wakeford," Victor said, shooting Charles a cool look. "Please. Go ahead."

Her single nod was short and efficient. "Thank you." She glanced to him, her smile softening a touch before she refocused on the other men. Her hands lowered to her sides, and his eyes were drawn to the incremental run of her fingers over her thumb.

"As I was saying," she went on. "Mr. Burns and I have engaged in a relationship that extends beyond professional. It is completely mutual. There was no implied threat or harassment, nor do I fear any from him." She waited a beat, inhaled. "I do, however, understand if this creates unwanted complications within the office. Although I'll have regrets doing so, if you'd prefer I resign, I will start sending out inquiries."

"No." Ryan thrust to a stand. "That won't be necessary." Ice formed in his veins as he dared the other men to override his assertion. Her declaration was unexpected and unwarranted. He'd leave before he let Brie sacrifice her job.

Her expression didn't change through her entire monologue, but it wavered now. Not much, but he caught the doubt and worry in the instant before she locked it back. She was doing this for him.

And that shattered him.

Heat roared in that space in his chest that used to be cold and empty. It pounded its demands, and he refused to shut it down. No, he couldn't shut it down. Not anymore.

No one spoke for a long moment. Charles's glower churned between him and Brie, but his bluster had diminished.

Victor finally broke the standoff with a brisk clearing of his throat. He sat forward, folding his hands on the table as he scanned each of them. "There is no reason for anyone to depart the company." He paused. "At least not yet."

Ryan opened his mouth to object, but Victor cut him off. "And I see no reason for that to change if everyone," he cut a glance to Charles, "remains professional." No one spoke to counter that statement.

Ryan released a relieved breath, his shoulders lowering from their tense perch, but he didn't relax.

Brie's smile was gone, in its place was the cool distance he'd come to respect during their hours spent deposing potential witnesses. But he knew how expressive she could be. How her smile could light up her face, and her eyes could flash with heat.

Victor huffed a short laugh, a smile blooming. "Thank you both for informing us of the situation." He turned his focus to Ryan. "I trust you'll let HR know, to keep things aboveboard."

He nodded. He'd planned to head there next.

"Charles," Victor prodded. "Do you have anything to add?"

The other man simmered in his own frustration before heaving a sigh. "I'd hate to lose either one of you," he finally admitted, the starchiness draining from him. "So please, keep it contained in the office."

Brie nodded, a courteous "of course" coming out.

Ryan, however, was done with the unearned reprimand. He let a sarcastic smile glide over his lips. "I have a sudden urge to turn into a hormonal teen and maul Ms. Wakeford over the boardroom table."

Brie's jaw dropped. Victor chuckled. Charles's scowl returned.

Ryan scooped up his items from the table, tucked them under his arm. "But I believe I can restrain myself until after working hours." He nodded to the men and escorted Brie from the room before he said something worse, like all the ways he planned to fuck her on that boardroom table soon.

If the two uptight men ever found out about the wild, dirty acts that'd been conducted on their precious cherrywood table, they'd both croak from heart attacks.

He stopped at the first free conference room, motioned for Brie to enter, and followed her in. Her giggle broke the second the door clicked shut. She slumped against the wall, her head tilted back to expose the long line of her throat.

He swallowed, his own laughter dying before it could fully form. She was so damn beautiful. The relief and shock glowed on her expression. This Brie took his breath away every damn time.

There'd been no hint of her professional cool all weekend. No pushing from her. No voiced concerns or unsaid expectations. They'd simply shifted into something deeper on a current so natural he barely understood it. Nothing in his life—nothing—had ever felt so right.

He should heed the warning for what it was. Something this good never lasted. Not for him.

She turned her head to shoot him a harmless glare. "I can't believe you said that."

He shrugged. "If they only knew..."

Her eyes widened before they dropped to a sultry promise that match the hushed tone of her voice. "Tell me, Mr. Burns. How many women have you ravished on that boardroom table?"

"None." He slid his fingers down her jaw. Her brow hitched up to scream her doubt. He shook his head. "That I can remember," he added. "Not after you."

Her sarcastic snort shot out as she shoved him away, grinning. She straightened from the wall and smoothed a hand over her suit jacket, her head shaking the whole time. "I'm not fooled by your bluff." She shot him a wink that took the heat from her words.

His smile spread easily. "Who said it was a bluff?"

Her expression turned serious, but with it was an understanding he couldn't decipher. "I don't want the details, but I'm also not naïve enough to believe that I'm the first woman you've...been with in the Boardroom." Her hand fisted, relaxed. "I get it. I just..." She glanced down, her hand fisting again.

He used his finger to raise her chin until she looked

to him. "Just what?" Nerves clashed with something new. Something light. Hope, maybe? Belief? Promise? Whatever it was, it'd been zigzagging around in his chest all weekend.

She searched him for a long moment, emotions rushing in and out of her eyes. She inhaled, held it. "I just hope that going forward, while we're together, I'm the only woman you'll be with."

Did she not get it? "You're the only woman I want. Anywhere." The only one he'd ever *truly* wanted—in every way. "You're not another Boardroom woman, Brie. You're mine now."

Relief flashed before it softened into something warmer, deeper. "Good."

Good. So much hung on that single word.

He trailed a finger down her jaw, tracked its path, marveling over the softness. He was close enough to catch her light scent that teased him with memories and more of those damn promises. The fear was there, scratching out his history, but he dismissed it.

Fear had lost its power over him the moment he'd embraced the strength of the darkness and solitude within that tiny, cramped closet.

"I expect the same." His voice had turned colder than he'd intended. Her frown told him he'd been too brisk, but he couldn't alter the facts. The thought of another man sinking into her lit a venomous anger he barely recognized.

Her lips quirked, those frown lines fading. "I accept your terms, counselor. With one addendum."

"That is?"

She patted his chest and slipped by him to reach for

the door. Her smirk was pure sex and cunning when she looked back. "I still get to be yours in the Boardroom."

And she still had the ability to shock him.

"Not a problem," he choked out. At all. His dick twitched, the desire racing south as expected with a declaration like that. But the tightening in his chest and the sudden loss of breath was different. "Should I arrange something?"

The sultry heat in her slow perusal left scorch marks. She bit her lip, let it roll out in the same blatant move she'd used that very first time in the Boardroom. It still worked.

She turned the door handle, gave a careless shrug. "If you wish." The seductress disappeared the second the door opened. Her expression went blank, her profile displaying her professional facade.

He stared at the open doorway, his throat dry, his erection demanding attention. Sure thing. He'd get right on that.

If you wish.

Just the thought of watching her come undone beneath him while everyone in the room raged with want and admiration made his dick ache. But knowing that she was all his, that she opened to only him, was free and sexy and so damn stunning. For him? Just him?

That— He swallowed. A shiver simmered under his skin and pranced on his longing. That was…everything.

He couldn't lose that.

Now the fear laughed. A big rocking roar that mocked his declarations, trampled his walls and threatened to expose the scared, lonely kid who only wanted to be seen.

Chapter Twenty-Six

"Hey, Brie," Lori greeted as she slid into the booth across from her. "How's it going?" She tucked her purse into the seat, stuffing it along with her trench coat into the corner. Her grin was big when she looked up. "Anything interesting to report?"

Brie barked out a laugh. Where did she begin? "Nothing that thrilling." It'd been weeks since she'd crashed her friend's apartment and had a minor breakdown. She counted back and realized it was closer to months. Wow.

"Right." Lori flipped open the bar menu. "And I'm not as dumb as I look."

"Are you sure about that?"

Lori flipped her off, her bright red nail gleaming in front of her smirk. "I opened the door for that one."

"You did."

"Fine." Lori snapped the menu closed and leaned in, her arms crossed on the table. "Give me the gossip."

Brie faked a deep thought. "Yeah, nope. I have nothing." She kept a straight face for a whole second before her laugh escaped.

Lori's scowl contained more annoyance than anger. She shook her head, arms crossing over her ample chest as she slumped back. "Not funny." But her reluctant smile said otherwise.

"I know." Brie shrugged, ducking her head. "Sorry." They both knew she was going to spill her guts, but it was fun to hold back. Especially when the info was so good.

She beamed inside. Her heart expanded every time Ryan looked at her. It fluttered when he touched her, even a graze on her arm or a considerate hand on her back.

Lori ordered a drink when their waitress stopped at their table. "Are you hungry?"

"A bit." She glanced at the time, which had the magical ability of turning her instantly ravenous. "I mean yes."

They ordered some appetizers and the waitress left. Their stare-down commenced a moment later. Lori was clearly waiting, but she wouldn't dig where she wasn't wanted.

Brie heaved an exaggerated sigh. "Fine." She rolled her eyes. "What do you want to know?"

"Truthfully?" Concern flowed over Lori's face. "I just want to know if you're okay."

"What?" She was shocked by that. "Yes. I'm fine." She frowned. "Why?" They'd texted since her meltdown. Lori knew she'd gotten over her initial embarrassment regarding Ryan and that Brie had gone back to work with no issues or comments from him.

"Because I'm your friend." Guilt made a quick appearance before Lori shrugged it off. "And I kind of feel responsible since I'm the one who got you into that situation."

The concern touched a soft spot in Brie. Again, this

was why they'd remained friends long after college had ended. "I made my own choices," she reassured her. "And I don't regret any of them." She didn't. Not one. "In fact, I'm really, really happy right now."

The truth fueled her grin and bubbled inside her. It was good to finally let her giddy free. She'd held it in, dampened it down and tried to remain calm. But here, now, she didn't have to.

"What?" Lori straightened, her mouth hanging open. She snapped it shut. "Good." She paused a moment, her head slowly bobbing. Her smile was warm and honest. "I'm happy for you."

The waitress dropped off her drink, and Lori took a sip of her lemon drop before continuing. "Now tell me what brought this on?"

"So..." She wrestled with the smirk trying to bloom. "I might be dating my boss."

Lori's eyes bulged. "Might? As in maybe or you are?"

Brie bit her lip, holding her secret in for a second longer. "I am?"

"Wow." Her stunned expression remained. "Now that's a development I hadn't expected."

"Me either." Not at all. In fact, it was the last thing she'd expect. Brighton definitely didn't approve, but that side of her was quieting more each day. Her mother's hold didn't reach her when she was with Ryan. He was separate from that world, an escape she didn't want ruined by her mother's conniving influence.

"And you're suddenly okay with dating your boss?" Lori arched a knowing brow.

She gave a shrug, her stomach churning. "Yes and no," she finally offered. People made a lot of assumptions, and although she put on a confident front before

Ryan and the other partners, it wasn't their judgments she feared the most.

"How'd it happen?"

"It just...did?" One return trip to the Boardroom with him and everything had changed. The whole thing was both fast and incredibly slow. "I mean," she went on when Lori scowled again, "we worked the case just fine together. I kept my lust controlled and stomped on the mortification when I realized he gave me no reason to be embarrassed."

"I told you," Lori shot in with a victorious smirk.

Brie wrinkled her nose, giving her friend the point. "And... I got to know him better." That was a major oversimplification, but it worked. "Then we might've made a visit to the Boardroom together—without the blindfold."

Lori choked on her drink, coughing madly as she scrambled for a napkin. Her glare would've taken down an army of timid students. And that only made Brie smile more.

"That was dirty play," Lori accused, clearing her throat one last time. She blinked, dabbing away the tears in the corners of her eyes. "I'll remember this at your next birthday."

Brie groaned, dropping her head. She imagined handcuffs, a blindfold and a golden dong for her thirty-first birthday. Her lips quirked. She could so see using every one of them with Ryan.

She glanced up through her lashes. "I think you've unleashed a monster."

"What do you mean?"

She blew out a long breath. "I mean," she lifted her head, "that Boardroom is damn addictive."

Lori's burst of laughter eased the knot of worry that'd lodged in Brie's stomach. "It is," Lori agreed. "I know exactly what you mean."

"It's…odd." Was that the right word?

"Why?"

"Because it's not supposed to be hot." She squirmed, hunting for an explanation. "Not in a room full of other people."

"Who says?"

"Everyone."

Lori screwed up her face in disgust. "You mean your mother and her high-society wannabes."

She snorted her agreement. "Am I that obvious?" Of course she was. A flash of shame nailed her chest. Not for what she'd just admitted, but for a lifetime of conforming to an ideal she loathed.

Lori shrugged her comment off. "The scorn just makes it hotter." An almost evil wickedness crowded into her eyes. "The supposed disdain. The superior judgment. The raunchy freedom that takes place right there under their righteous indignation." She rested her chin on her clasped hands. "Don't you think?"

Brie swallowed. There was something to that. That was how it'd started for her. A big FU to her mother. But now…

"I like being watched," she admitted on a hoarse breath. She stared at her friend, daring her to comment, yet dying for her response.

"It's empowering, right?" Understanding passed in a simple shared look.

Her smile ghosted over her lips, that tightness easing. "It is." Unexpectedly so.

"Sexuality is really damn powerful when you embrace it."

"That's deep."

"It's true." Lori sat back as the waitress delivered their food. She inhaled, her eyes falling closed. "That smells good."

"Can I get you anything else?" The waitress gave them a smile and departed when they said they were good.

"No, really," Lori said after a few bites of the artichoke dip. "Women have been using their sexuality for centuries. How do you think Cleopatra got all those men to bow to her? It's not new, by any means. We're just stuck in a fucked-up rut of male-dominated superiority specially aimed at stripping that power from women."

Brie gaped at her. She snapped her mouth closed, processing. "Now *that's* deep." She picked up her glass, studied the empty contents. "I think I need another drink for this discussion."

"Think about it," Lori went on, unfazed. "Men want sex. No, men pant, pillage and kill for sex. They bang their chests and flaunt their conquests to raise their standing among other men. But give them one strong woman," she held up a finger, "one, who understands that power and uses it against them, and she becomes the queen."

"I don't want to be queen," she countered, enjoying herself. Lori had been the one who'd initiated her into the art of random debate years ago.

"Neither do I," Lori agreed. "But the rush? That confidence that floods you? The knowledge that *you* can make them pant and groan in need?" She smacked her hand on the table. "Now *that*, I love."

Brie nodded, awed at the understanding when she really shouldn't have been. Not with Lori. "I was surprised by that part." She made a circular motion to indicate what she'd just said.

"I know." Lori took a bite of a chip, nodding. "It got me too, at first."

"It did?" She found that…interesting. Her friend had never lacked in confidence.

"Sure." Lori shrugged. "I don't think anyone really expects to get much out of group sex except sex." She raised her brows, daring Brie to counter her.

"I certainly didn't." She'd had no idea sex could be so…eye-opening? Amazing? Empowering. There it was again.

"It's not always like that," Lori cautioned. "I've had some meh experiences too, but not in the Boardroom."

"Like where?"

"Other clubs." She waved the question off. "They can be cool for general voyeurism and exploration, but don't expect any of them to replicate the Boardroom."

"I don't think that'll be an issue." She had zero plans to go orgy-crashing anytime soon. Her daring only went so far. "So, umm, how did *you* find out about the Boardroom?"

"A friend." Lori finished her drink and motioned to the waitress for another round.

"And what makes it so special?" Brie probed. Despite her three experiences in it, she still knew very little about it. She hadn't even talked in depth about the Boardroom with Ryan.

The emotion slid from Lori's face on a calculated fall that sent a chill over Brie. "I can't tell you that."

"Why?"

"Don't play stupid. You read the rules."

"But..." She clamped her mouth shut, frustrated and understanding at once. The NDA had been airtight. "I get it. Sorry."

Lori reached out to lay her hand on Brie's arm. "I'm not trying to be mean."

"I know. Really." It didn't dampen her curiosity, though.

"You understand the risk," Lori said. "I won't jeopardize my standing within it or the privacy of any member."

Brie was starting to get a clue at exactly how exclusive the Boardroom was. She'd had an idea, but she hadn't analyzed it. There hadn't been a need. And now?

"Can I ask, how does one become a member?"

Lori's head was shaking before Brie finished. "You already know more than you should."

"Why?"

"Ahh...because you just told me you're seeing Ryan Burns." Lori waited, expectation hanging once again.

Brie tried to follow the open-ended statement. "Nope." She shook her head. "I've got nothing."

Lori dropped her head back. "I have failed." She reared up. "Did I not teach you a thing about logical deduction? About connecting the dots and aligning facts? Think, Brie. Think."

What was she supposed to think about? Knowing too much? Sex? Ryan? "Wait." She frowned, thought back to their night in the Boardroom. The spontaneous one. "But I'd been a guest before."

"How many times do you think someone has the privilege of being a guest?"

"I hadn't thought about it until now." Because really, why should she have?

"And you went without the blindfold."

"So?"

"With Ryan Burns." She waited, eyes wide. Brie still had nothing. She shook her head, more lost now than ever. Lori slumped back, eyes closing. "I really *have* failed."

Brie couldn't stop the giggle that fell out. "I think you're being a little overdramatic."

The waitress set their new drinks down, and Lori snatched hers. "You're a lifesaver." She sucked down a long gulp. "Now maybe I can forget my horrible failure."

"The dramatics really don't work on you," Brie deadpanned.

Lori shrugged and took another sip of her drink. "You're probably right."

"I am." On this at least.

"Fine." She set her drink down, going serious. "If you really want to know more about the Boardroom, then ask Burns."

"Okay." She dragged that word out in confused understanding.

Lori rolled her eyes before leaning in, voice hushed. "He has the clout to grant you membership."

Membership? "I hadn't thought of that either." She'd understood it was an exclusive group, but actual membership? Like joining a gym? "Do you have to pay to be in it?"

"No." Lori looked seriously offended. "It's not a prostitution ring."

The lady sitting at a nearby table snapped her head around. Brie gave a tight smile, waiting until the woman looked away. "Nice," she mumbled.

Lori winced. "Just talk to Burns. I'm surprised he hasn't made you a member already."

"Maybe he has," she offered. Would she even know? "Unless I have to sign a double-secret, blood-binding contract or something. Maybe survive a trek through the valley of the dragons or, I got it." She clapped her hands, wiggling in her seat. "I have to pledge my first-born to the clan matriarch."

Lori stared at her, expression blank for one very long moment. "I give up."

"What?" She gaped at her friend. "You never give up."

"Well, I am with you." She finished the contents of her glass in an impressive display of irritation. She dabbed the corners of her mouth, disdain clear. "And on that lovely note, I have to go."

Brie grabbed her phone and checked the time. "How'd it get so late?"

"I am constantly wondering that myself." She laid some money on the table. "Do you mind taking care of the bill? I have to be somewhere."

"Where?"

"Somewhere," she evaded with a grin. "We'll talk soon." She frowned. "Well, maybe. Life always seems to get in the way."

"Agreed." She stood and hugged her friend. "Thank you."

"For what?"

"Being you."

Lori scoffed. "Well, that's easy." She patted Brie's arm. "We just have to keep working on you being you."

Brie dropped into the booth and watched her friend's departure without really seeing it. Brie being Brie. Who was the real Brie? The one in the Boardroom? The office? Or the one who appeared around her mother? Did she even know?

Yes. The truth rang with a clarity she couldn't hide from. Ryan was the one person who'd seen the closest rendition of the real Brie, and she was still a work in progress.

But she was really starting to like that version. A lot.

Chapter Twenty-Seven

Ryan maneuvered his car through traffic, his thoughts shifting between the road, work and the gorgeous woman sitting beside him. Brie stared out the window, her expression mellow.

He reached over to grab her hand. "Is everything okay?"

"Just thinking."

"About?"

"The Boardroom."

"What about it?" They'd been back for another visit last week and she'd been…stunning. Again. She reveled in the adoration more each time, which only made her more incredible.

Her hand tightened around his before she asked, "How'd you get involved with it?"

"A friend."

Her chuckle was heavy with cynicism. "That's what Lori said too."

"Lori?" He pulled up to the curb in front of the restaurant valet stand. "I thought you came with Jacob."

They'd never really discussed her initial visits to the Boardroom, but he hadn't worried about them. She was with him now, and that was the only thing that mattered. In truth, she hadn't been with Jacob even when he'd brought her into the Boardroom.

"I did."

Their discussion came to a halt as they exited the car. He gave the keys to the valet and came around to extend his arm to Brie. The evening light didn't hide the glow that rose on her cheeks or take away from the sophisticated cut of her dress. The deep burgundy color looked beautiful against her skin. The flowing material of the skirt brought a touch of whimsy that was balanced by the higher waist and halter top.

She wrapped her hand around his arm. Her touch sent a burst of pride through him. She was graceful and wanton wrapped into one amazing package, and she'd picked him.

"Do you attend a lot of these?" She glanced around the banquet room where the charity event was being held. She leaned into him, the subtle intimacy bringing a smile to his face, along with a need to protect.

"No." Normally, he would've sent a check and skipped the glitz, but he'd wanted to bring Brie. It'd been a long time—if ever—since he'd had anyone he'd wanted to bring anywhere. He glanced around the room. "There are some people I wanted you to meet."

"Oh?" Her eyes grew wide with overstated surprise. "Should I be worried?"

"I hope not."

He got them both a glass of wine and maneuvered them into a quiet spot along the wall. He nodded to a few people he recognized, but made no overture to extend the greeting. He had other things to focus on first.

"How do you know Lori?" he asked, going back to their earlier conversation. He assumed it was somehow connected to their mutual work in the legal field, but was there more?

"From college." She took a sip of her wine, studied him. "So you know her?" The word intimately was left off the question, and Ryan wasn't going to answer it.

He drew her out the side door to a brick patio. Heat lamps warmed the area and provided a quiet escape from the din of the banquet room. He found a secluded corner that gave them the privacy he wanted.

Her expression held a mix of question and concern when she turned to him. "What's going on?"

The narrow line he was walking seemed to shrink at her tone. He brushed her hair over her shoulder, appeasing his need to touch her. Reassure her.

"I'm aware of everyone who's in the Boardroom." He was exposing himself. The potential vulnerability dug into his gut, but he shut down the doubts before the old wounds were reopened. Brie wasn't his past.

Her brows dipped. "How do you mean?"

"I'm the legal counsel for the group." Trevor had brought him in at the very beginning, when it'd still been an idea played out among a small group in random arrangements.

Surprise shifted over her features before they settled into thought. "You knew who I was before you walked into that room the first time?"

"No." He hadn't. "Trevor handles the people details. My role is limited to the contracts."

"But I signed an NDA."

"Which Trevor approved and logged. I have the authority to see everyone's info, but I don't choose to know it." He ran his fingers down her arm to clasp her hand. "Too much knowledge is dangerous."

"That sounds ominous."

He chuckled lightly. "It's not that bad." He drew her in to press a kiss to her forehead. "I swear." A smile curled over her lips when he eased back. "But you understand the sensitivity that's required."

Her sigh was one of tired understanding. "I do." She glanced away. "I never would've gone if I hadn't been reassured multiple times of the privacy."

That guarantee brought in most of the membership. "I took the initiative to change your status from guest to member," he told her.

A hint of mischief sparked in her eyes. "I was wondering about that."

"You were?"

"Yes." She took another sip of her wine, turning away slightly. "Lori brought it up a little bit ago."

He tensed. "She did?"

"Don't get upset." She sent him a quick scowl. "She didn't tell me anything. She just told me to talk to you if I was interested."

"But you didn't." His accusatory tone slipped out before he could change it. He grimaced, cursing his suspicion when she'd given him no reason to feel that way. "Sorry. That was uncalled for."

"It was," she agreed, cutting him zero slack. But then she never shied away from calling him on his actions.

A foursome came out onto the patio, their conversation drifting over as they gathered around a cocktail table further down.

Brie watched them. "I just figured you'd approach me if something needed to be changed." She looked back to him. "After all, you're the one who already belongs to the group. You know the ins and outs. Not me."

"Brie." His voice held that tender emotion he couldn't articulate. He wrapped an arm around her, drawing her back in. "You're right." She raised a brow, her body still stiff. "And I did bring it up. Just now."

There was a long pause before she finally gave a low "true."

His smile pulled on the corner of his mouth. "So back to that," he went on before he messed up again. "Trevor wants to meet you."

She leaned into him, but the stiffness remained. "Who is this Trevor, anyway?"

"The Boardroom was his brainchild."

"Again with the ominous."

His low laugh broke through the bit of tension. "Not intentional."

She shot him a look. "You should work on that."

"It works well in the courtroom."

"Does this look like a courtroom?" She motioned to the patio.

"Brie," he growled, humor snaking in to lighten the gruffness. He hugged her closer, pressing his lips to her temple in a hard kiss. "Are you trying to drive me insane?"

Disbelief carried in her soft laugh. "No more than you're doing to me."

That sense of rightness surrounded him as he breathed her in. Every day was a new wonder with her, a new disbelief that she was with him. Yet in many ways it wasn't. Not when this connection right here wove through him to confirm what he was afraid to trust.

His phone buzzed in his pocket, and he reluctantly

stepped back to check it. He texted a response to Trevor before putting his phone away.

"You were wondering about Trevor," he started, finding her hand to lace his fingers with hers. "You're about to meet him."

"What?" Her head whipped around. "A little warning would've been nice."

"I just gave it to you."

She frowned. "And you couldn't have brought it up in the car? Or before you picked me up? Or earlier at—"

He cut off her rant with a hard kiss. She stilled, exhaled. He slicked his tongue over her lips, coaxed her to open them for a quick brush. He pulled back before the heat urged him to forget their location.

He skimmed his thumb along her jaw. "I didn't want you to get nervous."

Her brows dipped. "Why would I be nervous?"

He caught the movement from the corner of his eye as Trevor stepped onto the patio. Ryan gave her another quick kiss, hoping this went well, yet trusting she'd be fine. "Because he's been in the Boardroom with you."

"What?" Brie gaped at Ryan, comprehension struggling to take hold when he turned away.

"Trevor," he greeted, his hand extended.

Brie snapped her mouth shut, her smile in place when she turned. Her manners charged forward to gloss over the shudder that raced down her spine. *He was in the Boardroom with you.*

Ryan placed his hand on the small of her back. His touch normally calmed her, but right now, not so much. "I'd like you to meet Trevor James. Trevor, this is Brie."

Brie. Not Brighton Wakeford or even Brie Wakeford. Just Brie.

"It's a pleasure to meet you." Trevor shook her hand, his smile pleasant.

"You too," she managed to get out around her scrambling thoughts. Which time? When? Had he touched her? Put his lips on her? Or just watched?

Was one worse than the other?

"Have you been enjoying yourself tonight?" he inquired. Nothing in his tone insinuated anything other than polite social conversation.

"Yes." She smiled tightly, shooting a pointed glance to Ryan. "It's been full of surprises."

A laugh rumbled from Trevor. "I don't often hear that regarding him." He flicked his chin at Ryan. His smile was nice though, his manner joking instead of cutting.

Her defenses went up for Ryan. "That's odd," she mused. "He's constantly surprising me."

"Oh?" Trevor raised a brow, his expression a bit devious beneath the curiosity. "How so?"

With his humor and wit. The tenderness that hides beneath his cool exterior. His continued ability to make me feel cherished. All those answers flashed through her mind, but remained right there.

Trevor appeared to be quite charming. His devilish good looks were enhanced by the prominence of gray in his dark hair. The maturity only added to the overall appeal. But she didn't know him, even if he thought he knew her.

"Some secrets are better discovered on your own," she evaded, leaning into Ryan.

Trevor raised his glass in acknowledgment. "That is very true." Power emanated from him in the subtle hold of his shoulders and easy demeanor, but a perceptive calculation underscored it all. One her mother employed with cunning accuracy.

She let the expected laugh flow out, grateful that it didn't sound fake.

Ryan tightened his arm around her, his protection established and welcomed. Understanding flowed into her on the slight brush of his hand on her hip and the quiet assurance that flashed in his eyes.

He hadn't thrown her to the wolves. He had her back, just like she had his.

He shifted the conversation to mutual acquaintances with a grace that amused her. Ryan could charm when he wanted, and it wasn't always fake. The warmth in his tone and ease in his stance told her Trevor was someone Ryan regarded as a friend.

His diversion gave her a chance to regroup. Her shoulders slowly relaxed, the kink in her stomach easing with each breath. Yet the apprehension remained. Trevor was privy to some of her deepest, darkest secrets.

That same sick fear that'd crashed in when she'd found out about Ryan tried to set up camp again. But Trevor gave zero indication of having *any* knowledge of her, let alone intimate incriminating details. No lewd looks or innuendos. No dry remarks. Absolutely nothing to make her feel badly or exposed.

Trevor glanced toward the banquet room. "I suppose I should go mingle since it is my event." He shot Brie a smile, bowing slightly. "It's been a pleasure meeting you."

"You too." Her smile was genuine this time. She

waited for him to leave the patio before she turned to Ryan. "His event?"

"Yes." He took her empty glass and set it aside before he guided her toward the banquet room. "His corporation is a top sponsor of the charity, but it's also a personal cause for him."

Her respect for Trevor rose a little more. His open support and promotion of the nation's largest anti-sexual-violence organization could only be admired.

The crowd had increased significantly when they reentered the room, but Ryan guided her through it. He introduced her to many, some whose names were familiar through her work with the firm, and others who were important enough to be known in general. The amount of influence and prestige in the room was staggering. Her mother would drool with envy if she ever found out.

And then she'd be all over Brie to make introductions.

She was on her way back from the restroom when a familiar low chuckle reached her. Not exactly sinister, but practiced and fake like the bro-charm he applied to the three partners and the clients he schmoozed.

"Brighton," he called. She debated ignoring him, but manners had her turning around. "I thought that was you."

Her smile was pure professional courtesy. "Donaldson." She was fully aware of the associate attorney's first name, but they'd never crossed over to a first-name basis—until now, apparently.

His once-over ran from her head to her toes with a prolonged detour at her breasts. "I'm surprised to see you here." The insinuation being: she wasn't wealthy or important enough to be here.

"I could say the same." She kept her smile civil despite the revulsion congealing in her stomach. Months of working with him on the Palmaro case had exposed the smarm beneath his dressed-up front.

The flick of his brow highlighted his predatory intent. One she would've picked up on even if he hadn't taken one step too many into her personal space. "Nice job on bagging Burns." The lowered tone of his voice wasn't congratulatory. He snaked his fingers down her arm in a suggestive manner that left chills behind. "It's a shame I don't have a pussy so I could sleep my way to the top too."

Disgust rolled in a heaping mound that crawled up her throat and singed the back of her mouth. This was exactly what she'd feared would happen. And Donaldson was an ass. One who didn't deserve her time or response.

She turned to leave, but he grabbed her arm. His hand tightened when she tried to yank it away. Anger burned in her glare, yet she was fully aware of where they were. Causing a scene wouldn't help.

"Are you going to run to Burns now?" he taunted. "You can't handle a little office joking?"

"I believe the lady was leaving." The deep voice snapped into the conversation before she could respond.

Donaldson dropped his hold immediately, a fake grin flashing that screamed of male camaraderie. "We were just talking." He shot a wink that fell flat against the man's stone-cold glare.

"And it looks like she's done." He turned his focus to her, a hand landing on the small of her back in a reassuring gesture. "Shall we?"

Recognition lodged before she nodded. Her heart

ricocheted in her chest as he escorted her away. The man beside her was from the Boardroom. She didn't know his name or anything about him, but she could pinpoint his exact location in the room during her first unblindfolded visit with Ryan.

The one where he'd fucked her against the wall—and on the table.

"Thank you," she managed to say.

He shot a glare over his shoulder. "That man gives our gender a bad rep." His smile transformed his expression from intimidating to kind. "Ryan is over there." He motioned to the far side of the room.

Another round of tension bled from her muscles as he guided her through the people. They didn't exchange names, and he ducked away with a slight nod before Ryan turned to her.

Was this another benefit of the Boardroom? Lori had tried to explain it to her, and Ryan had already showed her that same courtesy, respect and sense of protection. But experiencing it with a man who was ultimately a stranger was empowering in a way she found hard to articulate.

She identified more men she shouldn't know but did over the course of the evening. Ones who'd stood along the wall and laid lust-filled eyes on her in the Boardroom. Her stomach twisted each time their faces clicked into context. And every time they either smiled politely or failed to acknowledge her at all.

And absolutely none of them left even a hint of the creepy slime that Donaldson had coated her in.

A sense of freedom crept into her bones and lifted yet another weight she hadn't known she'd been carrying. She got it now, what Lori had been trying to tell her. There was no shame applied to anyone in the Boardroom at any time.

Women weren't demeaned or looked down upon for participating. They weren't ridiculed for their desires, while the men were congratulated for the same thing. If anything, she'd felt cherished in those rooms. Respected.

And most importantly, what happened within those rooms didn't leave them—in any way. Not even through a flicker of recognition.

Unless your boss slips up and calls you by your scene name.

She grinned at that, the happiness dancing in her heart. She squeezed his hand, so damn glad he'd made that rare fumble.

Her smile was still in place, her head a little light from the wine when they departed. Ryan wrapped his arm around her after giving his parking stub to the valet. He nuzzled her ear in a tender gesture that sent goose bumps skittering down her neck.

"What's that grin for?" he asked before he kissed her temple.

She gave him a devious side glance. "I was just thinking."

"About what?"

She turned into him, lowering her voice. "The number of people in that room you failed to warn me about."

His confusion appeared honest. "What do you mean?"

Did he really not understand? "The other men. From the group."

There came the awareness. His wince held a touch of apology. "I honestly didn't think about it."

"Really?" How could he not?

"Really." He wrapped his arms around her waist, urging her closer. The intimacy flowed between them on the same easy note it'd held all evening. "I didn't. It's not a bro club or something anyone uses for ulterior motives." He gave a small shrug. "There's no back-slapping or locker-room talk about conquests. That's..." Repulsion wrinkled his nose. "Cheap. Trevor would never allow it. It'd be demeaning to the entire group."

And that right there made it unique to her world. "I find that utterly fascinating."

"How come?"

"Because I've never experienced complete acceptance without judgment. Not like that." Not even with her parents. Her father made overtures, but he'd never openly countered her mother's backhanded ridicule.

A gentle understanding broke over his face as he brushed a lock of hair behind her ear. "I believe that's why everyone guards it so fiercely. From what I understand, that acceptance itself is not unique within the world of the sexually open. But the ultimate trust among those who have a lot to lose? That's worth protecting."

It was. She got it now. And she felt privileged to be a part of it.

The valet arrived with his car, and he guided her into it before he got into the driver's seat. The comfort surrounded her as he pulled into traffic. Not from the car itself, but from the man who drove it.

She reached over to place her hand on his thigh. The need to touch him had woven its way into her until it'd become a necessity instead of simply a desire. Everything about Ryan was becoming a necessity.

And she had no idea how she was going to protect that—protect him—from the opportunistic claws of her mother. Or how long she could continue to hold her mother off.

Chapter Twenty-Eight

The distant click of the outer office door opening raced through the silence to lodge in Ryan's subconscious. He jerked up from his computer, frowned. A quick glance at the time had him rising from his desk. The office had been empty for hours, and it was too early for the cleaners.

He was around his desk and halfway to his door when he drew up, stopping. Brie strolled down the hall, hair flowing around her shoulders, a black trench coat wrapped snug around her. She held a plastic bag in one hand, her purse hitched over her shoulder. A smile lifted her face when she spotted him.

His heart did that weird pang-and-drop thing that should've seemed old by now. It wasn't.

"Brie?" He removed his glasses and rubbed his tired eyes. He'd been staring at the computer for too long. She was at his doorway when he slipped his glasses back on. "What are you doing here?" She'd said goodbye around the same time the rest of the office had emptied.

She lifted the bag. "I brought you dinner."

"Dinner?"

"Yes. Dinner." She strolled past him to set the bag on

his desk and her purse on the chair. The scent of something fragrant and spicy filled his office.

He inhaled, smiled. "You brought me chicken pad thai?"

She turned to shoot him a knowing glance. "It's your favorite, right?"

His brows dipped. "How'd you know that?"

She removed her coat and draped it over the back of the visitor chair before coming back to stand before him. She brought her lips to his in a soft kiss that teased the constant simmering want.

"I made a logical deduction based on your lack of variation the few times we ordered takeout." She raised her brows, that teasing mischief dancing.

"Your observation skills are stunning," he said dryly, but that warm glow in his chest spread a little further. She'd remembered his order. "How'd you know I'd be here?"

Her laugh hit his back. He braced for the sly comment or derogatory remark that used to come from his ex. Was this the start of the end with Brie?

"You usually work until nine, at a minimum," she said. He hunted for the hidden complaint in her tone but found none. "I made a lucky guess." Her expression showed nothing when he turned to her. Not until she cocked her head, frowning. "Is something wrong?"

He studied her for a long moment. Was she hiding her resentment or was he hunting for and creating something that wasn't there?

"No." He dropped into his chair and removed his glasses to rub his eyes again. "I'm just tired," he admitted. That must be it.

He blinked a few times and set his glasses on his

desk. Brie had moved around to stand beside him. She looked down, the corner of her mouth curled up in a tender expression.

She motioned with her finger. “Turn around.”

“Why?”

She shook her head and walked around behind him instead. “Do you always have to argue?”

“That was a question, not an argument.” He tried to turn his chair to track her.

The first touch of her hands on his shoulders stopped him. Then she rubbed, her fingers pinching the muscles that joined his neck to his shoulders.

His moan rolled out on the shot of relief that blasted through his neck. His head fell forward, shoulders rounding as he gave her more room. “That is…” Another groan rumbled up his chest and petered out in his throat.

Her soft laugh teased his ear before a kiss landed on the top of his head. It somehow managed to sink through his skull to feather down his nape and tighten in his chest. Damn it. Only with her.

The silence pulled around them until there was only her touch, rubbing the knots, teasing out the ache and hunting down the tension that lived in his shoulders. He removed his tie and undid the top buttons on his shirt at her urging, then her fingers dipped beneath his collar to heat his skin.

Every thought went to her firm, exploring touch as his muscles slowly relaxed. Heat spread down his back and across his chest with each new knot she uncovered and released.

Questions spun through his head. Why was she doing this? What did she really want? He didn’t ask, though.

He didn't want her to stop. Her touch was branded into him now, and he ached for it. At work, at home, in bed.

Their personal time together had been primarily limited to the weekends due to the hours he worked. But for the first time in his life, he was questioning his dedication to his job. Did he dare to have more of this? Of her?

She came around his side, her fingers trailing down his neck and jaw. He opened his eyes, resting back as he gazed at her under heavy lids. His blood heated more when he caught the wicked intent simmering in her eyes.

She nudged his legs apart, and he opened them willingly to allow her to stand between them. Fire smoldered beside the tenderness as she slowly dipped to take his mouth in an equally gentle kiss. He cupped her cheek, but followed each slow glide and swirl of her tongue as it found his and played. His heart started a pronounced beat that drummed out his slow fall into her.

She eased back, her eyes dark as she sunk to her knees. His breath hitched, his legs spreading wider. His dick went rock-hard when she drew her palms up his thighs to cup the juncture of his legs, her thumbs grazing over his balls.

He flexed his groin up, mouth going dry. Her eyes were full of intent when she tracked them over his chest to lock on to his. She wet her lips, but there was no calculation in the move. The lust and want telegraphed her plan in case he'd missed the blatant signals.

He dragged his fingers through her hair, mesmerized. She lifted her chin, following the gentle tug of his hand. He took the kiss he so desperately wanted, thrusting deeply to find the wanton heat only Brie held.

And like that, he was lost.

Lost in the wild, crazy free fall of lust and hunger until she cupped his erection, dragging her palm up the length. He ripped his mouth from hers and forced back the rampant wave of longing that one stroke had created. He let it flood his limbs and knot the desire deep in his gut.

He reached for her breast, cupping the fullness beneath her sweater, but she swept his hand away, urging him to sit back.

"Let me," she whispered.

Her eyes were so soft now. Something screamed from them that he didn't understand, not fully. How could he when it'd never been focused on him before? Not like this.

He forced a swallow if only to find some moisture for his parched throat. It didn't work. Nothing worked when it came to Brie.

She took over, undoing his belt with a slow precision that taunted him with every brush on his dick. His button was next, zipper right after. But she drew it down slowly, the soft purr another tease that rippled over his abdomen and wrapped around his balls.

Her lips were parted, a blush darkening her cheeks when she dipped her hand beneath his boxer briefs and grabbed his dick. He gasped, stomach clenching at the shock of heat and pleasure. She drew him out, her hand gliding up and down his length.

His eyelids dipped, but he refused to let them fall closed. Not when he had such a stunning sight before him.

She flicked her thumb over the cap, sending off a wave of sensation that shot down his shaft and landed another hit to his desire. Her eyes were full of lust when she glanced up. There was power there too, that awareness of what she was doing to him. He couldn't deny it either.

He lifted into her firm strokes, his hands gripping the armrests until his fingers hurt. The first slow drag of her tongue over the crown jolted the want higher. His back turned clammy and the air heavy with every little flick. She dragged the tease out, kissing, licking and stroking him until the hunger ate at his restraint and ripped apart his control.

"Brie," he whispered, hips jerking. "Fuck." His head fell back as his legs spread wider. Every movement was a silent request for her mouth. All of it. Around him. Drawing him in. Sucking.

Then the wet heat engulfed him, sinking down before she drew back up on a firm pull. His groan was ripped from somewhere near his groin. It blasted into the room with its sharp note of satisfaction. Blood roared in his ears. His pulse went wild. And he couldn't stop staring.

The top of his dick disappeared into her mouth with each dip. She fisted the rest of him, her hand following her bobbing motion to complete the effect. She slowed, licked the sensitive head before needling her tongue in his slit.

Another shot of pure pleasure raced to his groin and spread through his balls. Sparks went off when he squeezed his eyes closed, gasping for air as he fought back the orgasm that was building too quickly.

He forced his eyes back open, breaths ragged as he cupped her nape. Her hair feathered over the back of his hand to add another sensation to the plethora assaulting him. Longing crested with need to crash with want before it boiled into wonder.

This is just a blow job. Just a blow job.

It didn't matter how many times he tried to repeat those words, they didn't change the underlying awareness of how far he'd already fallen. He scrambled to stay centered, but it was useless. She pulled him under with her soft moans and purrs of appreciation.

The vibrations tickled over his dick and spread through that knot of desire cinched just below it. "Brie," he whispered in warning, tugging lightly on her hair.

She shook her head, glancing up to glare at him through her lashes. The fierceness in her intent slammed him back and stole his breath. And he wanted it. All of it.

She dropped down, taking him in. Her tongue worked that amazing spot just below the rim with a dogged determination that ripped away the last of his floundering control.

He thrust up, a thread of awareness making him hold back just enough to keep from gagging her. His world shattered on a blast of heat and pleasure that spun in a fiery, dizzying circle. He clung to Brie, gasping through his orgasm in choked grunts and clenched muscles until his lungs begged for air.

And still he stared at her, each of her rapid swallows pulling on him until he'd emptied everything into her. He fell back, sucking in air as his head slowly stopped spinning. He cupped her face, a hand on each side now. He had no idea how his hands had gotten there, but he couldn't let go.

She eased off him, a last lick catching his tip in a light flick that bordered on pain. He sucked in a breath, but didn't move to sit up. She watched him, her eyes large, lips swollen and red.

He stroked her cheeks with his thumbs and drew her up until he could claim another long kiss. The flavor of his come covered his tongue, and he moaned at the erotic blend.

Brie kissed him back, her passion smoldering with his until he was falling once again. Only with her. She was the only woman he'd ever lost himself with. He'd stopped questioning how weeks ago. Now the question was how long?

Would this last? Could it, really?

She broke the kiss, ending it with a light touch of her lips to his. He let his hands fall away when she hitched his underwear up to tuck him back in.

A raw chuckle cut up his throat as he nudged her hands away. "I've got it."

Her smile held that touch of mischief he was truly growing to love. "Are you sure?" She gave him a once-over, her doubt overstated.

He hauled her in by the neck and crushed another kiss to her lips. Her gasp was cut off by the hard drive of his tongue. She tensed, but that quickly gave way to a languid moan as she relaxed into him.

He nipped her lip before letting her go. "I'm sure," he said, daring her to challenge him again.

She laughed softly as she rose to her feet, but it wasn't mean-spirited. It didn't rankle his nerves or make the hairs on the back of his neck stand up.

A smile lined his lips as he shook his head. He stood, tucked everything into place and then drew her back into his arms. This kiss was slow and consuming. He poured his thanks into it, the lazy wonder knocking back the doubts once again.

Did she hear what he was saying? Understanding seemed to flow between them with each touch that skimmed his arm and breath that grazed his cheek.

He slid his hand up her side in a lazy path to her breast, but she shook her head, backing away. Confusion pulled hard on his brows.

"It's okay," she assured him, moving out of his arms. She gave his hand a last squeeze before she walked around the desk. "Tonight was about you."

"Why?" His brows pulled tighter, suspicion taking hold. "What do you mean?" He shoved his fists into his pockets, pulled them out to button his shirt up. About him?

A cold sheen of ice formed over the warmth in his chest. Years of being the butt of the joke, the poor kid in the front row who the other kids pretended to be nice to, only to ridicule later, rushed up to mock him. Every thought was irrational, yet there they danced, taunting him with his past.

Her movements were casual when she draped her coat over her arm and slung her purse strap over her shoulder, but she froze when she glanced at him. Concern overtook her expression as she slowly lowered her hand to her side. "What?"

"I—" He shook his head. "Never mind." He snatched his tie from his desk and yanked it around his neck.

Was he finally losing it? Had he picked up the wacky from his mother and the bastard from his father? Had the genes been ingrained in him from birth with no chance of reprieve? Had he not worked hard enough or long enough or…

"Ryan?"

He paused in the act of looping the knot in his tie, looking up. Confusion marred her forehead as she continued to stare at him. The sight punched at his guilt and knocked his doubts back a step. *Fuck. What am I doing?*

He let his hands fall to his sides, his tie untangling to hang from his neck.

It was Brie who broke the silence, asking quietly, "What's going on?"

How did he explain? Would she understand? Would it expose every flawed piece of him he'd tried so fucking hard to bury?

He shook his head. "Nothing. I'm sorry." He cleared the clump of grit from his throat, glanced away. That way he wouldn't see the hurt or disappointment in her eyes.

Her sigh dragged his gaze back. She ran a hand through her hair, drawing it away from her face. It fell in a cascade of silk to her shoulders. He knew exactly how soft it was. How it slid between his fingers to caress his skin.

"You're evading," she said, calling him on his actions when most scurried away.

His lip quirked at the corner. "Maybe."

"Why?"

It was his turn to sigh. His head fell forward, his defenses tumbling before he was ready. Brie wouldn't let him hide. Damn her for being…strong. Right.

"I warned you I wasn't good at this," he said, going for another evasion.

"What?" She flicked a brow up, arms crossing. "Receiving a blow job?"

His scoff cut through the tension and broke through

the irrational thoughts vying for validity. He pinched the bridge of his nose in an attempt to regain his focus.

Her arms were lowered, a soft understanding reaching out in silent reassurance when he glanced her way.

"This was about you. Nothing more. Just you," she told him.

Belief refused to take hold. "I don't—" He shook his head. For him?

A weariness wove its way into her expression. "I thought you'd be hungry. I thought you'd be tired, and I thought, maybe, you'd enjoy an act of kindness." She gave him a slight shrug. "That was it."

That was it. She wanted nothing in return from him.

"I'm going to go," she said, breaking into his scrambling thoughts.

She was at the door before he finally got his voice to work. "Thank you."

She looked back, winced ever so slightly. "Anytime." She searched him a moment longer before she left.

The sudden piercing ache in his chest nailed that cold space to remind him of what he had. Because it wasn't cold anymore. Not since Brie.

Not with Brie.

He caught himself when he dropped forward, his hands braced on his desk as he tried to find his breath. He'd never had this before, and he had no fucking clue how to accept it or what to do with it.

His ex had wanted her own things from him and their marriage. Her actions always came with an expected return. Every give contained a take he'd both understood and consented to. That's how life worked. That's how he'd obtained everything he had.

Until Brie.

"Brie," he called, his voice wavering on a husky rasp. He raised his head, his pulse throbbing with what he scrambled to understand.

"Brie," he called again, louder, firmer. He strode around his desk and was at his door before clarity struck.

"Brie," he shouted. His voice echoed through the empty office space, bouncing off the walls to highlight the acceptance hammering through him.

He needed her with him.

A shiver ran over his heart before the realization exploded in his chest. It fired the urgency driving him down the hall in long strides. He had to catch her. Stop her.

Make sure she understood what he was only beginning to comprehend.

Chapter Twenty-Nine

"Brie."

The call shot down through the office to stall Brie's hand on the outer door. She swung around. The light from the elevator foyer shone through the glass doors to provide a dim cast over the welcome desk.

"Brie."

Her frown deepened, concern flaring at the added emphasis in Ryan's tone. It rang of a desperate intent that didn't match the contained man she knew. Especially after his reaction just now.

She stiffened. Their communication had been off when she'd left, and she had no idea what to expect now. Was this what she got for being daring and assertive? What had she been thinking giving him a blow job in his office? The act had broken every professional rule, every rigid code of conduct. This had been a flagrant act of deviance that could've truly ruined her reputation if they'd been caught.

She couldn't hide behind the Boardroom either. This had been her own choice.

But she'd loved every damn second of it. The brazen freedom. The wanton control. The power that'd flooded her with each of his groans and reflexive hitches. Even the possibility of being caught or seen. The entire brash act had been exhilarating and shameless—until he'd withdrawn at the end.

But never, not even for one moment, had he made her feel cheap or less, like Donaldson had.

The entire incident had sent off conflicting bombs of excitement, annoyance and hurt.

She was reluctant to admit to the last one. Hurt led to disappointment which led to pain, and she wasn't ready to travel that path. Not yet. Not with Ryan. Her heart was too invested in them to think about it ending.

He strode around the corner, steps brisk, a determined look on his face. His tie spread in two strips of royal blue against his white shirt and winged under his arms. "Brie," he breathed, the note of relief confusing her more.

"What?" Had something happened?

"Damn." He swept her into a hug before she could prepare for it. "Brie." His arms wrapped around her to clamp her to his chest. A deep intake and release of breath cut a harsh path near her ear as he held her.

Confusion raced, but with it was relief. She held on, taking everything he gave. Explanations weren't needed. Not now. He was sorry. That much she understood.

"Brie." He set her down, his hands framing her face before he claimed her mouth. She opened without thought, her tongue finding his in the heated kiss. She stumbled blindly until her back hit the wall.

"Brie," he mumbled again, his lips trailing down her jaw. "Thank you." He nuzzled her ear. "Fuck. Thank you." His tongue traced a wet path over the shell before dipping in to tease the sensitive center.

A shiver raced between her shoulder blades on a path to her heart. She scrambled to hang on, uncaring of where her coat and purse fell. Her head buzzed with the overload of sensation and information he was throwing at her. Not in his words, but in the desperate crush of need pulsing into her.

"For what?" she choked out around the lump in her throat. She dug her fingers into his hair, passion rising up to blind her with hunger.

He shoved her sweater up, found her breast and rubbed his thumb over her nipple to send a wave of longing through her chest. Her gasp echoed in her head, but she needed more. Wanted closer.

"For coming here," he mumbled before taking her mouth in another hard kiss. "Bringing me dinner." He thrust back in, his tongue sweeping over hers. He shoved his fingers beneath her bra to cup her flesh.

She moaned into his mouth, her back arching to seek his touch. She couldn't think, not clearly. Was she missing something? What was he really saying?

"Thank you," he repeated again. "For giving without expecting anything." He plucked her nipple, teasing it until it ached for more, his face buried in her neck. "It's new to me."

Yes. That. More of that. His hips rocked, and she ground down on the hard line of his thigh. Need exploded in her core, her pussy begging for him. Just him. There was no one else. There'd never been anyone who could do this to her. Be this for her.

"I only want you," she panted between kisses, clutching his nape. She was here for him. That much she knew. She'd be here for him.

Be his.

That was the point. That was all that mattered right now.

Her skirt was bunched around her hips. The soft silk of his pants teased her inner thighs. He kissed down her neck, over her throat. Her head fell back to knock the wall. Reality tried to invade, but she only took it in and rode it higher.

They were in the entry to their office. Anyone could walk in. Catch them.

But he didn't care. Ryan didn't care.

And neither could Brie.

"This..." He drew his tongue up her neck. A low purr rumbled in her throat to communicate her desire. "Isn't..." He ripped away, jarring her from her daze. He grabbed her hand, heading down the hall. "Come here."

She stumbled behind him, her purse and coat left behind. She didn't question him. Not when her pulse raced and her body cried for him. Her heart jumped when understanding came.

He hauled her into the boardroom, slamming the door behind them. She was against the wall, his mouth back on hers before she had a chance to catch a breath. Yes. She fell into him, taking everything he gave and giving it back. The heated touches and wild caresses. The frantic drive that ripped moans from her throat and rumbled groans in her chest.

Her sweater came off, her bra next, and then his mouth was on her breasts. He cupped them, sucking her nipples and teasing each one with his teeth. She cried out at the intensity, yet wanted more. Still more.

This was wrong. Right. And so very naughty.

Her eyelids lifted, weighted lust holding them heavy. The room was lit only by the glow of the surrounding buildings. The darkness offered shadows and told secrets she longed to hear. The expanse of glossy cherry-wood spread down the room in a display of authority. The decadence and power vibrated from the pristine surface, touched off by the black leather chairs surrounding it.

Her fingers fumbled on the buttons lining his shirt, but she worked at them, her nails catching skin.

"Christ. Brie."

Ryan reared up, took her mouth. He caught her gasp and spun her around, ripping his mouth free. Fire and lust blazed in his eyes, but with it was something else. Amazement maybe? Fear? Need. They mirrored the very things racing through her. How could this be so good? So…perfect?

"I'm going to…" He hesitated. Her heart lodged in her throat. He wet his lips. His Adam's apple bobbed in a hard jump. He ghosted his fingers down the edge of her hairline in a touch so tender it sank to her heart and whispered of things she was afraid to hope for. He cupped the side of her neck, waited a beat before he said, "Love you."

Her world shattered into a million pieces of sizzling, joyous glee. Her eyes widened, lips parting, hope flying free.

"On this table," he continued, ripping a chair out of the way. He backed her into the table, the edge hitting her thighs. "Long and slow." He yanked the zipper down on her skirt, letting it fall to the floor in a forgotten heap. "Hard and soft." He drew his hand down her abdomen, shoved his fingers under her panties to run them through her pussy.

Her legs dipped, desire flaming on a hard clench

through her core. She rolled her head to the side, trembling with so much need.

He wrenched her panties down and then lifted her onto the table. He ripped the material off her legs in the next instant, her shoes going last. Another long, slow shiver prickled past her chest and under her skin.

She stared at him, stripped naked both literally and figuratively. She was incapable of holding anything back from him. How could she? When every touch reached her heart and brushed her soul?

He stripped his shirt off, tossing it aside. "I'm going to love you right here and remember it every time I sit in one of these chairs." He pulled his belt free. "I'll see you taking me in." He popped the button. "I'll remember the tight clench of your pussy around my dick." He tugged his zipper down. "I'll hear your soft cries and desperate pleas."

Her whimper slipped free. "Yes." She trailed her palms up his chest as he shoved his pants and underwear down in one motion, his erection springing free. Her mouth watered at the picture he made. "God, yes."

His kiss blew through her to confirm each word he'd said. The love flowed on every deep swipe of his tongue and each firm caress. This was the connection. This was the passion and understanding she'd sensed with him since that very first time.

He urged her back, his mouth never leaving hers until she lay on the table. The coolness chilled her heated flesh, prompting a flash of Boardroom memories. But this was different.

This was where they worked. No one was watching. No one would know—except them.

He stripped off the rest of his clothes, the light ghosting over him in a shimmer of shadows and highlights. Intent seared from his expression. His jaw cut a sharp line to define the edge of his face, and she lifted her hand to trace her fingers down it. Soft still. Smooth.

She feathered her fingers over his chest and then down to the thin line of hair that trailed below his navel. His stomach contracted, breath hitching. The short sprigs tickled her fingertips until she reached the thicker patch circling his shaft.

His groan carried the need trembling within her. She drew her fingers up the velvety skin of his dick until she reached the crown.

"Brie..." Longing and warning mixed in his tone to entice her further.

She locked her eyes on his as she ran her thumb over the slickness coating the top. A small tremble shook his chest.

His eyelids lowered, lips parting before he grabbed her knees, planting her feet on the table. A smirk curled on his lips when he trailed a finger through her heat. She sucked in a breath, pussy clenching. Want cried out in desperation. He copied her motion, circling his finger over her clit. Light, tempting and so damn slow.

Him. This was him.

This was the man she'd fallen in love with. This man right here, staring down at her with all the heat and passion he kept hidden from the world. But she loved all of him, every cranky, contained part.

He bent over, caging her between his arms. The tenderness radiating from his eyes drained her thoughts to just him. His lips brushed over hers as she wrapped her arms and legs around him, drawing him closer, but he held back, head shaking.

"I don't have a condom," he whispered. Regret hung on his words and echoed in his eyes.

The risks flew in and out of her mind in half a second. "It's okay. I have an IUD." She should be worried about other safety things, but the medical tests she'd submitted to the Boardroom had been thorough, and he was a member too. "It's just you and me, right?"

He nodded. "Just you and me." The meaning seemed to extend far beyond the current situation, solidifying intent in another level of understanding.

"Then we're good," she whispered, drawing him down. He let her this time, his tongue meeting hers in answering glides and deeper searches that were so damn right.

"We're good." His mumbled agreement came out between a gentle touch of lips and a quick nip.

His dick rode the hot crease of her pussy in tempting rocks until the urgency clawed at her. She dug her heels into his hips, tilting her pelvis up. "Please."

She could beg, plead and ask for whatever she wanted with him. He never judged. Never condemned. Never made her feel bad for what she wanted and who she was.

"Love me." Her words hung between them on a soft declaration.

He adjusted his dick, his focus pinning her down. "I will," he promised. He slid into her on a long, slow descent that filled her completely. Her breath eased out. Her heart contracted, expanded. "I do."

She stared up at him, lost. To him. To what they were and could be. "I do too."

"Brie..."

He took her mouth, driving hard and deep. Passion poured from him to melt her thoughts and bones. Each thrust rocked her back and brought her higher. Her blood sizzled, ecstasy building. Heat and fullness, desire and hunger—that was it. That was them.

She tangled her fingers in his hair, dug her nails into his shoulders, trailed them down his arm. Her lips were bruised and sore, but she went back for another kiss, another taste. She'd never get enough of him.

She'd never dreamed that her one night in the Boardroom would bring her here. To him. The freedom sang on her moans and rejoiced with each cry.

"Ryan." She could say his name now. He was just hers. Only hers.

Her heart fluttered around the pounding beat of her pulse. He shifted, dipping down to sink his teeth into her nipple. Pain shot deep before spreading wide. Her spine arched, head rolling back as she absorbed it, reveling in it. He pulled her nipple taut, letting go only to do the same to the other. Agony twisted with the pleasure, becoming one and the same. It surrounded her pussy, heightened her nerve endings and sensitized her to every touch, every breath, every whisper.

"Ryan," she breathed.

He stared down at her, nothing hidden. This was what she'd missed seeing those first times. That fire and want. The hunger and emotion. Him. It was still him. She might not have seen it, but she'd felt it. Known it.

A shiver, that strange, wonderful shiver, skittered over her heart and down her spine on a note of truth. She'd always known.

Desire speared her core when he found her clit. The hard, consistent rub spiraled her closer. It tore through her need until she teetered on the edge.

"Come, Brie." He grabbed her leg, hitching it up

from where it was locked around his waist. "Let me watch you." He plunged deep, lip curled, need and lust stamped on his face. "Fall for me."

Fall for him.

Her orgasm exploded on a silent promise and open declaration. She did. She had. Pleasure drenched her. Her pussy clung to his dick, spasms rippling through her core with each wave, blinding her until there was nothing left.

A harsh grunt crashed through the room. His fingers dug into her thighs. The table ground a painful line down her spine. The air was heavy with lust and sex.

She watched him through hooded lids as he came, grinding hard. The fierceness gave way to wonder before it softened to quiet amazement. She understood each emotion so clearly. They trembled over her skin and matched the rhythm of her breaths.

He braced his hands on the table, shoulders heaving. She lifted her hand to his chest to rest her palm over his heart. The solid, pronounced beat paced her own. He pressed his hand over hers, trapping it there. No words were needed now. She heard everything he said despite the silence.

The truth rang so clearly. She could embrace it now.

She'd fallen for him the very first time he'd touched her.

Chapter Thirty

Ryan paused in the open doorway to his patio, a coffee in one hand, the morning paper in the other. Sun streaked across portions of the concrete, the fall weather bringing less fog and pleasant temps.

Brie sat in the shade on a chair beneath the building overhang. Her legs were tucked up, his big white bathrobe wrapped around her. Her bare knees poked out between the part of the robe to tease him with memories of those legs wrapped around him, drawing him in. A coffee mug was cradled in her hands, her gaze focused on the distance.

His top-floor Mission Bay unit offered nice skyline views that included a small strip of the Mission Bay waterway. The neighborhood was still in the development stages, but the area was a nice mix of urban and tranquil. The constant hum of the city was diminished to the occasional car or boat horn and the distant echo of cheering fans from the baseball stadium.

Brie had spent more nights at his place than her own since that night in their office. The night he'd confessed to loving her right before he'd showed her on the boardroom table. His lips quirked. Remaining focused during Monday morning meetings had become damn hard after that.

She brushed a lock of damp hair behind her ear before she took a sip from her mug. Her phone dinged with a new text message. She reached for it on the table, brows dipping when she glanced at it. Her tight little scowl alerted him to the sender. It was the same pinched looked she got whenever her mother texted.

She typed back a quick response before returning her phone to the table. Her tired annoyance tangible when she sat back. The urge to comfort her swarmed up without thought or warning.

A hard twist knotted his stomach and encompassed his chest. He honestly had no idea how they'd gotten here. He'd been present for every moment. He could track the events and see the path, yet the logic didn't process.

Nothing in his personal experience said this was possible.

That didn't stop the contented peace from settling in his heart. Yeah, he did have one. It expanded every time he saw Brie and hitched each time she smiled at him.

The coldness that used to fill his chest had been replaced by a bright, shining warmth.

And he'd become a sap. Christ.

He hung his head, shook it. Nope. He couldn't get lost. Not in Brie. Life still existed, and he knew for a fact it wasn't all hearts and love songs.

With that sharp reminder, he shoved away from the doorway. "What time are you leaving?"

Her head snapped around, her smile faltering. "Around nine. Like usual."

The hesitation in her voice waved the red flag at his

dick behavior. He set his mug down before he dipped to kiss her, sending his apology into the hello that tasted of coffee and lazy Sunday mornings. Yet another thing he'd never expected to have.

The doubt was gone from her eyes when he pulled away. And there went that bizarre lift and fall that rippled through his chest and spread through every fiber of his body. How?

"No problem," he soothed, taking a seat in the chair beside hers. He picked up his mug. "I'm going to head to the office for a few hours." That was far preferred over attending Brie's family brunch—not that she'd ever invited him.

He shoved aside the irritation that tried to weasel its way in. Families were complicated. He didn't need to meet hers, yet the lingering, nagging holdover doubts from his childhood still nibbled at him. He wasn't good enough. He wasn't worth introducing.

He wasn't someone she could be proud of.

And he attributed every one of those doubts to his own insecurities. Brie wasn't like that.

"I should be done by one." She stared into the distance, absently nibbling her lip. "Do you have other plans for today?" Expectation lifted her brows when she looked to him.

"No."

"You can join me in my apartment hunt, if you'd like. I promise it'll be filled with disappointment, rejection and a few wows before the first two hit." Her attempt at levity fell flat.

"Why are you looking for a new apartment?"

Her sigh dragged the smile from her face. She curled into the chair more, shifting to face him better.

"My roommate wants her boyfriend to move in." Annoyance flashed in her eyes before it changed to dread. "And since the place was hers first, I can't argue."

"You could," he countered. "Did you sign a contract? We can—"

"Stop." She lifted a hand, laughter spilling out. "There's nothing to debate or fight. Really," she added when he opened his mouth. He snapped it shut, but his mind continued to spin through options and solutions. "She's a good person, and it's within her right to ask. Plus she's giving me time to find something else."

"Is she a friend?"

"Yes. But we're not super close."

They never talked about friends or their families, not really. He had nothing to offer in that discussion, and Brie never brought them up. Why? "I imagine you have a lot of friends in the area," he probed, curious. His ex had prattled on for hours about this connection or that contact.

She gave a dismissive shrug. "A few. I have more acquaintances than friends."

That, he understood. But… "I thought you might have more given you grew up in the area."

"I could say the same about you." She lifted a brow, the challenge extended.

His chuckle held an appreciative edge that managed to cut him with its sharpness. "I doubt your childhood was anything like mine." Harsh bitterness played in his voice and exposed more than he'd intended.

She lowered her feet to the ground, sitting forward. "Are you ready to share yours?"

He yanked his gaze away from her probing intent.

The lack of accusation or defensiveness in her voice only hit him harder. She was simply asking.

His hand tensed around his mug. "Not really." His leg started to bounce, but he stopped it almost immediately.

"Ryan." The gentle request in her voice got him to look at her. "It's fine." The truth of that flowed over him, from her relaxed pose to the understanding in her eyes. "I love you for who you are now. Not where you came from or where you're going. But you, right now, right here." She reached out to tap his chest. "You hide your heart behind your logic." She lifted her hand to touch his temple before she drew her fingertips down his jaw. "But I've felt it since the first time you touched me. That's all I need."

Honesty radiated from every pore as she silently dared him to argue. Could he when his heart was stuck in his throat and attempting to choke him? He cleared it away with a hard rumble, thoughts scattering.

He grabbed her hand, threaded his fingers with hers. The connection buzzed through him on a wave of disbelief before it settled into the peace. He released a slow breath, the hesitation exiting with it.

"Where'd you come from?" he mused.

"Walnut Creek." Her wink was all sauce that went with her grin. "From your standard suburban neighborhood, with all the expectations placed on the oldest daughter of two parents whose sole focus in life was to be better." The quick shrug said more than her words. "I was placed in that cart and shoved into the shiny glow of perfectionism before I was old enough to understand that it doesn't exist."

No, it didn't. Ever. "When'd you learn?"

Her fake show of humor fell away to leave behind

the old hurt. "When I broke my wrist doing a double back handspring." She twisted her free hand, staring at it. "My mom was more worried over the threat it posed to my standing as the cheer captain than the severity of the fracture." She scoffed, sitting up. "She didn't have to worry, though. I maintained my spot on the team, along with my homecoming-queen crown and the quarterback boyfriend." Her cheesy grin held a level of contempt he related to. "But that still wasn't enough."

He set his mug on the table and tugged her over until she was nestled across his lap, his arms wrapped around her, her head resting on his shoulder. The need to obliterate the obvious hurt radiating from her had him seething at parents he'd never met.

"How could it not be?" he asked, pressing a kiss to her temple.

"I wasn't valedictorian." Her breath skimmed over his throat in a soft kiss. "Or class president. And I didn't go to Berkeley or Stanford or any of the big state universities. And I'm only a paralegal. Not a lawyer. And—"

"Stop." He cut her off, hugging her closer. "I get it, okay. I don't agree with any of it, but I get it." The tension slowly dissolved from her stiff shoulders and tight muscles. He slipped his hand beneath her robe to rub soothing strokes over her thigh. "My parents didn't give a shit about what I did," he told her. "Just as long as they didn't see me." And he'd considered that a blessing. "The cigarette burns on my back are from the last time my father bothered to engage with me."

"Were you eleven then?" she asked quietly.

His soft huff held a dose of ironic mirth. "Yes."

He didn't know how to process her understanding or the fact that she'd connected his brief remark from weeks ago. He'd been eleven years old when he'd refused to react to the searing burns, one after the other, until the cigarette went out.

His arm tightened around her, his chest contracting. Brie was the first person he'd ever shared that tidbit with. His ex had never asked.

"I hear there's a nice balance somewhere between those two extremes." She rubbed a soothing stroke over his chest, her empathy communicated without the overdose of sympathy and analyzation.

"There is?" he joked. He was done thinking about the past when it did no good.

She gave a slow nod. "Yeah. I've even seen it."

"Where?" He jerked to the side, mock surprise in place when she scowled at him.

"On TV," she deadpanned. She held a straight face for a beat before her grin took over. "And a few friends in high school who had normal, attentive parents," she conceded.

"They really do exist," he mused, using the mystical Santa Claus tone. Yet another thing he'd never been allowed to believe in.

Her nod was slow and solemn. "They're a very rare species, though. They're only found in remote locations and under specialized conditions."

"Such as?"

"Full moons and the summer solstice."

"Of course."

Her lip twitched, her smile itching to break free. "Of course."

His chuckle escaped before he captured that wavering smile with his lips. He filled the kiss with empathy and understanding, trusting she heard him. Because she got him like no one else ever had—or had even tried to.

And that was a gift he was still learning to trust.

Warmth crept into Brie's blood and circled through her on a slow hum of contentment. Ryan teased her tongue with light grazes and gentle nips before he eased back.

She slicked her tongue over her lips, savoring the lingering tingle. That flutter in her chest mimicked the shiver that spread beneath her skin. How had she fallen so hard? Time had slipped by on the cyclical pace of weeks that'd flown into months that'd become seasons. Fall had arrived and with it came new opportunities instead of endings.

"I should get dressed," she said with regret. Missing the nine-thirty train wasn't an option.

Ryan slipped his hand up her thigh to graze his thumb through her pussy. "Are you sure?" Speculation played on his face when her groan fell out. He pressed on her clit, eyes smoldering.

"Yes!" She shoved his hand away, laughing with her own regret. She sat up, tugging the robe around her. "As much as I'd love to stay and fuck you all morning, I can't." Not if she wanted to keep her mother off her back. She cupped his face and kissed away the frown that'd formed. "Sorry," she whispered as she started to rise.

He tugged her back down, kissing her again. The urgency pumped into her, lighting her up and shifting that constant, flickering flame to an inferno.

"Ryan," she whined, ripping her mouth from his. "I have to go." The *tick, tick, tick* of the clock hammered in her mind with the warning bell of her mother's quiet wrath.

He stole one more kiss before he let her go. "Fine." He dragged his hand down her leg as she stood before he adjusted the obvious erection tenting his shorts. "I'll just take care of this by myself."

"You poor, suffering man," she commiserated, running a finger up the rigid line before she walked away. His dry laugh followed her into his condo to set her heart fluttering again.

Her grin was still on her face when she slipped her flats on twenty minutes later. She fluffed her hair in the closet mirror and checked her sundress. Would her mother comment on the deep cut of the neckline or the bright red color?

"You look beautiful."

She spun around at Ryan's voice, the tenderness spreading to wrap her tight. She flicked her eyes over him. Even in a loose T-shirt and basketball shorts, he was sexy. His hair was still damp from his shower and he'd shaven, like he did every single morning even though he could get away with not doing so on the weekends.

"Thank you." Every dismissive comeback disappeared under his honesty. She let her mother-induced insecurities go. She liked the dress, and that was all that mattered.

She stopped in front of him when he didn't budge from the closet doorway. He stared at her. Thoughts floated around his dark eyes in obvious waves that had her hesitating.

"What?" she asked, laying her hand on his chest.

Dread twisted in her stomach. Was he going to ask

to join her? To meet her parents? He hadn't yet, but it was only a matter of time, right? That's how relationships worked. Meet, fall in love, meet the families… And she couldn't get herself to take that next step. Not when it could ruin everything they had.

"Do you have any friends you can move in with?"

Her mind jumped to the topic with an added hitch that came whenever he dove into a subject without warning. He always had a purpose, a defined intent.

"No. They're all married or have roommates."

"Are you looking to live alone?"

She shook her head. "I can't afford it." Even the studios were out of her budget or in undesirable locations.

"So you're going to live with a stranger?" The lines in his forehead deepened.

"Hopefully, they won't remain one for long." She dismissed his worry, urging him to move so she could get by. "I really need to go."

He let her pass, but reached out to grab her arm before she could move away. She looked back, irritated. "Ryan?" Was this where he dug in and asked why she hadn't invited him to brunch?

"Why don't you move in here?"

His question sputtered about in her brain without taking hold. "What?" she finally managed to get out around her exaggerated guilt.

He stepped up, framing her face with his hands. "Move in here. Live with me."

Her pulse jumped. A swarm of nervous butterflies took flight in her stomach and tickled another string of hope. "Live with you," she repeated, still not believing his words.

A smile slid over his face, amusement lighting his eyes. "Yes."

She grabbed his wrist, needing the support to hold her steady. How did he just lob that at her? And smile? Him. Ryan Burns. The man who had a plan and path for everything?

"Why?" Her suspicion was tossed out on a volley of doubts.

His sigh was weighted before he drew her into his arms. She went, if only to get away from the overwhelming intensity of his gaze. "And I thought I was the suspicious one."

"You are," she mumbled, circling her arms around his waist.

"I know."

A kiss landed on her head and even now, it sunk in to knock against the insecurities that still held strong within her. "I'm just trying to understand," she explained, easing back to see his face. "Where'd this come from?"

"Where'd you come from?" he countered, chuckling. He brushed her hair back, cupping her neck, his thumb caressing that tender spot just behind her ear. The touch was so casual now. Normal and almost expected. When had they come so far?

"I thought we covered that earlier?" she quipped, the lightness saving her from crumbling.

He puffed out a single note of amusement. "We did."

"So?" She left that hanging, waiting. A part of her really needed to hear his explanation. She didn't need him to swoop in and save her, if that was what he was trying to do. It was just a roommate. She'd be fine.

"Stop overthinking this, Brie." The amused quirk

of his lips countered the vulnerability that flashed in his eyes.

He rubbed a finger over her forehead, the tension leaving as he did, which irritated her too. He shouldn't be able to do that. But he could.

Was that all part of this love thing?

"It was just an offer," he went on, his gaze shifting to track the movement of his thumb. "You're here every weekend. You have clothes in my closet and a drawer in the bathroom." True, but that was still a far stretch from living together full-time. He looked back to her, truth exposed in the dark depths. "Plus, I like waking up with you in my arms." *Oh...* "And seeing your scowl before your first cup of coffee in the morning."

"I don't scowl," she interjected.

He lifted a doubtful brow, which she glared at.

"And curling up next to you after a long day," he went on. "Breathing you in as you fall asleep."

She swallowed, feeling herself fall all over again. But this was huge. "I need to think about it."

His brows dipped just slightly before they flattened back out. "I understand." Did he, really? "No pressure. I promise." A crispness had come back to his tone, one that said the topic was over. He'd made his points, now it was her turn to counter.

But she didn't have anything. Not yet.

She lifted up to give him a quick kiss. "I have to go. Really." She caught his hand, giving it a squeeze. That strange shiver spread up her arm to tease her heart with acceptance. This was right. He was right.

But a leap this huge required thought, not impulse, right? Or at least the presumption of thought. Her heart was already screaming hell yes. But what about work? Her mother? Her career? Would the respect she'd worked so hard to achieve be dismissed behind the assumption that she'd slept her way to her position? Exactly like Donaldson had said.

Brighton cringed. That conservative, always perfect, do-the-right-thing side of her cramped around her floundering freedom.

Hadn't she already faced these issues?

Brie had danced at an event dotted with area attorneys, fucked in a room filled with area executives, became a member of the Boardroom, formally informed the company partners of their relationship—didn't all those actions scream yes as well?

But what would her mother say—do—when she found out about Ryan?

The pros and cons fluttered in and out of her head the entire train ride out to Walnut Creek. And each mile that brought her closer to her mother, the mantle of Brighton crept in until Brie was crushed beneath the identity that still held so much power over her.

She slipped the white sweater out of her purse, tugged it on over her sundress, buttoning it until her cleavage was covered and propriety established. Her hair was pulled back into a low ponytail, her expression schooled, her thoughts shuttered before she stepped off the train. Reserve in place. Decorum plastered on.

Her bitter resentment buried so deeply there was zero chance of it slipping out.

But it was still there.

Chapter Thirty-One

Brie shoved through the doors of the courthouse, shoulders back, satisfaction humming. Ryan had just nailed down the closing details on the Palmaro case. The final settlement between the two parties had left their client happy, which meant Charles would be too.

She glanced at Ryan, heart skipping along with the nerves that plucked at her courage and laughed at her insecurities. "Nice work," she said as they waited to cross the street.

The area outside the Civic Center Courthouse was busy with the typical midweek flow of people heading in and out of the multiple government buildings clustered around the plaza.

"Thank you." He flashed a quick half-smile. "Same to you."

Pride flared as they crossed the street. The hours they'd both dedicated to the case faded into the background now that the parties were in agreement. It didn't always work that way, which only made the wins feel bigger.

She snuck another glance at him. The sun tugged out the lighter shades hidden within his dark hair and added a glow to his cheeks. Or was that the extent of his display of excitement?

He guided her around a group of people pointing at City Hall, his hand placed on her lower back. It fell away moments later, but that touch still made her heart hitch. That little lift and fall of recognition.

Her blood warmed too. It pumped through her on an added beat of awareness. None of that had faded since the beginning. If anything, it continued to grow stronger.

And she'd hesitated.

The why of it baffled her now. Two days later and her heart still screamed *yes* to his offer. He hadn't pushed or questioned her either. Did he care or was he simply being Burns? Logical. Distant. The consummate professional upholding his agreement?

The scent of food from the small line of food trucks parked on the edge of the plaza drifted over to tempt her nose but not her hunger. Her stomach was too knotted to allow even the thought of food to be desirable.

She hooked her briefcase higher on her shoulder, took a deep breath. "Yes," she told him, cutting a quick glance his way before refocusing on the enclosed glass building that housed the elevators to the underground garage. "I'll move in with you. If the offer's still open."

"It is." The quick drop of the two words held zero insight to his thoughts. "Are you sure?"

His strides didn't falter nor did hers. But the world filtered away until there was only him, walking beside her, making one of the biggest leaps of her life.

"Yes. I am. Are you?" Her pulse made a double-time attack on her throat that outpaced the click of her heels on the sidewalk. They were doing this. Here. Now.

"Yes." He touched her arm, slowing. She came to a stop, nerves leaping in every direction when she turned to him. His love blazed down at her when she finally met his eyes. His lips quirked, amusement mixing with tenderness. He ran the back of his fingers down her jaw before he drew her in, his whispered "very" ghosting past her ear.

Relief collided with her flailing nerves before joy took over.

She squeezed her eyes tight, her arms coming around him to finish the embrace. The rightness snapped in the second she was enfolded within his strength. That shiver spread on a confirming note around her heart.

Every reason for her hesitation was gone now. Poof. Eliminated beneath his certainty.

"Brighton?"

She jerked back, her head whipping around to find the source of the voice. *No. It can't be. Not here. Not now.* Fear slammed in the second her doubts were confirmed.

"I thought that was you." The high tone full of fake sincerity scratched over Brie's nerves to leave them raw and exposed.

"Mom?" she choked out, thoughts scrambling. She inched away from Ryan in an automatic need to distance him from her mother's daggers. "What are you doing here?"

She went in for the false hug that chilled the warmth that'd only just been there.

"Nice catch, honey."

The soft whisper in her ear sliced a path of revulsion to her heart. She pulled back, her smile plastered on despite the bile crawling up her throat.

"Why haven't you told me about him?" The admonishment came on another soft note meant just for her. A smile laced with condemnation broke the perfect plane of her mother's face. She cut a glance to Ryan, her once-over not so subtle before she christened Brie with her silent reprimand.

Rejection pulsed as she stared at her mother. She couldn't look at Ryan, not when even the slightest indication from her would send her mother into full predatory mode. She appeared so...pleasant. Her hair was perfectly arranged. Her suit tailored perfection. Her smile soaked in honey behind her power-red lipstick.

Brie's smile tightened. The threat breathed down her neck to draw her defenses out. They snapped into place on a blink and small flick of her chin.

She wove her arm around her mother's shoulders, attempting to turn her away from Ryan. "I love the suit," she said, shifting the focus from herself. "Is it new? The cut looks great on you." Flatter, preen and dodge. She ran a hand down her mother's arm. "I could use some new suits myself."

"Thank you," her mother said, accepting the compliment before she waved Brie off in a move of false embarrassment. "I picked it up a few weeks back."

"Brighton," her dad broke in, stepping up behind her mother. The stiff hold of his smile could've been understanding or impatience. "This is a surprise." His gaze slashed to Ryan, his meaning implied.

Dread pooled into a sick muck that coated her lungs. She sucked in thin breaths, her smile threatening to crack.

"We were just handling a case," she evaded, motioning to Ryan who was now feet away. Her parents looked at her with expectation that forced her manners to comply. “Mom, Dad, this is Ryan. We work together. You caught us celebrating a big win.” She rattled out the string of sentences on a rush of panic followed by a forced laugh.

Her gaze skittered between the three of them, her heart so leaden each beat was a pronounced thump. “What are you doing here?” she went on before her dad could even lift his hand to greet Ryan. “Do you have time for lunch?”

She flashed a glance at Ryan, a silent plea going out only to crash on the stone wall of his expression. Gone was the love and affection that’d been there just moments ago. In its place was the calculated blankness that gave away nothing. It froze out opponents and dumbfounded charmers with its complete lack of emotion.

And it was directed at her.

A chill swept over her, sinking into her bones. Her skin prickled with the anxiety choking off her air. A counter heat spread over her limbs and down her back in a proclamation of the gigantic mistake she’d made—was still making.

She’d messed up. Alarms blared a clear warning, yet she had no idea how to change course. She wasn’t prepared for her worlds to meet. Couldn’t Ryan understand? Couldn’t he see her panic? Hadn’t he heard her when she told him about her mother? About her life?

“Hey, Burns!”

The call broke through the tension on a snap of reality. The world crashed in to bring another horrific threat.

Jacob strode up, a polite frown tugging his lips down. “Sorry to interrupt,” he said, glancing between them before he refocused on Ryan. "I was wondering if you had a moment." Inquiry met concern as his brows drew together.

"We should get going," Brie managed to say, her voice sounding distant in her own ears. "I'll meet you back at the office." She tossed the last out to Ryan without waiting for a response.

The zero acknowledgment from Jacob didn't stop the clash of her worlds from exploding into a fiery ball of doom in her head.

"Mom, Dad," she urged, nudging her mother forward. "There's a nice place just around the corner. The salads are perfect." Because a bunch of greens tossed in a bowl with some other items could be imperfect, right? "Why are you down here, again?" she prattled on, each step away from Ryan a victory and a conviction. "You didn't tell me you'd be in the city," she added in an attempt to shift the guilt.

Awareness bit down her spine in little digs that drew blood, but her sense of wrongdoing slammed against a rock of defiance. She drew her shoulders back, insisting silently that she was doing the right thing. It'd be okay. He'd understand.

Hell, he'd never implied or hinted that he'd like to meet her parents, not once.

Her mother allowed Brie to urge her along, but her shoulders were stiff, and her jaw held that glacier edge of disapproval. Her voice was low and sharp when she spoke. "That was very rude of you." Her nostrils flared her contempt around the frosty gloss of the smile that remained. "I can't believe you brushed him off like that." Her eyes darted over her shoulder in an unneeded reference to whom she was referring.

Brie caught her dismay before it managed to unhinge her jaw. She clenched her teeth, refusing to give her mother more ammunition.

"It's a gorgeous day," she said instead, her throat aching with everything she wasn't saying. "How long—"

"Brighton," her mother snapped, stepping away from Brie's guiding arm. Her glare was laced with menace. "I'm not stupid. I know exactly what you're doing. What I don't understand is why." She turned around, and Brie followed her lead, the pending doom burning the back of her mouth.

But Ryan was gone.

She scanned the area, her pulse racing in a mess of regret and relief. Her fingers itched to dig out her phone and text him an explanation. An apology. A plea for understanding.

Would he answer?

"Joanne," her dad soothed. "It's none of our business." He shot an apologetic smile at Brie.

Her mother whipped around. "It's our daughter. Of course it's our business."

"There's no business to be in," Brie interjected. "Really. I have no idea what you're talking about." Her confused tone was Emmy worthy. She held her expression in the crafted bafflement that'd worked since her teens.

The light changed, and her mother stalked through the crosswalk three steps ahead of them. Her dad drew her into a side hug that managed to slow the darkness that was engulfing her. "You should head back," he told her. "I'll handle your mother."

Brie had to swallow to keep the sudden rush of tears from climbing higher. She blinked, blew out a breath. "It's fine."

"It's not," her father chided. "It hasn't been for years."

Her head whipped around. She studied him, lost in the past yet trapped in the present. "What do you mean?"

He lowered his arm so they could thread their way between the oncoming pedestrians. Her mother continued her sulking stalk until she yanked open a door and stepped inside, apparently picking the restaurant.

Brie came to a stop, grilling her dad with her eyes as he did the same. "There's nothing wrong," she insisted, uncertain why she was doing so. It just was. They all pretended nothing was wrong in order to keep the balance. That was how it worked—how it'd always worked.

A light breeze picked at the ends of his gray hair to ruffle them to the side. "I owe you an apology, Brighton." He brushed her hair over her shoulder in a touch reminiscent of times when she'd been dressed in her kitty-cat nightgown, waiting for a hug goodnight. The action tugged on the fragile strength holding her emotions together.

She shook her head, not in rejection of his words but of what they could mean to her stability. "Are you getting a divorce?" she burst out. "Is that why you're here?"

Her father's dry laugh held amusement, not bitterness. "No, honey. We're not. It was just a meeting with our lawyer over our estate." He glanced to the restaurant. "Believe it or not, I do love her." The warmth in his expression declared as much. "But," he went on, "I love you too. And I believe I've held back too often when I should've spoken up. My lack of assertion has hurt you."

Her head was shaking before he finished. "Don't say that." She laid a hand on his arm. His cashmere sweater slid under her palm with the same softness layered into his voice. “I’m fine.” She was a grown woman. Her father’s responsibility had ended years ago. Her mistakes and hurt were all on her now.

“I know who Ryan Burns is.” Fear zoomed back in to rip at the comfort her dad had established. “I referred you to Charles,” he reminded her, but there was no reprimand in his tone. “I’ve lived long enough to recognize love when I see it, and that hug was more than a simple celebration.”

Panic zinged back to shred her lungs. She struggled for air, but refused to let her father see her distress. “Where are you going with this?” She couldn’t deny his statement despite the self-preservation that said she should. Not when she longed to share her joy with him.

You were supposed to be able to do that with your parents.

Blue eyes so like her own stared back at her from behind his glasses. “Don’t let your mother’s ambition ruin what you have with him. Not if it’s real. Not if he makes you happy. And Brie…”

The use of her nickname broke the dam that’d held her tears back. They roared up her throat to slam into the backs of her eyes with a force she couldn’t control. She tried to blink back the burn before she dashed the first few away. She sniffed, swallowed, averted her eyes to hide her pain.

“Honey.” Tender love enfolded her as her father wrapped his arms around her. “Brie. Sweetie. What have we done to you?”

Her father had been the first one to ever call her Brie. Others had followed, but never her mother.

“You haven’t done anything,” she told him around another sniff. She managed a weak smile as she pulled back. “Except love me.” His giving nature had been her salvation. The years had aged his appearance, but he was still the dad who’d worked long hours and commuted even more to give his family the security of a stable home. They’d never stressed for anything even though her mother had insisted on the best of everything.

And in her own way, that was how her mother showed her love. She’d wanted the best for Brie, she’d simply failed to understand that her definition of best wasn’t the same as Brie’s.

Her dad shook his head, a sad frown adding wrinkles to his forehead. “I should’ve stepped in—”

“Don’t, please.” She dug through her briefcase for a tissue. “The past is done. And really,” she shot him a smile, “it wasn’t so bad.” No. It’d been pretty blessed. Especially compared to Ryan’s.

His sigh held a weight she couldn’t dislodge for him. She could barely carry her own demons right now.

He tucked his hands in the pockets of his slacks, a grim smile curling his lips. “I was going to say, you looked happy before we interrupted you.” He paused a beat, and Brie finally gave him the confirming nod he was waiting for. Her smile grew at the admission. His own grin followed and some of that weight seemed to lift from him. “Good. I’m happy for you.”

“Thank you.” There was the joy. Her dad knew about Ryan and the world hadn’t ended. She took a deep breath, her lungs expanding with the freedom it brought.

“Does he treat you right?”

She chuckled at the dad question. “Yes. He does.” The memory of how right slid in to wrap her in another hug. He loved every side of her like no one ever had. She bit her lip, hesitated, then took the plunge. "I'm moving in with him." Her stomach twisted in the half-second it took her dad to respond.

"You are?" Surprise lifted his voice, but there was happiness in it too. "Then I think I'd better get to know this man before he sweeps you away."

Her eyes darted to the restaurant door, doubts rushing in.

"I'll handle your mother," he reassured her. "I promise. Just don't let us keep you from him. And please, don't keep him from us." The flash of hurt in his expression had her second-guessing every reason she'd created to keep Ryan away from them. "I'd like the opportunity to get to know the man who makes my daughter happy."

Oh…and the tears were back. Shame washed over her in a sneak attack that left her chest tight and her heart sore. She'd done that, hadn't she? She'd kept Ryan away from them because of her own fears and… embarrassment.

She hadn't wanted Ryan to meet them. No. She hadn't wanted Ryan to see her around them. She conformed to her mother's expectations every damn time. How would he see that? He'd given her power when she'd been stripped naked in a room full of men, yet she was afraid to be her own person around her mother.

Not anymore.

She started for the restaurant, but her dad laid a hand on her arm, stopping her.

"Don't," he said, reading her intent. "Not today. Nothing good will come out of a confrontation today." His wisdom sucked the life from her burst of determination. He gave her another hug that managed to heal some of the battle wounds scarring her heart.

He released her, keeping his hands on her shoulders. "Go find that man of yours and apologize. I got the distinct sense that he didn't take your dismissal well." He chuckled softly, stepping back. "I know I wouldn't have."

Her regrets slammed back in to remind her of the damage she'd inflicted on Ryan. How had she done that to him?

He'd told the other partners about her. He hadn't made her into a dirty secret to be hidden away. But that was exactly what she'd done to him.

Pain seared her heart as another wave of panic took hold. It nestled beside the mortification that slowly revealed the truth of her actions.

She'd shunned Ryan for absolutely no reason.

The man who'd worked his whole life to dig himself out of a bad situation. Who'd achieved so much. Who was an amazing wonderful person. Who'd become everything to her.

Who she'd refused to acknowledge in front of her parents.

What had she done?

Chapter Thirty-Two

The bottom of the glass stared back at Ryan, the contents diminished to a few ice cubes, a trace of clear liquid and a squeezed lime. He motioned to the bartender for another round, his thoughts limited to that act alone.

The numbness had dug in to block the potential pain. Right. His harsh scoff got a skeptical look from the man hunched over the bar three stools down. Ryan didn't care. Nothing mattered.

He accepted the drink with a nod, switching out the empty with the full glass. A television blared a baseball game, but the commentary was lost on him. He'd learned the rules of every professional sport and could comment on any play or team in a way that'd make someone think he cared. He didn't.

His drink slid down his throat on a glide of satisfaction that did little. It only succeeded in filling the emptiness with reminders of how he'd gotten here. Every step, every move, every calculated action he'd made had been to get him as far from this seat as possible. Yet here he sat.

The atmosphere consisted of foggy beer signs, musty beer-soaked floors and a clientele that eyed his suit with disdain. Perfect. He resisted the urge to flip every blurry-eyed, attitude-ridden drunkard off. They had no clue—none—about him.

But who did?

His harsh laugh garnered more looks from his fellow bar bums. His cool glare succeeded in getting every one of them to look away. He could take on any of them if they wanted a fight. He'd learned that too. How patience worked to his advantage. How to go for the soft spots, dodge, use his feet. Street fighting didn't have rules.

A body slid into the stool next to him, but he refused to look over. There was a half-dozen other stools available, and he was well aware of why the two on either side of him were free. He'd made damn certain the custom-tailored suit didn't dull the fuck-you vibe radiating from him. It screamed in his chest and vibrated through every nerve ending that protected the numbness.

If he didn't feel, he couldn't hurt.

Trevor signaled the bartender. "I'll have what he's having." He motioned to Ryan.

Ryan sipped his drink, resentment slithering into the emptiness. "Thanks for coming," he stated, his eyes locked on the television.

"You went high-class for this meeting."

He shrugged. "It fit my mood." He'd walked into the first place that hadn't screamed pretentious or tourist trap. He'd chosen well.

The bartender delivered Trevor's drink with a nod and a quick departure. His scruffy beard and ripped flannel over a black T-shirt with a faded band logo matched the atmosphere.

Ryan hadn't owned a flannel shirt since his college days. His closet was now lined with suits, slacks, dress shirts and enough ties to rotate over two months without duplicating. And what had it gotten him?

Trevor took a sip of his drink. "Really? Lime and soda?"

He gave another shrug. He might be sitting in the damn seat he'd avoided his whole life, but he refused to fall farther.

"Are you going to tell me why we're here?"

His answer sat on the back of his tongue in a weighted heap. He swallowed down his hesitation. There was no other way. "I want out of the Boardroom."

Silence greeted his declaration. Tension wound its way through his shoulders and up his neck the longer he waited. But he kept his eyes focused on the TV, his peripheral vision catching Trevor's movements.

Trevor took a drink, set his glass back down. "No."

Ryan snapped his head around. "It's my choice." Anger wiped out the numbness in a flash of heated fury. "You can't say no."

"Then why'd you tell me?" Trevor arched a brow.

"Courtesy." He scoffed, head shaking. "Forget it." Why'd he bother?

"Nope." Trevor flicked a smile when Ryan glared at him. "You brought it up. Now we discuss."

"There's nothing to discuss. I'm out. I'm just giving you warning instead of being a dick." He could've been. Maybe he should've been. That's what everyone expected of him.

Trevor's slow nod wasn't one of agreement. "What brought this on?"

He choked on the answer. Fuck. Nope. That wasn't coming out. "It's time," he evaded.

"Just like that?"

"Yes."

Trevor gave another nod. "I'm going to assume this has something to do with Brie."

He wrapped his hand around his glass, clenching it. "No."

"Liar."

"Dick."

Trevor lifted his glass, holding it out in expectation.

Ryan glared at the glass before shifting his gaze to nail his friend. His smirk was classic Trevor. Arrogance backed by confidence earned through his steadfast dedication to everything he did. Add in his fucking sense of intuition that enabled him to read people with barely a glance, and Trevor James was deadly.

Ryan's sigh fell out in an annoyed gust. He clicked his glass to his friend's, a reluctant smile releasing a wave of tension before he took a drink. His shoulders lowered, and he dropped his head forward to stretch the back of his neck. "What time is it?"

"Five."

"Huh." He'd successfully blown off his first afternoon of work in his entire life. That was kind of pathetic, only he couldn't decide in which way. The fact that he had blown off the day over a woman or that he'd never done it before.

"Are you going to tell me what's going on?"

Brie. Fuck.

He scrubbed his hands over his face and let the sick swirl of angst and hurt engulf him. He shouldn't care. Her dismissal shouldn't have gutted him like this. Her… He swallowed hard to keep the ache in his throat from growing. He'd known better than to open himself up to this. The pain in his chest laughed at his blind stupidity. Or had it been wishful thinking?

And wishes were for gullible kids who believed in fairies and magic—something he'd never fallen for.

He rubbed his eyes, squeezing the bridge of his nose in an attempt to pinch back the headache throbbing behind his eyes. "I relearned a valuable lesson today," he finally admitted.

"Which one was that?"

Ryan lowered his hand to study his friend. Trevor glanced his way, mild curiosity his only visible emotion. That calm regard hid a depth of intelligence that'd impressed him from the moment Trevor had struck up a conversation at a charity event. His pinpoint characterization of both the event and the attendees had created the bond that'd led to Ryan's participation in the Boardroom.

He'd been involved with the group since its founding, his legal skills the asset Trevor had sought. Ryan wasn't blind to that, but somewhere over the years Trevor had morphed into one of the few people he trusted.

"That trust is easily broken." He'd trusted Brie too. He'd thought they understood each other, but now... He shook his head, rubbing a hand over his chest. The clenching throb beat hard and deep through the numbness he was struggling to hold on to.

"It is."

Trevor's agreement yanked a snort from Ryan. "So why do we bother giving it out?"

"To keep us grounded."

"How?"

"Because it forces us to take risks and allows us to

believe that there are still people in the world worth giving it to."

He stared at him, thoughts spinning out. "And when we find out there's no one left?"

His sarcastic scoff showed a flash of resentment that tainted his voice. "Then you become a bitter old man who believes the world is his to control."

Or his to abuse.

Ryan stared at his drink, his past rearing up in a flash of drunken scenes and angry scorn. He hadn't become that exact man, but had he become a different version of him?

"I can't remove Brie from the Boardroom," he said after a moment. "And I can't stand the thought of seeing her name on scenes without me." Fuck. The truth twisted the knife in his chest until it was lodged deep between his ribs.

"Is there a reason why you think that would happen?"

A logical one? No. Unless he completely walked away from her. Was he ready to do that? His head was shaking before he realized he'd answered himself.

No. He wasn't.

"Fuck." He braced his head in his hands, digging his fingers into his skull until his pulse thumped beneath his fingertips.

Trevor ordered another round for both of them before he spoke. "I think this is good."

Ryan jerked up. "What kind of a fucked-up statement is that?" His scowl dug deep into his forehead.

Trevor jiggled his glass, lifting it to shake an ice cube into his mouth. The crunch reached Ryan with the casual nonchalance it was clearly supposed to project. A lazy smirk lifted Trevor's lips when he finally looked to him. "How long have we known each other?"

"Almost ten years." He knew that without thinking only because Trevor's friendship was the longest-standing one he had. The few college friends he'd claimed had faded away after graduation, and his colleagues had never progressed past that status.

"And in all that time, I've never seen you this worked up over anything," Trevor said. "Not even your divorce."

"And…?"

His smile spread in a show of understanding. "Being human is good."

Ryan snorted his disgust. He took his fresh drink from the bartender, stirring the contents for something to do. "I think you're losing it, James."

"Nope." Trevor flashed a grin. "I'm pretty sure it's you in that boat right now."

Ass. He focused on the TV, thoughts circling around Trevor's words. That wasn't the first time someone had implied he didn't have feelings, but it'd never bothered him before. Yet the fucking mess of anger, disappointment and…loss was tearing him up. This was exactly why he'd kept his distance from everyone.

"Emotions make you vulnerable." He stated the fact without preamble or expectation of comment.

"They do," Trevor agreed. "But life is empty without them."

He dropped his head, chuckling at the pointed accuracy. He'd never considered himself lonely, had never identified the emptiness that'd surrounded him, but he saw it now. Brie had filled his world when he hadn't been looking. And now…

He could wallow in his own misery or get off this chair and go talk to her.

"I don't know what happened between you two," Trevor said. "But forgiveness is a part of love."

Ryan held in his snort for a long beat before it burst out on a choked laugh. He stared at the man who was as much of a bachelor as Ryan had been. "Did you really just say that?"

Trevor's eyes grew wide in mock surprise, lips quirking. "I did." He wiggled his glass. "It must be the drink."

His mouth quirked in a half-smile at the lame joke.

"Have you talked to her?" The humor left Trevor's tone, making a quick shift back to serious.

He shook his head. "No. Not yet."

"I suggest starting there."

"You are full of words of wisdom today." Sarcasm dripped from his voice.

Trevor lifted that damn brow of his that managed to have a language all its own. "I'm assuming that's the real reason why you called me."

There was no way he was going to admit to that. He'd never phoned a friend for help. He wasn't even sure he knew *how* to do that. Yet here Trevor sat at five o'clock on a workday.

"Thank you." The statement came out flat, but he meant it.

"Any time." Trevor finished his drink on a tumble of ice cubes and a fake contented sigh. He checked his watch, flashed a grin. "I have another appointment."

"Jacob caught me today," Ryan said, changing the subject as Trevor slid from his stool. "He has a special request he wanted to run by me."

"And?"

He gave a dismissive shrug. "I'll send you the details. It's been done before, but not to this extent."

A frown etched into his brow. "Is it legal?"

"Yes."

"Why'd he go to you?"

"Because it'd require a new contract."

Trevor's brows hitched up before he nodded. "I'll take a look."

Ryan watched him depart. His strides were long, carriage strong, confidence emanating from him on a subdued air. He'd tried to imitate that exact vibe since he'd put on his first rack-purchased suit, but he'd never been able to pull off the natural ease that came from being born with privilege.

He stared at the ballgame once again, thoughts tracking everywhere and nowhere. The pain in his chest had dimmed to a dull throb that reminded him of what he could lose. The bitter rage was gone, but its nasty residue left him drained, both mentally and physically.

His body ached when he'd done nothing more strenuous than lift his glass all afternoon. Memories dipped in of the cramps and numbness that'd infused his limbs after he'd been locked in the closet for hours. All night sometimes.

Would his parents be proud of him now? Were they even still alive?

Loathing wrenched his stomach. He'd stopped caring about them long before he'd left home.

But Brie obviously cared about hers. Maybe that's what hurt the most. Knowing that after all he'd worked to achieve, he still hadn't been good enough to meet her parents.

Fuck.

Chapter Thirty-Three

The distant ding of the elevator sounded down the hall on a muted ring of hope. Brie turned her head, her optimism long faded. The repeated ding over many hours had signaled the return of what felt like every person who lived on the floor—except Ryan.

Her heart caught, squeezed when he rounded the corner. His head was down, shoulders lowered in a dogged expression of exhaustion that soaked through her. Sympathy wound with fear, but it didn't rouse the overstated emotions that'd consumed her when she'd arrived. Her tears had drained her energy, leaving her empty when they'd dried.

Time had muted her initial panic. Contemplation had softened her personal beratements. Logic had dulled her fears until there was only mellow acceptance left.

He'd either listen to her or not. He'd forgive or not. Understand or…not.

Her heart gave another clench at the thought. She wanted to believe that what they had was strong enough to survive her mistake, but that belief had wavered the longer she'd sat there.

He lifted his head. Slowed. Her chest tightened, held.

His guard went up with a visible tensing of muscles

and flattening of his expression. Weariness lined his face, though. The weight of the day pressed on him in a way she'd never seen before. Not even after an eighty-hour work week.

He'd removed his tie at some point. The top three buttons of his shirt were undone, his sleeves rolled up. His suit jacket was tossed carelessly over his shoulder. The rumpled state of his hair proclaimed the multiple hand swipes it'd endured since she'd last seen him over seven hours ago.

She swallowed, her own expression immobile. Her heart wept, though. Tears rolled from it in silent mourning for what she'd done to him.

He continued forward, his eyes never leaving hers as he approached. Nothing changed on his expression, though. Not a flicker of his thoughts came through to give her a hint of what was next. She had no idea what showed on her own face. Doubts raced, questions flew, and her fear rose once again to choke her with all she could lose.

He came to a stop beside her. Fatigue flowed off him as he stared down at her. She could only look up from her seated position and wait. Did he see how sorry she was? Did he want to hear her explanation? Her apology?

"I'm sorry," she whispered, desperation and remorse thrown into each soft word. "I didn't mean to hurt you." But she had. The visual proof of how much tore at each little piece of her heart. "It was about me. Not you."

The air vibrated with the awareness that never left with him. It hummed over her skin and screamed the discord. It sat on her conscience along with the guilt that'd berated her since the moment she'd dismissed him.

His sigh came from somewhere deep when it fell

out. The echoing silence of the hallway magnified each hard thump of her pulse as she scrambled to interpret it.

Then his expression softened. His eyes closed. His head fell forward just a tad. Hope leaped in her chest before he turned away. That same hope crashed in a burning heap when he pulled his keys out of his pocket and unlocked his door.

Her mouth moved, words formed, but refused to come out. Panic clashed with her growing resignation to leave her frozen. She tried to swallow, but there was nothing there. She tried to catch a breath only to come up empty.

He looked back to her, extending his hand in silent expectation. Could he… Was this… That same wonderful awareness sped down her arm to embrace her heart the second she grasped his hand.

He helped her stand, her throat parched for words that would make things right before he led her into his condo. The silence slapped out at her, but with it returned hope. The synchronized tap of their shoes on the hardwoods welcomed them into the darkness as he drew her down the hallway to the kitchen. Only there did he drop her hand.

She tried to speak again, yet the timing wasn't right. Not now. Not yet. He wasn't ready. That knowledge eased into her understanding on the whispered notes of comfort.

This was them.

There'd be no emotional outburst from him. No accusations or loud condemnations. He hadn't walked away. He hadn't shut her out, and he wasn't now. He was simply collecting himself.

She owed him that time.

Relief wove through the pain binding her heart to allow a long, slow breath. He set his jacket and briefcase on a bar stool, tossed the keys on the island. He ran a hand through his hair before he moved to the fridge. The bright light glared briefly through the space when he opened the door to grab a bottle of water.

She blinked, waited.

The urban location meant that full darkness never fully descended, not with the plethora of windows in the dining and living area. She was used to this too. He often moved around the apartment using only the glow from outside.

After hours of uncertainty and dread, a tentative peace settled into her when he grabbed her hand and drew her into the living room. Sorrow was still there, along with regret, but gone was the numbing fear that she'd lost him.

He sat on the couch, head falling as he set the water aside. He seemed to sink into the cushions in a display of vulnerability he showed to so few. Did he know that? Were his defenses a conscious action or purely reflexive based on years of needing to protect himself?

She sat her purse on the coffee table and lowered herself onto the couch beside him. Another piece of her heart broke, yet it was woven into a bigger blanket of understanding. He did hurt. He did love, and he cared far more than he let anyone see.

Her love for him deepened in that moment. He had no reason for letting her into his home after the way she'd treated him, yet here she sat.

Tears stung her eyes and tickled her nose. Explanations throbbed in her throat yet in her heart, she understood he didn't want them. Words were empty if they weren't backed by actions.

He'd taught her that on that long-ago night when he'd wrapped his arms around her and somehow touched her heart.

She eased his hand from his lap, clasped her own around it. Warmth flooded her on contact. She inhaled, savored it. The gentle squeeze of his hand shuddered over her on another wave of relief.

Her head fell forward. Tears slid down her cheeks in a mix of gratitude and shame.

"I'm sorry," she whispered. Every drop of her misery was poured into the words. She squeezed his hand, silently begging him to hear her. "I'm so, so sorry. I didn't mean to hurt you. I panicked. I was trying to protect you from—"

A sharp tug on her arm had her falling into him. He released her hand to wrap his arms around her, drawing her to his chest. She squeezed her eyes closed, lip quivering as she held back the sob scrambling to break free. She refused to dump that on him. Her guilt was her own to bear. Her own to resolve.

"My mother," she mumbled against his chest.

He rubbed a hand over her hair before he lifted up to press a kiss to the top of her head. Her heart contracted around the love bursting from it. How? How had he forgiven her when she'd barely gotten an apology out?

But it flowed through her, that gentle quiet that breathed his meaning into every fiber of her being. It eased through her pain and grazed by her guilt before whispering over her heart. He loved her—still.

"Thank you," she whispered, making a quick swipe at the tears on her cheeks.

This was love. Real love. The kind that made mistakes and forgave imperfections. The kind that understood when one stumbled and offered support instead of ridicule.

His arms tightened around her for a long beat before he released a tired exhale. His voice was low when he said, "You forgave me for something far worse."

She frowned. "I did?"

His soft puff of amusement ghosted through her hair. "I was certain you'd never speak to me again after you found out I'd been in the Boardroom with you."

"Oh." She'd forgotten about that. Another wave of gratefulness crept through her. "I'm so glad I did."

"Ditto."

She sucked in a deep breath to fill herself with his scent that was now home to her. The light fragrance was darkened with the underpinnings of stale smoke and sweat, but it was still him.

"How long were you out there?" The deep vibration of his voice rumbled through his chest even though the words were barely audible.

"A while." Would it help to admit she'd been there since early afternoon? No. "You wouldn't answer your phone. Carla said you called in sick." When he'd never done so before. That bit of information was provided to her on a questionable note and implied reprimand.

"I needed some space."

"I know." Which was why she'd waited. "Can I explain?"

"Will it help?"

"I don't know."

He dragged his hand through her hair, let it slip through his fingers. The comforting touch melted through the chill that'd gripped her to remind her how close she'd come to losing this—him.

"I deserved better than that," he said. There was no anger in his tone, just tired truth.

"You did. You *do*." She shifted around to see him. The hurt remained in his eyes, but it was littered with old pain she longed to heal. "And I will." She sniffed back a new wave of tears.

His calm regard was almost worse than a round of angry yelling and harsh accusations. The silence exposed more of her own guilt without the relief of fake indignation or defensive walls.

"I'm sorry," she told him one more time, the words for her as much as him. "In my head, I was protecting you. I know that sounds crazy, but my mother had her claws drawn the second she spotted us, and I wasn't prepared. I wasn't ready to share you with her. Not yet. Not when—"

She bit her tongue, squeezing back her fears. When what? When… She swallowed. "When I'm ashamed of who I am with her." There was the deep dark truth. It swarmed over her with its crushing admonishment. She hated the person she became to please her mother.

She'd been raised to believe that the person she was free to be with Ryan was the one she should be ashamed of. But she wasn't. She'd never been, not even that very first time.

A shudder raked her, the guilt building in layers over her remorse.

"Brie." The empathy in his voice gutted her further.

She shook her head. "No. This isn't about me. This is about you. About what I did and how I hurt you. You never hid me. You've never made me feel bad about anything. Not the Boardroom. Not the wild public sex or my professional reserve or my work ethic or intelligence or our relationship or…anything." Her voice dropped on the last word, her burst of indignation fading with it.

And with it came another note of clarity: If all of that was true, then what did she really have to hide from him?

He might have secrets in his past that she was still uncovering, but she'd been hiding her present from him, and that was so much worse. "I'll introduce you," she said in a rush. "You can come to brunch, or we can have coffee or—"

He laid a finger over her lips to silence her rambling. Compassion and sadness blared in his gentle touch and tender gaze as he cupped her jaw. The darkness masked the color of his eyes but not the sincerity. Each gentle swipe of his thumb on her cheek was a small stroke of acceptance and forgiveness.

"I thought you understood by now," he whispered. "I love every part of you, Brie. Full stop."

"But you haven't seen all of me."

The corner of his mouth quirked up. "I could argue that."

His dual implication pulled a smile from her. "I was being serious."

"So was I."

The fact that he could joke, that he was joking with her, was just one more thing that lifted her heart and let her believe in what they had.

"I'll meet your parents when *you're* ready." He brushed his lips over hers. The impact rammed through her to obliterate the crushing weight of her admission. He searched her for a long moment before he sat back, drawing her down with him until she was cuddled against his chest once again. The steady beat of his heart slowed her own until she finally relaxed into the calm.

"I don't ask for much," he said after a while, his soothing strokes on her arm never stopping. "I expect even less. My parents ensured that I understood nothing was freely given, even love. Especially love." He huffed a bitter laugh before he went on. "I'm going to make mistakes too. I'm going to react based on my past, and you're going to have to remind me that this is the present."

"Is that what happened?" she asked. "My rejection reminded you of theirs?"

He was silent for a moment before a low "yes" came out.

The admission added another punch to her guilt. "I honestly didn't intend that."

"I know." He drew his fingers through his hair in that absent way she loved. "But it still hurt. And," he went on before she could apologize again, "it took me a while to sort through it."

"Where'd you go?"

"To a bar."

She frowned. "You don't smell like liquor."

"I didn't drink." He took a breath. "I wanted to. I thought about it. But I promised myself I would never be him." Contempt edged his tone as he spit out the last words. "Only to wonder if I'd become a shinier version of the same bastard."

His self-deprecating snort cut through the room. There was that hurt boy she wanted to hug and soothe. She was years too late to reach the boy. But the man… she had him.

"Why would you think that?" she probed.

"In case you missed it, I'm not really known for my warm and shining personality." Sarcasm laced every word and brought a smile to her lips.

"You're plenty warm with me," she told him, serious. "But I'm not so sure about the shiny part. Can you describe it for me?"

He swatted her hip in joking reprimand. "Behave."

"But if I'd done that, we wouldn't be here right now." And that thought brought a wave of thanks to her mother. Without her dogged demand for perfection, Brie never would've dared to be imperfect.

"On second thought..." He slid her around so quickly she could only gasp and hang on until her back was on the couch. That devious grin she loved curled over his lips as he came down on top of her. "Go ahead." He claimed her mouth in a long, slow kiss that took away the doubts and fears that'd festered all day. His breath heated her lips when he whispered, "Be very, very naughty, Brie. I'll be right here with you."

And he was. He had been since she'd made that wild, daring step into the Boardroom, and he was still here. "Thank you," she whispered. *For loving me. For understanding me. For letting me be Brie.*

He dropped another kiss on her lips, the touch so gentle, so tender it spoke directly to her heart before he whispered back, "I'm not going anywhere."

Her grin lit up her face as she drew him into a kiss, beyond grateful they'd found each other. She'd gone into this crazy wild adventure under the safety of blindness, only to be grateful for how much Ryan saw.

But she saw him too, and she'd never let him doubt that again.

Epilogue

Ryan sat his tablet on the table when Brie stepped onto the patio. His breath stalled, his heart doing that strange flutter as he took her in. Would he ever get used to that sensation? The kick to his chest when he saw her? He hoped not.

The red sundress hugged her curves to perfection before it flared out at her hips. The thin straps led to a V-neck, displaying a hint of cleavage that while still tasteful, was more than she usually showed. It was damn sexy in that understated way that was so her.

And right there, on prominent display, was the sinful little mole beneath her collarbone that'd tempted him from the very beginning.

He drew her down for a kiss before she took a seat in the chair next to his. "You look beautiful," he told her. There were times when he still couldn't believe she was here, that *he* was here.

"Thank you." She gave him a once-over, her smile suggestive. "You're looking nice yourself."

"Sure," he said around a brief chuckle. His standard suit-and-tie wardrobe didn't have a lot of variation, but the praise still warmed him, as did the appreciation in her eyes. It was her look more than her words that embraced his heart and reminded him he was loved.

And that was a sensation he was still learning to trust.

She reached over to take his hand, her gaze wandering over the view. Her hair fell around her shoulders in a glossy flow that never failed to lure him in to feel its softness.

"Are you ready for today?" he asked, brushing his thumb over the back of her hand.

"Yes." Her response was firm and confident. "You?"

"Yes." And that was a response he'd never thought would be true. But everything was different with Brie. He was even getting used to that. But in this case, him meeting her parents was a bigger step for her than himself.

After the debacle in front of the courthouse, he'd come to appreciate Brie's demons. They might be dressed up nicer and come with smiles, but they still haunted her.

His hours spent at the bar that day had finally brought that truth home. She'd forgiven him and, more importantly, had trusted him again after she'd discovered he'd been in the Boardroom with her. His lie of omission had been huge to her, yet she'd seen past his mistake to see Ryan. How could he not look past hers that day to see Brie?

Their pasts were a part of them, though. He'd tried to outrun his only to discover he was creating an empty future. But not anymore. Not with Brie.

The low hum of the city blended with the soft flutter of the breeze to create a quiet he cherished. Brie had moved in with little fanfare and even less upheaval. Her belongings had merged with his in the same way that her life had blended with his—with only a few hiccups and an understanding that escaped words.

"Should we go?" he asked. The decision was completely hers. He understood that unlike his parents, hers were still important in her life. She loved them, and he'd do whatever he could to make that easier for her.

He'd supported her through the multiple discussions she'd had with her mother. Ones that'd ended in tears and others that'd left a smile. Their relationship was a work in progress, but then weren't they all?

She inhaled, held the breath before releasing it in a slow exhale. Her nod was firm when she made it. "Yes."

He squeezed her hand before they stood, then drew her in for a soft kiss.

Her whispered "thank you" floated out to embrace him with her love. She understood him like no one ever had. Each touch and action since her first Boardroom visit had formed a communication he still marveled at.

"Always," he whispered back. He'd always be there for her. She'd won his heart when he'd sworn his didn't work. She'd shown him how wrong he'd been.

The drive to Walnut Creek was made in the comfortable silence that often settled between them. She pointed out a few buildings and places that held memories as they drove by them, along with the exit that led to her childhood home. He didn't comment a lot, only held her hand and listened.

That small, distinctive run of her fingers over her thumb occupied her other hand. It was the tell that'd given away her identity so long ago. The habit wasn't necessarily related to nerves. He knew that now.

She directed him off the highway and to the country

club, adding more memories. "I practically lived at the club in the summers," she mused. "Mom had my sister and I in every activity. Swimming, tennis, golf..." Her smile was soft. "We did them all. I once had a pretty mean backswing." She shot him a smile. "I bet I could take you in a match."

"I'm sure you could," he agreed with a laugh. Golf had been the one sport he'd learned to excel at and only because deals were made and negotiated on the course.

He pulled into the long drive leading to the clubhouse. The overstatement of privilege spread out around them, from the manicured greens to the multitude of tennis courts and the parking lot packed with luxury vehicles. The distance from his childhood in East Oakland was enormous, but he wasn't there anymore. No, he hadn't been there in almost two decades, yet his past remained a part of him. Just like Brie's did.

He left the car with the valet and followed Brie through the building, her hand tightly clasped around his. He had her back. He wouldn't let her be hurt, but he also wouldn't do anything to hurt her. This was her show.

"Morning, Kayla," Brie greeted the hostess with a smile. "How are things today?"

"All's quiet on the Western front," Kayla quipped, the classic reference far outdating her apparent age. Her grin was welcoming when she flashed it at Ryan, her quick once-over executed with efficiency. "But I'm thinking we may have some excitement soon." She raised a brow at Brie, her smirk knowing.

Brie's laugh was light as she glanced at him. "I'm hoping not too much." She squeezed his hand, a bit of the tightness leaving her features.

The outside patio was packed with diners enjoying Sunday morning brunch. Brie greeted a few by name, waved at more, her smile never wavering.

Once again, he was awed by her grace and beauty. No one here would ever see the bold, lascivious Boardroom woman, but he knew her and loved her.

Her hand tightened around his as they approached her parents' table. He'd spotted them the second they'd stepped outside. Her mother's instant frown communicated her disdain, but he wasn't sure over what.

Her father stood, his smile welcoming. There was no ice or distance coming from him, unlike the frosty chill held beneath her mother's smile.

Brie glanced at him, her smile wide and confident. Yes, he loved this side of her too.

"Mom, Dad," she said, warmth flowing from her voice. "I'd like you to meet my boyfriend, Ryan Burns." She flashed a beaming grin at him, and he was utterly lost to her.

Brie had come into his awareness on a gasped sigh and a blind trust that'd left him humbled and foundering. She'd brightened his life and exposed a part of him he'd been afraid to acknowledge. But he'd done the same for her.

They were a team now. A couple.

And he treasured that in the same way he treasured her. With his whole heart.

* * * * *

Thank you for reading BLIND TRUST!
More scintillating stories from The Boardroom are coming soon, including SIGNED OVER, the newest Boardroom Memo short, coming in July 2018.

And read on for an excerpt from AFTER HOURS, book one in THE BOARDROOM *series from Lynda Aicher.*

The folder had to be in the boardroom. There was no other place she could've left it.

Avery Fast plowed down the empty stairwell, engrossed in her thoughts as she backtracked her way through her afternoon. She'd already checked the smaller conference room, the break room and Carmen's desk. And that'd been after she'd torn her own desk apart and scanned her boss's.

As the executive assistant to the financial controller at Faulkner Investment Group's San Francisco office, a lot of confidential information flowed through her. Her boss, Gregory Conwell, counted on her to keep the data secured, and she had never let him down in the eighteen months since she'd been in her position.

And she wasn't about to now, either.

Her heels tapped on the stairs, the echo bouncing around the cavernous concrete silo. The single flight wasn't enough to work off her frustration. She brushed her bangs away from her eyes as she swiped her badge through the reader and yanked the heavy fire door open with a grunt.

The Faulkner offices were spread over two floors of a high-rise in downtown San Francisco. A staircase near the main entrance offered a grander connection than the fire stairwell she used, but it was also out of her way. Efficiency was crucial right now.

A clammy sheen had built up on her heated skin the more her panic deepened. Had someone taken the folder from her desk? Why? Who? Had she even brought the folder to the meeting in the boardroom that afternoon?

Doubt twisted with the knot constricting her chest. She didn't remember doing so, but... The preliminary quarterly numbers were in it. The ones no one saw until they were verified, rolled up and strategically manipulated. The raw data wasn't for general consumption, especially the payroll details.

Her stomached roiled at the thought of having to explain what happened. What if someone had found the folder and shared the information with others? Her job would be toast—along with her reputation.

Why had she printed them anyway? Oh yeah, Gregory had asked her to. Why couldn't he keep everything online in the age of digital everything?

The office doors along the darkened hallway were closed, the lights off behind them, but a dim light shone from the open door of the conference room. She'd sat on the far side, near the end of the table during the meeting. Could someone have set the file on the coffee credenza? Or maybe it was still on the table, if she'd even left it there.

She was out of options. It had to be there.

Her brain stalled about a second after her feet did in the boardroom doorway. Her mouth fell open. *Oh my...*

The boardroom wasn't empty after all. Nope. Not even close.

She scrambled to comprehend what she was seeing while knowing exactly what she watched: sex. Wanton, hedonistic, erotic sex. A woman and *two* guys.

But here? In the office? On the boardroom table?

Heat raced up her back to engulf her chest and neck. Blood roared in her ears, accelerated by her racing heart and the strange desire blasting through her.

She blinked once, twice, but the image remained. Propriety told her to look away. No, she should run away. What was she doing standing there? *Walk the hell away. Now.*

But she didn't move.

The scene was…unbelievable. Unreal. Wrong. And so damn hot.

A single lamp on the credenza provided a soft glow to the room and dulled the edges of the threesome along with their actions. Their reflections were hazy shadows in the large windows along the outside wall. The lights from other buildings and the streets far below provided an open backdrop and little protection from prying eyes.

Like hers.

She should go—before they noticed her. She should.

She searched for moisture in her mouth. Swallowed hard. Slowly wet her dry lips.

What would it feel like to be that woman? The one splayed on the table, naked except for her black stilettos? Her eyes were closed, her red lips parted in a silent sigh, or would that be a cry of pleasure? Her black hair was spread in a messy array across the wood, her wrists bound by two thick cuffs over her head. She was lean yet curvy. Beautiful. And totally lost in what was being done to her.

Her back arched, a soft moan escaping to flow with a sultry lethargy through the room. It swirled around Avery to drag her deeper into the eroticism. Avery's breath hitched. Her nipples puckered with sharp tingles that raced to her pussy.

The men were feasting on the woman. That was the

only way she could describe it. Both of them. At the same time. A guy in a dark suit had his back to Avery, his head buried between the woman's spread legs. Another in a white dress shirt and navy tie was sucking on a nipple while rolling the other between his fingertips. He stretched back, the tip clearly caught between his teeth, and the woman's back arched impossibly more. She squirmed, another purring moan tumbling out before a gasped "Please."

Yes, please. Avery's back bowed in time with the woman's, her nipples aching for the same attention.

It didn't make sense. She'd never enjoyed porn. And she'd certainly never considered going to a live sex show. Yet...

She swallowed. Inhaled. The heavy scent of sex and arousal flooded her, adding another layer of stimulation. She sucked in another long, slow breath. The hedonism flowed through her to dislodge every concept of conservatism or impropriety she held.

A low growl—yes, growl—from one of the men tore through the room. Raw, fierce, exalting. No man had ever made that sound with her.

A soft whimper of want tumbled out before she realized it was there. *Oh, God.* She clamped her mouth shut, fear charging in. Had they heard her?

She took a step back, prepared to flee. Guilt sped in, yet it wasn't enough to make her go. She'd be mortified if they caught her, but what would they do next? Would the men switch places? Would they fuck her? Both of them? At the same time?

Her pussy clenched, lust swarming hot and fast from her core. Her head spun with so many desires she couldn't process them. She shifted her feet and bit her lip to keep quiet.

She'd never had a guy who'd been that devoted to her pleasure. Ever. Let alone two.

The woman gasped, her legs spreading even wider. The man between her legs pumped his arm, a low sucking and squelching sound emanating. Avery's eyes widened on another inhalation. She couldn't actually *see* what he was doing, but she didn't need to.

Her pussy pulsed again. Her nipples tightened even more. They ached to be touched. Her hand inched up before she clenched her fist and forced it back to her side.

The woman on the table turned her head. Her eyes fluttered open as a soft cry bled from her lush lips. She closed her eyes only to reopen them, her focus squarely on Avery.

Oh, shit.

Her panic pounded out a frantic SOS in her head, yet she remained trapped in the moment. A sultry smile curved over the woman's ruby-red lips, her hooded eyes conveying the pleasure the men were giving her. Passion overrode logic along with every ounce of self-preservation Avery had. Heat flashed another wave of want over her chest and burst into an aching demand between her legs.

She gripped the doorjamb, her head swaying with the heady sensations. The eye contact made the whole experience intimate. Like she was supposed to be there.

But she wasn't.

The woman wet her lips in a slow pass that screamed seduction. The movement swiped out at Avery in the tease that it was. And for some damn reason, she wanted to tease her right back. Her tongue pushed at her teeth, but she kept them tightly closed.

This was insane. She'd never been sexually attracted to women. Not really anyway. Not enough to act on it.

But…

What am I thinking?

She jerked her gaze away, determined to leave only to freeze again.

Another man stood in the darkened back corner of the room, arms crossed over his chest, feet spread in a power stance. And his eyes were locked squarely on her.

Her muscles seemed to petrify along with her thoughts. She had no doubt that he'd been watching her the whole time. He didn't move either. Not even a flick of his lips or brow. He simply stared at her. Waiting.

Embarrassment doubled down on the lust blazing through her to set Avery on fire from head to toe. Heat flamed over her cheeks before sinking down her neck—and she still didn't move.

His face was shadowed, but she didn't need the florescent lights to know exactly who he was: Carson Haggert, the chief technology officer for *all* of Faulkner.

And possibly one of the sexiest men she'd ever encountered.

His tie was loosened, suit jacket gone, shirtsleeves turned up to expose his forearms, but he still emanated that all-consuming authority that prickled over her skin whenever he was near. It consumed her now, sucking the truths from her and exposing every lascivious thought running through her mind.

The exposure trembled down her legs, and she locked her knees to stop it from showing. A high whine of unabashed pleasure winged past her in an unnecessary reminder of what she'd walked into. The pace of the sucking sound increased with the woman's panted breaths and soft moans.

"Make her come."

The hard command shot from Carson to crack through the mounting tension. Avery flinched, her lips parting in confusion. His focus was still squarely on her. Did he mean Avery was supposed to make the woman come? Or were the men supposed to make Avery come?

Three short cries were followed by a long, drawn-out note that left no doubt about who was supposed to make whom come. And she wasn't included in the party. At all.

She was the intruder.

The uninvited observer.

The one risking her job by standing there.

That last thought finally got her moving. Mortification set in the second she spun around and fled down the hallway. Her heart pounded in another flight of panic, this one dogged by fear.

The closed office doors sped by, her pace increasing the more reality reemerged. She'd just watched an illicit sex game play out in the boardroom. And she'd been caught doing so.

She threw herself against the crash bar, slammed through the fire door and flew up the stairs as fast as her heels and pencil skirt allowed. Her hand squeaked against the metal railing when she gripped it to turn on the landing. The door slammed shut below, and she flinched, tensing. She shot a quick look back, at once fearing Carson had followed her while hoping he would.

And then what? Would she be fired? Threatened into silence? Harassed?

She yanked on the door handle when she reached her floor only to stumble forward when it didn't open. Of course it was locked. She jerked up, her arm throbbing, and fumbled for her ID badge clipped to her waist. Her hand was shaking when she finally swiped her ID through the card reader.

She dashed to her office, her head swiveling the entire time. Would Carson show up before she could leave? Would he cut her off at the exit? Block her flight of embarrassment?

Force her against the wall and lay a hot demanding kiss on her?

Right. Like that had a chance in hell of happening.

It took more precious seconds for her to grab her purse, lock her drawers with fingers that refused to cooperate and swipe her coat off the rack before she could flee the office entirely. Her pulse rate didn't decrease one iota the entire time.

Not when she peeked around the corner in the hallway or tried to quietly tiptoe down the wooden staircase near the office lobby. Not when she bit her lip and seemed to wait forever for the down arrow to light up on any one of the bank of elevators. Not when the ding of arrival pinged through the silence to signal her freedom.

And not when she caught a glimpse of Carson Haggert staring at her from across the lobby, a knowing smile curling his lips as the elevator doors closed.

She clenched her purse tighter, adrenaline flying through her system to leave her sweaty and chilled at once. Her mind reeled, thoughts scrambling in and out before a single one could take hold.

She wasn't naïve or exactly sheltered, but this stuff didn't happen to her—or anyone she knew. Nothing in her thirty years of life had prepared her for this. Not one thing.

The rapid click of her heels across the marble-tiled lobby echoed through the open atrium to highlight her flight. The security guard studied her, a brow raised in unasked question.

"Night," she managed to croak out over the scratchy dryland that'd overtaken her throat. The chilled dampness hit her in the face the second she shoved through the revolving glass door. She sucked in a deep breath and slipped into her jacket before the foggy air could sink into her bones.

The sidewalk was fairly empty, which made the air seem colder and the shadows deeper. She laughed at herself, yet the quick tap of her heels didn't slow. A glance over her shoulder showed a few people huddled into their coats, chins tucked low against the chill. But no Carson, even though she'd half expected to see him.

Expected or wanted?

God, she *was* being naïve and stupid.

The fluorescent light buzzed under the protective cover of the bus shelter that provided zero protection from the curling wisps of fog. Her silk shirt clung to her back, and a shudder overtook her entire body. Goose bumps broke out on her bare legs despite the erotic warmth that still encased her. She huddled further into her trench coat, but it didn't help.

How had she gotten herself into this mess? If she'd left the boardroom when she'd first realized what she'd walked in on, then she wouldn't be so screwed. No, if she hadn't misplaced the reports in the first place, she wouldn't have returned to the office to hunt for them only to stumble into an illicit ménage à trois.

Images of the steamy threesome combined with the commanding presence of Carson crashed in as the bus pulled up. Another shiver trembled down her, ending with the tight clench of her pussy around the unfulfilled want.

No. No way. There was no way she'd ever be able to do something like that. She shook her head in an attempt to clear the visuals scorched into her memory. It didn't work. Would they be imprinted forever, tormenting her with ideas and longings she'd never dare act on?

She didn't glance at any of the other passengers on

the short ride home, instead opting to stare unseeing out the window. What would they think if they knew what she'd seen—done? Would any of them care?

The events of the evening were finally sinking in when she trudged toward her building. A warm yellow glow lit up the window of her little two-bedroom condo. The curtains shifted, and then the shadowed outline of her two cats appeared as they perched on the window ledge to greet her.

There. That was her life.

One that didn't include office sex scandals or orgy-fests in the boardroom. Would that be classified as an orgy? Probably not, given there—Stop!

She stomped up the four flights to her condo, determined to put the night behind her. She wouldn't think about any of it. Not tonight. Not tomorrow.

Not ever again.

Right.

And what would happen when she saw Carson Haggert at work?

Don't miss AFTER HOURS by Lynda Aicher, available now wherever Carina Press books are sold.

www.CarinaPress.com

About the Author

Lynda Aicher is an RWA RITA® Award finalist, RT Reviewers' Choice winner and two-time Golden Flogger award-winner who loves to write emotionally charged romances. Prior to becoming an author, she spent years traveling weekly as a consultant implementing software into global companies until she opted to end her nomadic lifestyle to raise her two children. Now her imagination is the only limitation on where she can go, and her writing lets her escape from the daily duties of being a mom, wife, chauffeur, scheduler, cook, teacher, cleaner, and mediator. You can find her online at: lyndaaicher.com.

Facebook.com/lyndaaicherauthor.

Twitter.com/lyndaaicher.

Bookbub.com/authors/lynda-aicher.